3,OOO
Miles

3,000 Miles

Jason Schneider

J. Schneider

MISFIT

ECW PRESS

Published by ECW PRESS
2120 Queen Street East, Suite 200, Toronto, Ontario, Canada M4E 1E2

LIBRARY AND ARCHIVES CANADA CATALOGUING IN PUBLICATION

Schneider, Jason, 1971-
3,000 miles / Jason Schneider.

ISBN 1-55022-686-X

1. Title.   II. Title: Three thousand miles.

PS8637.C44T47 2005   C813'.6   C2004-907033-9

Editor for the press: Michael Holmes / a misFit book
Cover and Text Design: Darren Holmes
Author Image: Shannon Lyon
Typesetting: Mary Bowness
Printing: AGMV

This book is set in Goudy

The publication of 3,000 Miles has been generously supported by the
Canada Council, the Ontario Arts Council, and the Government
of Canada through the Book Publishing Industry
Development Program. Canada

DISTRIBUTION
CANADA: Jaguar Book Group, 100 Armstrong Ave., Georgetown, ON L7G 5S4

PRINTED AND BOUND IN CANADA

ECW PRESS
ecwpress.com

For Candy

I will not forget that this kid killed himself for something torn T-shirts represented in the battle fires of his ripped emotions, and that does not make your T-shirts profound, on the contrary, it makes you a bunch of assholes if you espouse what he latched onto in support of his long death agony . . .

—Lester Bangs, "Peter Laughner," 1977

1 Marcel
La Forest: September 6, 1994.

Like everyone else, I'm leaving town after another Labour Day weekend. It used to be that I couldn't wait for all the idiot tourists to get out of here and stop pretending that they're communing with fucking Nature. Whatever. I don't even know why I'm wasting my energy thinking about that shit now. I don't have to say I'm from here anymore. Pretty soon, I'll be bitching about big city people. Even though I'll probably become one of them.

Don't get me wrong, there are many things to love about La Forest. One thing I'll definitely miss is the woods. City kids get the street, we get a bunch of trees. It's all still survival of the fittest. That must be why I hate the summer crowd so much. This is our turf, we earned the right to live here. Not like you shitheads who get in your parents' cars, bribe someone to buy a couple cases of beer and then floor it for three hours without caring about anyone else on the road. Your only reason for being here is to see who can drink the most and shoot the most stuff.

I've seen it every year and still can't figure out why it's such a big deal. But fuck it, like I said, I shouldn't be wasting my time thinking about it. Today I'm leaving my parents' house on Ste. Marie Street. They're not taking it very well, but they know, after all that's happened, I have to go. It won't be long before they're back to their routine — drinking and playing bridge with the Delormes. Anyway, they've got my little brother to worry about. He'll be following in my footsteps soon, I'm sure.

I don't go for most of that Indian spiritual shit, but I believe I'm at the point in my life where I have to take a journey. Otherwise, there's not much point in going on. I sound like such a fucking jerk saying that, after what they did. I never approved of it, but in the last few weeks, at least I've come to accept it. Everyone's looking for some kind of way out, but most of the time when we find it, we're too scared to open the door. Now, when I think of those guys, I remember the nights in the woods when we'd take our girlfriends there and lay on the banks of the creek, just listening to it trickle by. I never appreciated that creek until I heard a song with a line about the sound of rushing water in the dark that really got to me. I think the best I've ever felt was when Monique and I were there one year at the beginning of May, before the mosquitoes got too bad, feeling her warmth in the middle of the night while the water drowned out our nervous laughter.

There were never enough of those nights, though. Labour Day would always come way too soon, which meant just one more bush party, and maybe a bigger bonfire to mark the occasion. Our parents even wanted to get in on it. Then, almost overnight, the trees would be a different colour and we'd begin numbing ourselves for the long winter ahead. The process would take hold when we went back to school, reverting to our natural roles: the headbangers, the stoners, the slackers, the bullies, the nerds, those-most-likely-to-succeed. There weren't many in the last group, and there was a little bit of the rest in all of us.

No one from our town ever really accomplished much, because everyone always had to work so fucking hard for next-to-nothing. The town started as little more than a logging camp, back in the days when guys worked in the bush eight months of the year and the rivers carried logs downstream to the big mills that made furniture, roof beams and hockey sticks. Someone finally decided to build a mill right here so families didn't have to be separated and, voila, La Forest was born.

Everybody worked at the mill when my father was my age. He hasn't worked in five years but he still goes down there to chat with the guys during their lunch break. All the older folks talk about the mill constantly, but I don't think it's ever seriously come up in a conversation I've ever had with someone my age. That's because when we were born, the mill didn't need people anymore. It's not that I'm bitter, I couldn't imagine myself working there anyway, but after the mill stopped hiring I think everyone knew things were going to be very different.

The mill still can't be ignored, though. First, there's the constant noise. And it mostly makes paper now, so there's a lot of chemicals, something that made people uneasy when I was a kid. Some old-timers started getting cancer, and there was a lot of talk about organizing a lawsuit, but nothing came of it. They were all too spineless to bite the hand that fed them, and that broke everyone's spirit.

The worst part is still the smell. We're all used to it, except in the summer when the plant shuts down for two weeks. We wake up one morning and realize what fresh air is. That's the best time of the year, when we can finally get away from our families and enjoy life a little. But the smell always comes back. It creeps up on us while we sleep, waiting to ambush us when we open our windows in the morning. The night shift starts to pump it out all over again, twenty-four hours a day, until the mill shuts down again at Christmas. When my relatives come up from Montreal, their first reaction is always, "Oh God, that smell! I don't know how you can live here."

We just do. My father came home with chemicals all over his coveralls, while cousins and neighbours died of cancer.

None of it mattered. This was our home.

I guess another thing I'll miss is Sergio's, makers of the best pizza I've ever had. There isn't much fast food here, so Sergio's is the most popular hangout, and he deserves it. One time, I was eating there with some friends when a half-dozen motorcycles pulled up. The place was packed, and everyone got really nervous because we'd all heard of the gang wars that go on in the city. But the riders turned out to be three men and three women, and they immediately searched out Sergio. He treated them like long-lost family. I understood one of them say, in English, "We came all the way from Ontario for one of your pizzas."

Andre was with me, but he didn't know much English so he

didn't laugh. He seemed genuinely uninterested in the scene as it played out.

"What the fuck's with you?" he asked.

I translated, but he still didn't laugh. As we each took another bite, I heard him mutter "Fuckin' animals" under his breath. I stared at him until he noticed, then quickly turned my attention back to the bikers. I realized I'd never had an opinion about outsiders until that moment. The summer mostly brought families on camping trips, while the other seasons brought hordes of hunters and fishermen. We were always told not to stray too far into the woods after that fall when Robbie Delorme was accidentally shot by these guys from New Brunswick. They thought he was a quail or something. His family did all right in the end, the hunters paid them off in exchange for not pressing charges. Actually, I think a lot of people got jealous about it. Every now and then I'd hear my friends' parents say, "You behave or I'll send you out in the bush with antlers on your head." The first thing Frank Delorme did was quit his job at the mill and cash in his pension. Then he bought a new car, a new stereo, a satellite dish and every other cool thing you can imagine. He got Robbie some stuff, too, after he recovered.

It was normal for Andre to not be impressed by unusual things, like having bikers invade our favourite hangout. We'd been friends forever, and not once did I remember him ever being surprised. He wasn't an overly negative guy, he just never seemed interested in anything outside our little world. Even when it came to girls, I never saw him go out of his way to make a play. Then one morning, I came to school and Sylvie was on his arm like she'd been born there.

Andre never talked about his family either. His father worked at the mill but wasn't really part of the regular crowd that hung out at the Lion Rouge on weekends or went fishing in the summer. The family lived in one of the small, wooden houses a few blocks from the main street on Cartier Ave. and kept to themselves. From the few times I'd gone over there, I remembered only a rusty Chevy

Malibu on blocks in the front yard and a collection of old snow-mobiles littering the back. I assumed Andre's dad was a mechanic, but when nothing ever seemed to move at their house, my perception changed. I couldn't imagine how they survived.

Andre did have an older brother who was pretty cool. Michel was in Grade 12 when we started high school. He and his friends tolerated us since there weren't many other kids to hang out with. My parents already hated Michel because of something that happened when I was eight. I'd heard him recite an obscene version of "The Night Before Christmas" and asked him what a few words, like "cunt" and "rape," meant. He told me to ask my mother. She nearly killed me and I couldn't understand why. Michel would also bring porn magazines to school and explain to us what everything was, and how it worked, while his friends busted their guts. After a few years we all wanted to grow our hair like him and wear leather jackets. By then he'd moved on to telling us about Gene Simmons spitting blood and breathing fire; Alice Cooper puking on stage and eating it; Ozzy Osbourne biting the head off a live bat. The priest couldn't hold our attention anymore.

Those of us who were lucky to have cheap stereos started hanging around the only place to buy records, which was the big supermarket where everybody shopped. Every few weeks, Andre would grab one of his brother's metal magazines and the two of us would search the bins for any name or title we recognized. Nobody had to tell me my parents would disapprove of this music, I knew the first second I heard it. I decided, then, to keep my listening confined to my headphones, and the tapes carefully stowed away in my bureau. Everything was fine for several weeks, until I brought home an LP of Iron Maiden's *Number of the Beast* and my mother freaked out over the cover, the same kind of hellish doodle I was trying to create myself in my schoolbooks. I tried to explain that I wasn't serious about what she thought was Satan-worshipping, and my father must have convinced her that it was only a phase.

The scene at school was changing, too. Michel and his friends no longer merely tolerated us, and it felt great to see the shocked faces of the teachers the first time we walked into the classrooms with our newly customized jean jackets stitched-up or magic-markered with the names of our heroes. Until then we'd all been obsessed with the Montreal Canadiens, and the names Guy Lafleur, Ken Dryden and Larry Robinson dominated our conversations. I can look back now and see how we were all conditioned to believe that our greatest accomplishment would be to become a soldier in the endless war against the Maple Leafs.

Remembering this stuff has been the biggest help for me in dealing with what went down. I'm nearly through it all, and it's plain to see how one thing naturally led to another. First came the music, then the drinking. The first time I ever saw someone really drunk was at Mario's house. He was a friend of Michel's and didn't mind people coming over to play video games in his attic. It was everything I wanted my room to be: the walls covered with posters, a big, loud stereo, bottles, pipes and pornography out in the open. A strobe light completed the effect.

The night in question wasn't out of the ordinary, except that Andre was getting ribbed a little more than usual by the older guys. It was the normal big brother/little brother stuff, which went on all the time, but that night Andre was in the mood to fight back. Empties littered the room, and a bottle of Canadian Club someone had stolen from their dad's liquor cabinet was almost gone. They were goading Andre into taking a swig but he just sat there sipping his bottle of 50, the rage visibly building on his face. The conversation started to drift, but Andre suddenly spoke, as if he'd been struggling with the words for a long time.

"Make me a fucking drink. Anything you want."

I swear he sounded like a cowboy and his eyes never strayed from the poster of Jimi Hendrix above his brother's head.

Some guys burst out laughing, as Michel eagerly obliged.

"Holy shit, this is gonna be fun! Oh no, don't get up, we'll bring it to you."

Andre didn't react to the sarcasm. He remained statue-like, and I asked as casually as I could if he knew that at the very least they were going to piss in it.

He shrugged it off. "Hey man, we came here to have fun, didn't we?" His brother and the others returned after a short time, Michel carrying a large German beer stein with a lid that concealed the mix.

I asked what was in it but was ignored. All eyes were fixed on Andre as he gripped the heavy mug with both hands. He gave a quick glance at Michel's stupid grin, popped open the lid with his thumb and then took a short sip. He recoiled, wincing, as the attic exploded in laughter.

"It would probably taste better with a nipple," one of them blurted.

"Come on, you didn't even taste it," another said. I couldn't laugh, and sat detached, trying to figure out why Andre was going through with this pointless exercise. He finally took a man-sized gulp and brought the stein away from his lips with what looked to me like a twisted gleam in his eye.

As he took three or four more gulps, I scanned his face for signs of a transformation. By this point, Michel and the others were being distracted by someone's brand new copy of Guns 'N Roses' *Appetite For Destruction*, and its cover, a cartoon depicting a ravaged and bloody young girl slumped against a wall. Mario had cranked up the stereo, and a loud debate had started about what tracks were best. I kept watching Andre's eyes, and saw they were nervously darting around the room. He began grabbing at unseen objects.

"I think it's time for a refill," he slurred to no one in particular.

The older guy sitting next to us heard this and laughed out loud, prompting Michel to return his attention to his brother.

"Jesus, he's fuckin' toasted! Mario, you gotta let him crash here tonight, I'm not taking him home like this. We'll both get killed."

"What was in that?" I yelled, before Mario could answer.

"Relax. Your little buddy's fine," Michel said. "He's ready to have some fun now. Why don't you join him?" I looked again at

Andre, leaning back in his chair, his eyes glassy and heavy. I had never seen anyone get so wasted so quickly.

I didn't want to, but I left him there that night. This was Michel's handiwork, and I figured he'd pay for it somehow. When I called their house the next day, their mother told me tersely that Andre was still asleep and he'd call me when he woke. I didn't talk to him again until school on Monday when he shrugged off my concern. He did tell me Michel had told their parents he had food poisoning. I couldn't imagine them buying it.

Whenever we'd meet at Mario's after that, Andre came prepared with a hefty amount of beer and the two of us would try to drink it all. He'd hooked up with Sylvie during this time — and Monique and I began our brief infatuation — but they always avoided going to Mario's, probably for good reason. We couldn't hold our booze, and at least one of us would always end up puking on the street before we got home. When we weren't scheming ways to get booze, we were talking about music. Mostly it would be the Satanic references, until one day Andre mentioned in passing that he was buying a guitar. He had gotten his parents' permission to sell his hockey equipment, and they were taking him to Quebec City to pick one out.

He came home with an imitation Fender Telecaster, a tiny Peavey amp and a guitar-for-beginners book written in English. He told me he didn't have to understand the words, the finger positions were all he needed. I didn't hang out with Andre much after that. I really didn't see him anywhere but at school, where he and Sylvie were usually locked onto one another. He'd invite me to his house once in a while, when he had figured out some rudimentary thing on guitar, and I pretended to be impressed.

Gradually, we drifted into different cliques. I couldn't stand Michel and his friends anymore. They were into smoking hash and Andre was becoming a dopehead. I'd started playing Dungeons & Dragons with a group of guys that included Richard and Serge, two other old friends who were usually around when Andre was busy.

MARCEL

None of us thought the game was a big deal. I didn't even know who the first person in town to acquire it was. We just played it like we played Monopoly when we were kids. But soon word started going around that kids in the States were freaking out because of it, getting into all kinds of weird devil-worship stuff. Our parents confronted us about what went on when we got together to play. Séances? Ritual sacrifice? It was all bullshit, and we told them in so many words. City kids were fucked-up on crack and getting molested by priests. No wonder they were committing suicide.

Suicide. Now that was a nasty word in our town. It was common knowledge that it was slowly wiping out the nearby Rez. Those kids had less to live for than us, incredibly, and had resorted to sniffing the gas pipes that heated their houses. Nobody talked about it much, "None of our business" being the usual excuse, but when the hard times hit the mill, my dad starting getting more funeral calls than usual. I remember him telling my mother he'd have to buy a new suit if it kept up.

We continued to play the game, while the rest of the people we knew were getting stoned, but it was still something we had to keep from our parents. I guess that's what made it exciting. One night, there was a problem finding a house, so I had to resort to calling Andre. It was a Friday and he was at home with Sylvie, practicing his guitar. I never heard her complain about anything he did. After a little persuading, he told me we could go over to Mario's attic. I was hesitant, but agreed to meet him there in an hour.

The rest of the D&D crew got together at my house and we set out for Mario's, which was about five blocks away. He met us at the front door, and we could hear that a crowd was already there. I asked Mario again if this was going to be all right, and he told us not to worry, that he'd had way more people up there before. When we got to the top of the stairs and passed through the small wooden door, I saw Andre and Sylvie. They were drinking beer and taking hits off the joint that was being passed around. Setting up the board proved to be a bit of a hassle, and we got little help from the older guys who made fun of us for playing a board game. But after about fifteen minutes of observing, they warmed up to the concept, like it was a Slayer album come to life before their eyes. Andre, particularly, was intrigued and sat quietly behind me, analyzing the various moves.

We played for three hours that night, and Andre hung in all the way. His brother and the others gave up quickly and turned their attention to formulating drug deals and messing with Mario's new compact disc player. He was the first guy in town to get one. We didn't have a chance to examine it until we stopped playing, but occasionally I'd notice Andre's head whip around when a heavy song from one of Mario's pile of CDs came on. I remember we all kind of paused when we heard this odd punk tune. Its chorus went something like, "I feel stupid and contagious. Here we are now, entertain us."

Andre was present every time we played D&D from then on. He had hit it off with Richard and Serge when he'd noticed the Iron Maiden T-shirts they had bought from a head shop during a hockey tournament in Toronto. Both of them played on the town's all-star team, which competed against other teams from Quebec City. Every year, the town held a big event when money had to be raised to send the team to a tournament. Usually it was a bingo night or a dance with a raffle that had to make up the difference for whatever the mill would donate as the team's sponsor.

The year the team went to Toronto was the furthest Serge and Richard had ever travelled, and it was all they could talk about when they returned home. The team had blown every game, as we'd expected, but with all the money raised, the guys got to stay in a hotel right on Yonge Street, where they took over a dozen rooms, just like a real pro team. They would tell stories about breaking curfew and walking around until two in the morning, baiting hookers, spending hours in the arcades playing video games they had only dreamed about and gawking like the country boys they were at the skyscrapers and the CN Tower.

The funniest thing I remember them saying was about a group of them trying to enter a strip club, and they all got in except for Richard, whose ripped jeans failed to meet the dress code. What the other guys saw were real, live naked women for the first time, some with rings in their nipples, belly buttons and vaginas. That's all they would talk about — rings in vaginas.

They ended up buying a whole pile of cheap T-shirts from bargain bin stores, hoping to impress everyone back home. It impressed Andre, and he impressed them with his musical knowledge and recent drug experiences. By now, Andre had begun seeking out others to form a band. One of his brother's friends was a drummer, and he was in the process of persuading Mario to pick up the bass. Rene's drum kit soon became a fixture in Mario's attic, taking up the space where we'd put the D&D table. It didn't matter. We were losing interest in the game as the pressures of our final year of high school mounted.

Andre called me one night to come for rehearsal. He said it would be the first time they had all played together. I was curious, and a little bored, so I said okay. He met me at his front door and didn't allow me to step in. I suddenly realized the only reason he invited me was to carry his amplifier. It was a cold night in early November. We had been getting snow for about three weeks and the sidewalks were slippery. I shifted the small, but surprisingly weighty, speaker cabinet between my two frozen hands.

All the way to Mario's, Andre talked non-stop about what he wanted to do that night, then rambled on about his dreams of stardom. He hadn't decided on a name yet, it was too early for that, but he figured they could quickly get into the emerging death metal scene in Quebec City. He said Rene had been going regularly to the clubs. It would be easy. All they had to do was write about 12 songs and record them. After that, they could start playing shows.

We got to Mario's, and I had to make one last effort to get the amp up the stairs. Andre didn't think of helping me. Instead he warmly greeted his bandmates, who were already helping themselves to a case of Blue that Mario had provided, along with a small baggie containing a couple of fair-sized chunks of hash. For once, I was glad to be offered a toke, and it eased my exhaustion. I melted into a beat-up chair with a beer and watched the trio tentatively set up and check sound levels.

Rene was ready behind the drums but Andre was having trouble getting in tune. Mario wasn't even sure how to tune his bass. For several long, grueling minutes the only sound was a high-pitched *ping-ping-ping* as Andre repeatedly checked the lower strings on his Telecaster. Finally, he looked satisfied, and gave Mario a serious glance. I couldn't believe that Andre was giving orders to a guy we all admired and feared. Andre was definitely in control of whatever this would be. Mario plucked a few choppy notes and shrugged his shoulders. Andre wasn't happy and told him to hand over the bass. He carefully tuned the instrument again, methodically playing the part, I assumed, that Mario was supposed to have practiced.

A tense silence followed. They were ready to start, and I noticed the one thing missing was a microphone. Rene counted in and they launched into something vaguely resembling 1950s rock-and-roll. Rene kept fairly even time while the other two struggled to keep up. Mario was soon completely lost, in the end adding only infrequent bursts of wrong notes. For his part, Andre was playing pretty well, until he tried to solo. He attempted several flashy things we'd seen guys do in videos, with little success. Still, by the time Andre signalled the end, they no longer resembled three stoners, but a group of road-hardened rockers coming offstage after their final encore at the Colisee.

I brought out three fresh beers and passed them around. The guys smiled tentatively as their bodies reabsorbed the rush of energy they had just released. I half-jokingly said something about the song being good but needing a little work. Andre played down the remark with hostility, claiming it was just the first song they'd learned and they had to get it out of the way. A few awkward minutes passed as Andre tuned his guitar some more and the others wondered out loud what to do next.

Mario fooled around with some riffs that resembled "Smoke on the Water" or "Iron Man," I couldn't tell which. Andre suddenly broke in with the chords to the song we had heard the first night we were over to play D&D.

"Guys, you remember that Nirvana tune?" Mario keyed in right away but Rene looked confused.

"I just figured it out the other day," Andre continued. "You know, the one that starts out quiet then gets loud then gets quiet again?" Andre illustrated this by playing the chords again after dramatically stomping on his new distortion pedal. He must have felt good seeing us all look impressed.

"Wait a minute, I'll go put it on." Mario took off his bass and moved to his stereo. He quickly scanned his CD rack and pulled out one with a picture of a baby chasing a dollar bill under water. The sound that came out of the speakers wasn't as loud as Andre's amp, but it was far more powerful. We listened in silence until the final strangled scream trailed off into nothing. I spent the time reading the CD booklet and immediately noticed the resemblance Andre had to the guy in the middle of every picture, who must have been the leader of the band.

He was scrawny, with greasy blonde hair evenly framing his sneering face. In one blurry shot, he gave the photographer the finger. Somehow I felt that that finger was also meant for people like me, people who didn't understand what this was all about. Not yet, anyway. I was turning my back on Andre and he would have given me the finger, too, if it mattered to him. He was building his own world now, a world that no one, not even Sylvie, seemed able to penetrate.

The guys tried running through the song a few times, but it didn't amount to much without vocals. They also tried a few of the metal songs we used to listen to before they packed it in and devoted the remainder of the evening to drinking the rest of the Blue. For the next few hours they talked about what the band should be. Rene wanted to call the band Dogs in Heat, and play death metal like his heroes in Quebec City. Andre didn't seem into that, and talked more about the songs he had been writing. Eventually, he was persuaded to play one or two.

They weren't metal — I couldn't imagine Andre growling out unintelligible lyrics — they were more like that Nirvana song, slow and deliberate with melodies that made his adolescent voice crack when he reached for high registers. The others guys smirked drunkenly as Andre stumbled on his own cumbersome language. At times, it gave me chills, dwelling on the hopelessness we were both feeling.

After each tune, Rene and Mario condescendingly clapped and said, "Bravo." But an uncomfortable silence followed Andre's last song, until it was broken by Andre's question, "You guys ever think what death is like? I mean, all these bands sing about hell but do you think it's really like that?"

We were all shocked out of our stupor.

"That's all bullshit man," Mario said. "Don't you know that it's God's job to keep people from going to hell? If you believe in God at all then he knows you're a good guy and you'll go to heaven. Don't be a jackass." The rest of us laughed cautiously, but Andre still looked troubled.

"Then, why does everyone freak out when somebody kills themselves? Maybe he doesn't even belong in this world, you know? Like, remember Robbie Delorme? If he had died, I bet his parents would have still cashed in. They knew that it was all part of God's great plan to make them rich."

"What's his plan for you?" I asked.

"I don't know, man. Sometimes this place just gets me down, you know? We can pretend to do all this stuff with the band but it's never going to amount to anything unless we get out of here. I've been thinking about moving to the city."

Richard and Serge had just started their first year at Laval and had their own apartment. I figured Andre was thinking of them as his connection to get set up there, so I asked if this was true.

"Yeah, I went to see them last week and they were cool about letting me crash with them for a while, just to see if I can get anything happening." I waited for him to elaborate, and in a few seconds he continued. "I might work on some songs or get a job at a record store. Anything."

"Come on man, you're not serious, are you? You're gonna have to sell that new shit I've been mixing up if you want to survive," Mario said, hardly concealing his joy at this sudden opportunity.

"Well, maybe that's what I'll do then." Another uncomfortable silence followed, until Mario bumped into a table and an empty bottle rolled off. It didn't break.

"I gotta go home Andre," I said. He silently struggled off the couch, chugged the rest of the beer in his hand and mumbled something to Mario about jamming again in a couple of days.

An icy wind greeted us when we hit the street and erased any trace of drunkenness that may have remained. I carried his guitar case this time. Andre emitted occasional grunts over the weight of the amp, and I noticed the plug dragging in the snow. It was too cold to have a normal conversation. I clumsily offered, "You're right man, there is too much death around here. If you want to go to the city, that would be cool."

He laughed. "Of course it would be cool, I just don't know what to do about Sylvie."

"What about your parents?"

"Fuck them. My dad's so far gone now, he doesn't even notice when I leave the house. My mom spends all her time trying to get him to act halfway decent. Michel only comes home to sleep. He's making more money dealing hash than my dad's made in the last three years. There's no room for me here, man." It almost sounded as if he choked up but it was probably the cold. There wasn't really much more to say, so we remained silent until we got to Andre's house. Covered with a fresh layer of snow, the abandoned cars and snowmobiles appeared even more ghostly. All I could think about as we approached the door was what Andre had been saying about his life here. I imagined what could be going on inside, and for some reason felt compelled to investigate. But Andre just took his guitar case from my hand and said he'd see me in school on Monday. I walked home feeling thankful that I could once again put my hands in my pockets. But they never did warm up, not until I got home and put them in front of the wood stove.

I did, in fact, see Andre at school on Monday, and pretty much every day after that until the end of term. He wasn't in class much, though. He'd taken up his brother's position as the school's chief dope dealer and was doing good business. The band finally made its debut in front of everyone at the community centre's New Year's party. By this time, Andre was singing his own songs, as well as a bunch by Nirvana. He had also grown to look even more like that band's leader, Kurt Cobain. Many others had as well, myself included. I hated to admit it, but Andre's tastes still rubbed off on me. Kurt's vacant face and greasy blonde hair were everywhere. It was even more amazing to see flannel shirts and Kodiak boots become essential fashion accessories. For us, they'd always been what you wore to survive the cold.

One day, Andre cornered me by the arena, furious that Serge and Richard had gone to Toronto to see Nirvana play at Maple Leaf Gardens and hadn't even bothered to buy him a ticket. This crisis passed quickly, though, and Andre went back to making regular trips to see the pair in the city. Sometimes he'd take Sylvie, but mostly he'd go alone, hidden vials of Mario's homemade meth paying for the trip. I didn't know anyone who was really doing it, but I guess Mario had a connection somewhere, and people were getting off on it.

I stuck to beer when I was at Mario's, especially after the night when, for a laugh, he spiked Andre's drink with that shit. The band was jamming when Andre began babbling and moving nervously around the room. We panicked, and figured playing a song might focus his energy. He put on his guitar and launched into a maniacal solo. The other guys tried to follow him, creating a deafening slab of noise I'll never forget. Andre came down a couple of hours later and Mario's experiment was deemed a success. Andre wasn't even angry.

Not too many other people had the guts to try the stuff, though. They were content with hash that came from God knows where — I could never be bothered to find out, but it never stopped coming. All winter, Andre sold meth in Quebec City and split the profits with Mario. Andre took his share and bought a car, which made the weekly trips a lot easier. It was an old blue Chevette with a standard transmission and the first signs of rust showing on the frame. Andre would drive me and whoever else to school just because he could, and I guess everyone was impressed. Everyone else with a license drove their fathers' old pickups.

Andre said he was ready to move to the city as soon as Richard and Serge finished their final exams. They were going to stay down there and work, so they decided they could all get an apartment with the help of Andre's drug money. It seemed like a pretty good plan.

Then came that Friday afternoon in early April. I'd just come home from school, satisfied that I was one week closer to the summer. I grabbed a Coke from the fridge and turned on MuchMusic. There was a Nirvana video on, so I turned it up. Then the veejay came on and said Kurt Cobain had stuck a shotgun in his mouth and blown his brains out.

I thought of Andre and wondered if he'd heard the news. I waited to hear more facts before I called him. There were the mystery stomach pains, and the suicide note: "In the words of Neil Young, it's better to burn out than fade away." He'd been dead for days before they found him and his wife, Courtney Love, was unavailable for comment.

I got on the phone but Andre's mother said he'd already gone to Quebec City for the weekend.

2 Andre
Quebec City: May 7, 1994.

Rich and Serge say I can live at their place for as long as I need to. Famous last words. It's right near campus so it's close to work, and it isn't that bad, I guess. I mean, I've never lived anywhere else, so what do I know? I miss Sylvie like crazy, but there's no way her parents would ever let her live with me, even if that's what she wanted. At least they care about what she does. My parents didn't even ask how long I'd be gone. It didn't matter, all I took was my clothes, my tapes, my guitar shit, some food. But it would have been nice if they had at least, you know, wondered. The first thing I bought was a futon, which seemed better than sleeping on the guys' couch. They have everything else, like appliances and a TV and other things I hardly use. I have to be out on the street most of the day if I want to make any money. Word got around fast about Mario's stuff, so I can pretty much work as hard as I want.

The guys haven't given me a hassle about anything yet, as long as I keep the stash out of sight and make sure no one phones while they're asleep. They work during the day at a campus coffee shop, which they tell me isn't all that tough because there aren't many students around during the summer. But when they come home, all they do is bitch about having nothing to do. Actually, most nights after I come home, we just sit around, drink beer and listen to music.

I'm starting to think my parents were right, that I'm completely useless. The band was a fucking disaster. All Rene wants to play is death metal, and Mario can't even remember three chords. I ended up selling my gear the second week I was here. I couldn't bring myself to play anymore, but what pissed me off most was that I only got about half of what I paid for all that shit. I tried telling the guy at the music store that I had the same distortion pedal that Kurt used, but he didn't care. I came close to taking the money and scoring some heroin, but I stood by my decision not to get high. It's bad enough selling this shit to survive, especially to kids. I don't need the extra grief of doing it myself.

I can't stop wondering if Kurt felt that way, too. Did it cross his mind that his depression was being transmitted to everyone who listened to him? Maybe offing himself was the only unselfish thing left. It makes sense to me, but people don't want the truth. It's all in the fucking music, and I still listen to that shit every day. In fact, if I didn't have my walkman, I don't know what I'd do, having to deal with all the downtown trash. The kids are okay, and once in a while I'll meet someone with a Nirvana T-shirt who at least can carry on an intelligent conversation. If it wasn't for the music, I swear I'd kill someone sooner or later.

That's probably as good a reason as any for taking myself out. It's only a matter of time. Just the other day I heard about a kid who jumped off the Jacques Cartier Bridge with Nirvana in his walkman. It seems so obvious, but for some reason I can't bring myself to do the same thing. I cross bridges every day, and find myself feeling dizzy now that the rivers are flowing again. I could be carried out by the St. Lawrence into the ocean, and never be seen again. But then, I could just as easily jump in front of a bus. I'm also starting to see more and more guns on the street and I'm torn about getting one. What's the point when I'd ultimately just use it on myself? I'm sure Kurt had the same argument with himself, which is why the only bullet I want in my head is the same one he put in his.

I guess what it comes down to is, if I won't be remembered for how I lived, I might as well be remembered for how I died. In a way I have to admire all those guys who've jumped off bridges, just for having the guts. But what did they ultimately accomplish? Years from now, people will dig up the newspaper articles — "Copycat suicides, claiming that Cobain's death pushed them over the edge." I can't be a part of that. Kurt's life was worth much more to me. It was worth more than what all the newspapers and tabloids said about him. What it meant was something I can't put into words, something beyond being a product or a lifestyle that was sold to me. I have to explain that somehow.

The only way I can see doing that is death. All society wants is famous corpses. The more that pile up, the more product gets sold. But we're the ones buying the stuff and if we're gone, well, the whole fucking system goes to hell. It's logical, isn't it? The only problem is figuring out how to make a statement without looking crazy, which rules out jumping off a building or a bridge. The more you suffer, the more others will suffer with you. Like, when I was a kid, I remember hearing about IRA hunger strikers on the news, or Tibetan monks setting themselves on fire. Sure, they died for a cause, but the point is, everyone remembers. Mario always said the coolest way to go out would be driving a 1967 Cadillac El Dorado convertible into the Grand Canyon with The Doors' "L.A. Woman" playing on the tape deck right at the "Mr. Mojo rising" part.

My car is the only thing of value I have anymore, so it needs to be involved somehow. I think everyone understands that it's a symbol of freedom, and that's what's ultimately important, right? I mean, those guys in *Easy Rider* bought it on the road and that was pretty cool. There was another of my dad's favourite movies, but I can't remember the title. All I remember is there's this guy driving a souped-up Challenger or something, and he's on the run from the cops in the desert. The best way they can think of stopping him is by blocking the highway with two giant bulldozers, but he didn't think twice about slowing down.

I could crash my car, too, but then you run the risk of ending up paralyzed. That would suck. I don't want to burn to death either, that would look too evil, and I'm through with Satanic shit. It's fun for a while, but one day you realize you don't have the guts to go all the way. I've heard there are guys out there actually sacrificing cats and dogs. Who wants to get caught up in that? No, whatever I do has to be pure. People have to see how an innocent boy has been corrupted by their sick society. It's not just an act of rebellion, it's a condemnation of the values they hold dear. Everyone who tries to change the world dies doing it.

I finally tried explaining this to Richard and Serge the other week, when one of them asked why I'd been so quiet. They must have thought I was nuts, because they both laughed. That's just like them, I suppose. Ever since they've been here at university they look down on everything connected with back home, including me. It doesn't really bother me because I'm the same way, but they make me feel like an idiot a lot of the time. They're definitely not any smarter than I am, no matter what shit they learn in class.

They liked my idea of going on a trip, though, kind of like a farewell tour. I figured they would. All we ever talk about is going someplace where we can at least imagine ourselves having fun. Most often, we talk about Toronto and walking up and down Yonge Street, like those guys did on their hockey trips. And stopping in at the strip club that wouldn't let Rich in. We'll pound down six or seven beers, then take a bunch of the dancers back to our hotel and fuck the shit out of them.

We've also talked about going to New York or Boston, somewhere where we can score some premium dope, and then hit a club with a kick-ass band. We'll offer them some of our stash, then they'll take us on for the rest of the tour, with backstage passes every night.

We talk about corny shit, too, like seeing the sun come up over the Rocky Mountains. Come to think of it, there are tons of things we want to see. We were taught that a lot of our ancestors were forced out of the country around the time of the Plains of Abraham, and they went down to Louisiana. I guess that's how Mardi Gras got started. I hear they still speak French down there and that New Orleans is a lot like Quebec City, except the bars are filled with transvestites and you can see live orgies onstage.

Then there's Seattle. We're all in agreement, we have to get there eventually. I don't really know what's it's like, but we have to see the city that was Kurt's home, although I already explained to them that I don't want us to seem like those blind morons who go there looking for some kind of answer. I know the answer, and as soon as I figure out a way to express it, we'll all be free. Rich said we'd probably be better off going to Las Vegas, where we could at least get legal hookers. I said, yeah, what the hell? Let's try everything, just as if a doctor told us we have six months to live.

One of Kurt's songs I play all the time is called "I Hate Myself And I Want To Die." Serge called me a nihilist for agreeing. I had to look it up. I guess it means I'm filled with self-loathing, that I don't believe in anything. He also said I'm afraid of living. I told him to look around. Just about everyone is afraid of living. I'm not. And I'm also not afraid of dying. I want to live so much on the journey we're going to take that it would be pointless to try to live any more when it's over. I felt like a fucking preacher saying that to them, and I think that's what finally convinced them to go. Suddenly, both of them wanted to be nihilists, too. We all have grown to love the word, actually. I've never really thought of myself as an *-ist* before — it's kind of cool.

The next thing I know, Rich pulls out this overpriced atlas he had to buy for geography class, and we're spending the rest of the night planning a route. They started kidding around about going back home one more time to say goodbye. I actually thought that was a perfect place to start. I haven't seen Sylvie in nearly three weeks, and a part of me is aching for her. I don't have to say which part.

The two of us have everything in common, but most of the time I treat her like shit. She sticks by everything I do, though, not like other girls I've known. Richard was so pussy-whipped when I first got here, I thought the phone was welded to his ear. Serge has never had a girlfriend as far as I know. I can tell because when we talk about sex, he just nods and smiles, pretending to understand what I'm saying. Sometimes, he turns away in disgust, just for a split second, when my stories get more graphic.

I've never done any of that stuff to Sylvie, though, and I've never said I did. She doesn't deserve to be degraded that way. She's a saint. I don't know how I'm going to tell her about what I want to do.

Rich has already told his girl, Anne-Marie, that we're going on a trip that should last about a month. I yelled, "Don't bet on it," when I heard him explaining it to her over the phone, but he ignored me. I figured she asked him why she wasn't allowed to come along when he said, "Honey, this is a guy thing. We've got to blow off some steam after living together through this year. Exams were a bitch. You know how it is." I gave him a smile and a thumbs-up when I heard that. This was the first sign of balls I'd seen on him. As long as they're along for the ride, things will come together eventually.

We marked out all the stops once the route was settled. We're going back home first to say goodbye, then we'll come back here to close up shop and hit the Megadeth concert at the Colisee. Serge has had tickets for over a month, so it would be pretty stupid to bail. It'll make for a good going-away party, too.

It's a full month since Kurt died, and I can't wait any longer. I don't have any loose ends to tie up, and I keep telling Rich he doesn't have to pay the rent anymore. I'm hoping nobody breaks into the apartment while we're gone, but I guess that doesn't matter either. It does remind me that at some point I should make a will. One night a while ago, we actually talked about who would get our stuff if we kicked off. It's surprising how you never decide these things when you're young. Who would want all our crap, though? It's mostly just odds and ends and old, worn-out clothes. What would anyone do with it?

While still thinking about this, I tell the guys to pack their shit now, because I don't want to stick around any longer than we have to after the concert. I'm still too worried that they might chicken out.

The Friday morning we leave is chilly for May, even though spring is in full bloom around our block. I get up before the others to get the car ready. I'd forgotten about it as we made the other preparations, until last Wednesday when it wouldn't turn over. I had to spend $300 to have the starter replaced. Cars have a way of making you believe in God. They're capable of instantly wiping out your life, or at least reviving your survival instincts if you're stranded on the side of the road in the middle of nowhere. I guess that's why I see so many crucifixes and rosaries hanging from rear-view mirrors.

I always travel light and I'm urging the other guys to do likewise — the Chevette never could be called a luxury car. I've limited them to sleeping bags and all they can stuff into their knapsacks. Rich has a Coleman stove and some cooking utensils that include a small pot, forks, spoons, knives, a small kettle for boiling water, mugs and bowls.

Serge is bringing a cooler because he and Rich still drink a lot of beer. I'm giving it up, since I'll be doing most of the driving and I can't afford to get pulled over. He's also bringing his ghetto blaster, and a travel case with about 25 tapes. I figure we'll get sick of them before long, but there's no point in saying so.

As I warm up the car, Rich pisses me off immediately by going back for one last look around the apartment. He returns with a smile that gives away the enthusiasm none of us want to express out loud. He and Serge play rock-paper-scissors to decide who's going to ride shotgun. Rich wins, rock beats scissors. Serge complains that he's cramped in the back seat, but I shut him up when I tell him that means he's in charge of the music. He puts on Black Sabbath's "Paranoid" as I pull the car out of the parking lot and swing it north through downtown.

The extra weight proves to be a strain on the engine. I hadn't expected that. It takes some effort to get into fourth gear but it begins to relax when the speedometer finally approaches 100 klicks. We're on the Trans-Canada running through the suburbs, six lanes of anonymous asphalt walled-in by concrete and the constant stream of other vehicles. This is now our home.

It isn't long before we reach the exit that takes us back to La

Forest. It's just a two-lane highway that cuts through some boring countryside. But on this morning, the first signs of spring warm me as we roll past an endless succession of farms specked with unusable, rusting machinery. I try to take in as much of this glorious scene as I can while the guys attempt to carry on a front-seat/back-seat conversation without much success. The initial roar of the car's small engine has settled into a consistent purr, but it's still annoying hearing them repeat almost everything they say. It doesn't help that Serge has the radio blasting as well. Music still takes precedence.

Once they chill out a bit, the drive becomes a breeze. Every little detail on this stretch of road triggers a memory. Most of them aren't worth mentioning, except maybe the truckstop that kind of marks the halfway point. That was where, one day, Sylvie found a $50 bill when we stopped on our way to the city. We'd just walked out after having lunch, and I went to the phone booth to make a call. When I came out, she was standing there holding the bill between her first and second fingers and waving it at me with a childish grin on her face. She said some trucker must have dropped it. I asked her if he'd dropped it in her underwear, which, not surprisingly, ruined the rest of the day.

Just then, Rich asks me what I'm going to do when I see her again. It's a shocking coincidence that leaves me silent for several seconds. All I manage to say is, "I don't know, man." I can tell that the guys are secretly hoping Sylvie will snap me out of wanting to destroy myself. They don't believe I'll do it with her still in the picture, but I'm way past that now.

As always, the first thing we see when we approach the town are the fumes from the mill. People just keep burning up their lives in there. Of course, no one bothered to decide what we were going to do when we arrived, so there are a few tense moments until I direct the car toward Rich's house, the closest one. I figure we can get a free lunch, because Rich's mom is one of those housewives who's devoted her entire life to her kids.

Sure enough, she appears at the screen door wearing an apron and warmly invites us in. She's right in the middle of preparing soup and sandwiches for Rich's little brothers, who are still in high school. As we remove our shoes, she gives both her eldest son and Serge a peck on the cheek. I get a forced hello. I've never been good with other peoples' parents.

We sit at the big kitchen table, me at the head with Serge on my left. Rich takes his regular spot. His mom calls to Guy and Raymond, and the two boys appear from the living room where they were watching TV. We're given our bowls and then a choice of sandwiches from an enormous platter that's placed in the centre of the table. Rich never realized how good he had it.

There's the expected small talk as Rich's brothers seem genuinely interested in his progress at Laval. He tells them how he did on his finals, and the other stupid shit about campus life I've heard dozens of times already. During a lull, he finally decides to drop the big news of our trip. Actually, Rich's mom forces it out of us after her habitual window-gazing picks up on the overloaded car in her driveway.

"Are you boys going on vacation or something?"

"Well, yeah, Mom, that's kinda what I wanted to tell you. You know, school's over, so we got the idea of going out west for a few weeks, just to blow off a little steam, eh?"

"Oh," she hesitates. Her son has been out of the house for a year now, so it's painfully obvious she's learned to let go a bit. It's also obvious by the look she gives him that she doesn't approve. "I hope you haven't forgotten anything," she manages.

"No, um, I don't think so." I try hard to enjoy the food, but the sudden tension ruins my appetite. Rich starts scrambling for the right words. "We're just going to be camping and sightseeing, nothing big. I'll call whenever you want me to."

The next ten minutes feel like an eternity as we polish off every scrap of food on the table. Serge and I keep glancing at each other to make sure we finish at the same time. At that moment, we both slowly get up and Serge says he has to see his parents. Rich can't hide his anxiety and awkwardly shows us out. His mother maintains a stony silence and watches our every move. I tell Rich I'm going to see Sylvie tonight and I'll call him in the morning. As he sighs in agreement, I get the impression he doesn't want to be left alone with his parents. Serge adds that he'll try to come back later but can't promise anything. I imagine his folks probably will want him there all night, too.

Serge gets into the passenger side with genuine relief. He leans the seat all the way back like he's in his dad's La-Z-Boy after Thanksgiving dinner. The car is warm and starts like a gem. We sputter out of the driveway and head to Serge's house, by the arena, five minutes away. His mom is working in the front garden when we pull up and she gives us a big smile and wave. She's another great mother, but Serge is her only child. This time I don't want to be around when he explains the trip. I don't have a reason to stay anyway, so I repeat that I'll call him in the morning and leave him standing in the driveway with his knapsack after giving his mom a courtesy wave.

I don't want to go home. They aren't expecting me. They'll automatically think something is wrong and give me the third degree. I'm not up for that. I want to see Sylvie.

I pull into the donut shop and sit down to think things over with a cup of coffee. Eventually, I decide to call her, but as I'm dialing I realize it's mid-afternoon and she's still at school. I sit there for the next two hours, cranking myself up higher on caffeine. Since I stopped getting high, coffee is my only addiction. Most of the time I feel like I'm immune to it, but right now I can feel the veins pumping in my left hand.

She'll be home by five. By that time, the clock is moving backwards. I get on the phone at the stroke of the hour. It rings three times and her mother picks up. She says Sylvie just walked in the door and is in the bathroom. I'm too nervous to call back, and ask if I can hold. She sounds out of breath when she finally gets the phone.

"Hello?"

"Hi, it's me. I'm back for the weekend."

"God, thanks for telling me. You don't call for two weeks and suddenly you show up and expect me to drop everything just like that? Maybe I'm busy."

"Baby, don't play that game. I've got to talk to you. Can I come over, or can you come down to the donut shop?"

"We're eating now, I'll ask my mom." There's silence for a few seconds. "She's setting a place for you. Leave now."

I don't care that she's pissed, I'm just glad to see her again. It's good to get another free meal, too, even if I have to endure more stress from her parents. We get along fine, but I always knew they hoped their daughter would wise up and dump me before she got to university. I figured it would happen, too.

After the meal, Sylvie instinctively begins doing the dishes, so I help her as her family retreats to different rooms. I ask what she wants to do tonight. She doesn't know. I suggest going to the community centre and playing a little pool. She nods.

The community centre was created to keep kids off the streets. You could always shoot pool, play video games, watch movies in the lounge, and every Saturday they would get a DJ for a dance party. It also turned out to be the perfect place to do drug deals and make out. We arrive and sit in a corner of the lounge where *Back To The Future* is just starting on the big-screen TV. I buy a couple of Cokes, which doesn't help my caffeine buzz, and prepare to tell Sylvie about the trip.

"Why do you have all your stuff in the car?" she asks, before I get the chance.

"That's what I wanted to tell you. Serge, Rich and I are going out west for a while." I feel a scene coming on before I even get the words out.

"What? But you just got back. You don't call me for two weeks and now we're not going to spend any time together? You're a real fucking prince, you know that?"

"I know, I'm sorry. There's more to it than that. I can't live here anymore. We're going out to scope out some new things. When we find something cool, I'll come back and get you and we can get out of here forever." I hate lying to her, but I know she'll never leave this town. At least not now, not under these circumstances. She's heading for great things; I'm not, and that's that. She starts to cry, and I have to deal with it. Fortunately, the few others watching the movie don't give a shit.

She pulls herself together and says, "I can't stand being away from you like this. I worry about you out on the streets. I mean, it's one thing to be the big hustler around here, but you can't live like that in the city. I can't live like that."

"I know. That's why I have to find something else and you have to keep doing your thing. One day everything will be all right. Let's get out of here." We go into the other room with the empty pool table and sit on the couch. Time drags on and it feels like I could hold her for the rest of the night. But soon people I haven't seen in a long time come in and the small talk gets grating. I take Sylvie out to the car and we sit in silence for several minutes.

"Have you seen your parents?" she finally asks.

"No. And I don't plan to either." I leave it at that, and trust that she understands. I know she just wants to break the silence. I finally suggest going to the cemetery behind St. Joseph's, always a popular make-out spot. We haven't been there since last summer, and I fully expect her to reject the idea, but she nods weakly while turning to look out the window. After parking at the dark church, we walk behind it into the yard marked with gravestones dating back to Confederation. Whenever I've come here I've always been careful in choosing which stones to sit at, but it's too dark to read. I head straight to the large one near the top of the hill where the final rays of sunset can still be seen. We don't speak at all. The babbling creek is all I hear, and I think about who else might be lurking. Maybe Marcel is here with someone, too, running his hand up her thigh, exploring her mouth with his tongue.

The thought turns me on. I reach my hand to Sylvie's cheek and brush her straight blonde hair from her eyes. I move in for a kiss and she willingly accepts it. This is the best I've felt in months. My hand moves down to her small, firm breasts and lingers there until the obscene feelings overtake me and I move down to the wet spot on her jeans. This causes her to start running her fingers through my hair and up and down my back. At these moments I can't help but feel proud that I'm the only guy Sylvie has ever been with. I've always respected her virginity, but for some reason, I choose this moment to make a case to go all the way.

I also tell her that I love her for the first time. She pulls back and stares at me for several seconds before replying, "Do you?"

"Well, yeah, haven't you been waiting for me to say that?" She sees right through me.

"I don't want you to go so soon. Why can't we talk about what we really want? I'm not going to have sex just because you're leaving."

I think about what I really want, and it's her. "I don't know what I want. What do you want?" Copping out so quickly, I'm ashamed.

"Right now, I just want to be happy, and the only way that will happen is if you're happy," she says. "I'll be going away, too, at the end of the summer, and I want you to go with me."

All I can say is, yes, I'll go away with you, and we hold each other in silence once again. My gaze turns to the emerging stars and I recall the countless hours I've spent staring at them. But I also remember the bodies buried beneath us and I wonder whether they're actually up there in the heavens, looking down. The sexual urge disappears. Sylvie's head is on my chest, and after a few minutes I think she's asleep. Then she stirs and asks me where I'll be spending the night. I say I might as well stay here. It seemed funny to me, but she doesn't laugh. I tell her I can always stay at Mario's. He's expecting me anyway.

We get up, dust ourselves off and walk back to my car. I don't want this to be the last time I see Sylvie, but for some reason I think it will be. She's living in the future and I'm living in the present. It stands to reason that two such beings cannot coexist. Like Kurt said, *I'm not gonna crack.*

The streets are deserted as we drive to Sylvie's house. I estimate we were out for three hours after we pass the youth centre and see only a few stragglers hanging outside the closed front doors, looking to make one last score. As I'm pulling into the driveway, Sylvie asks if I feel like coming in for a while. I don't, but remember I still need to call Mario. Her kitchen lights up in an eerie fluorescent glow as I reach for the phone. Mario picks up after one ring, and straight off he says he's preparing the stash that's going to finance the trip. He sounds fucking wired, so I just tell him I'm coming over and hang up. Sylvie looks unbelievably gorgeous leaning back against the sink, all sleepy-eyed, with tussled hair and her T-shirt clinging to her torso. I indulge in one more momentary thought of groping her.

"Will you call me tomorrow?" she asks.

"Yes," I say. We hug like children and I make my way to Mario's.

He shows me in, still blathering a mile a minute about how the process is going. I'm far too tired to hear about it and try to get comfortable on a recliner that now occupies the corner of the attic where the drums used to be. I wake up to a strong chemical smell, which makes me turn down his offer of coffee. Mario has been working through the night, and the room is littered with empty bottles of ephedrine, beakers and dishes we stole from chemistry class, and lots of other shit I'm afraid to know about. I'm in awe of his efficiency.

The room is now a full-blown meth lab, with only a few Hendrix and Zeppelin posters left to remind me of what it once was. Mario has actually convinced his parents they cannot enter without his permission. They're beyond senile anyway. He could say he was building a nuclear warhead in here and they wouldn't blink.

He continues to work throughout the day as we negotiate our deal. He's going to give me four ounces to start, which I presume will see us to the border. His cut will be 50 per cent, but he says he'll understand if I need some extra cash to get out of a jam. Once. I tell him there's no chance of that. He'll be getting back thousands.

As soon as he receives the cash, he'll send the next shipment by courier to the post office in Royal Oak, Michigan — a suburb of Detroit — where we'll pick it up. I try not to show my discomfort with this arrangement, and he assures me he's done it loads of times. If they ask any questions, all we have to do is pretend we're tourists picking up a care package from our parents. Mario keeps reminding me to start working on my English, too, and by the third time, I'm ready to punch his fucking teeth out.

Crossing back into Canada won't be a problem, he insists, as long as we stay out of trouble. He warns me about going to Vancouver, but I tell him I'll send back the money as soon as the stash is gone. It takes some convincing for him to believe we're coming back.

Mario assembles the package as I go to my car to retrieve the empty tote bag I brought along to carry it. On his advice, I've also picked up a moneybelt. He said that most guys who go for your wallet in a pinch are happy if they make off with a couple hundred bucks. Always keep a little bit of money in your wallet, but keep the rest in the belt. To get at that, he said, they have to kill you. He warned me not to carry a weapon, though, especially in the States. I resisted the urge to tell him that having a gun would probably be the worst thing for me. I'd never been in a spot that I couldn't talk my way out of, so I wasn't really worried. Mario thinks I should do whatever the buyers tell me to do in the States, because they'll probably find my accent funny. They'll all be wanting to impress the other homies by hanging with a real live French guy. If I did something aggressive, though, they'd whack me for sure. Who wants to be ordered around by a frog, right?

We discuss other possible scenarios for the rest of the afternoon: dealing with cops, the border guards, American slang. It gets to the point that I want to leave right then. After noticing the time, though, I remember to call the guys. We make plans to meet at the youth centre for the weekly dance party. I'm not that interested in going, but I agree, since this will undoubtedly be my last opportunity to see everyone. I know Sylvie is waiting to hear from me, too, and I eventually get the better of my fear of seeing her again. I call and tell her I'll pick her up at eight.

As I'm on the phone, Mario brings up some food — grilled cheese sandwiches and Kraft Dinner. He mentions that my brother will be coming over to get high and watch the Canadiens/ Nordiques play-off game. I shrug and tell him I've just made plans for the night. I love my brother, but he always was the biggest loser in town. I haven't seen him since Christmas, but I assume he's still scamming workman's comp and using half of it to fry his brain. Good for him. As much as I need Mario's help, I despise everything he and my brother represent. I don't blame them for how they live, I just hold them responsible for making me exactly like them. They used to be my idols, but now they're pathetic, pretending they're still the baddest guys in town. That's my future, too, and I can't escape it.

Sylvie is waiting at the door when I pull up. She's wearing a short black skirt, black stockings and my old leather jacket. Her hair is teased and her eyes and lips are lined with black. She tears into me for wearing the same clothes I had on yesterday. I calmly tell her I slept in them. I don't give in to her petty anger, I'm already on the road.

I hate dancing and I especially don't want to tonight. Sylvie seems to understand. I talk to a few people but ask more questions than I answer. What I do make sure to tell them is what they want to hear: "Yeah, I've been busy. The city's cool. Great clubs, great bands. I'm going back tomorrow." Nobody needs to know anything else.

I need a place to stay again and Rich obliges. We have to leave early, I say. I drive Sylvie home and kiss her several times in the car. She asks me to come in and I say no, but not without a lot of guilt.

She cries but eventually gets out. She stands stationary in my headlights, waving like a moron as I back out of the driveway. I drive to Rich's and collapse, fully clothed again, on his guest bed. I'm such an asshole.

3 Serge
Montreal: May 9, 1994.

The phone wakes me around nine. It's Rich saying he and Andre will be picking me up in a half-hour. It's so good sleeping in my own bed that I've almost forgotten the trip. As I refresh my memory, I replay last night in my head and realize what an ass I am for not making a move on Chantal. What the hell happened? One minute I'm talking to her, and the next minute I'm heading home. "I've got to get up early tomorrow." Jesus Christ.

Whatever. Today's the first day of the rest of my life and all that shit. I should just get ready. When Andre says he'll be somewhere, he'll be there, on time. My parents are up to go to church, so breakfast is waiting for me. I inhale a plate of scrambled eggs, bacon and toast as my mother lays into me about why Andre can't wait until church is over. She's on the verge of tears. I give her some lame answer about being on a tight schedule. None of us have been to church since we've moved out, and I'm not about to start now. In a way, I kind of regret it. Who knows, maybe it really helps when you're ready to kick. But I really don't miss it at all. There have been too many Sunday mornings where I've been glad to sleep until noon. I couldn't have talked Andre into doing it anyway. His mother will be there, and I know he doesn't want to see her.

The Chevette pulls up just as I down the last of my orange juice, and I grab my knapsack. It's strange, but I feel a change come over me. It's as if my parents are suddenly out of my life for good, and whatever I do from now on isn't their concern. I'm just a normal guy doing normal guy stuff.

My parents stand beside the car as Andre and Rich help me load my gear into the hatchback. My mother hugs me, and my dad says something predictably lame before they both go back inside. I take one last look as they linger in the doorway — they're just two people I happen to know. Rich and I play rock-paper-scissors again for shotgun and this time I win. Scissors beats paper. Rich is excited but Andre seems moody and tired. I ask him jokingly if he's okay to drive. He says he'll be fine once he has a couple coffees. There is no argument about making that our top priority.

Sunday mornings are the only time when the donut shop is empty, at least until after church, and that's not a bad thing. The rush of escaping town is making me jumpy. Apparently, Rich and Andre have had breakfast as well, so we just order coffees and get right into talking about the dance. Rich starts up by bugging me about flirting with Chantal. "I'm telling you, it was a sure thing, man," I say. "Why'd you drag me out of there?"

"It was for your own good, pal. You know she just broke up with Pete. He was ready to kick your ass if you touched her."

"Yeah, but she was all over me."

"Bullshit! She was so drunk she would have slept with Andre. Ain't that right?" Andre is still drowsy and responds with an inattentive nod. It's clear that he's had a hard night without much sleep.

"How'd things go with Sylvie, anyway?" Rich asks.

Andre takes a long gulp from his mug before saying, "Well, you know, there was no easy way to do it. She's got her life to live, I've got mine."

"You'll get together again," I say. Neither of them respond.

Andre buys another coffee to go and we get on the road back to Quebec City. The weather is still good. It's getting warmer every day; a good omen. Rich puts on a Megadeth tape in preparation for the concert tonight, and it perks up Andre even more. There's no traffic, so he pushes the car in time with the music and even starts tapping his hands on the wheel along with the drum fills. Whatever happened last night must already be fading into memory.

The sun beams right on us, eventually making the car unbearable. I have to put an end to the music by rolling my window down, the onrushing air briefly bringing relief from the stifling heat. But my euphoria doesn't last long — the lack of conversation forces me into inane thoughts. Why *do* dogs always stick their heads out of car windows? I roll mine back up just in time for "Symphony of Destruction," and we all reflexively bang our heads.

I savour the moment, but at the same time, the immensity of the trip weighs on me. There are thousands of miles of unknown territory to cover. We are driving across a continent, a huge portion of the earth's land mass. We are going to see things our families only know from TV, and most of them will pass us by with little more than a glimpse. As all this settles on my mind, I turn to look out the window and begin concentrating on the landscape. Like the song says, *this land was made for me* — and there it goes, at 120 kilometres an hour.

Every time a new song starts, Rich says something like, "I'll bet they'll play this." I respond, "Yeah man, that'd be cool," or, "No way, that's a piece of shit." I can sense Rich trying to enjoy these early moments of the trip, too, but deep down I know his heart isn't in it. He wants to be with his chick, or even at home with his mom. One of the saddest things I ever saw was the look on his mother's face the day we left for university. The funny thing is, he was just as broken up as she was. They must have stood there crying and hugging each other for five minutes while my parents and I waited in the van. It was embarrassing. He'll do anything for anybody, and that's why I know he's partly going on this trip to please Andre. Rich really does admire him.

We reach the outskirts of the city by late afternoon. Andre wants to determine exactly what the plan is, which leads to some tension. Rich suggests hanging out at the apartment but Andre disagrees. He doesn't want to see that dump again, he says. Apparently, the road is our home now. Andre looks tired again, so I say something about stopping for food. "You can rest for a while. Rich and I can slam down a few beers before the show." This makes some sense to him, so he turns the car in the direction of the closest tavern, which happens to be in a strip mall a few blocks away.

Once inside, Rich and I order burgers while Andre gets some poutine. He finishes it quickly, then goes out to the car to sleep, leaving the two of us to drink our beer. It's been kind of a tradition for us to get wasted before a concert. Like when we saw Nirvana in Toronto. We both got so shitfaced on the bus down there that we had to piss in the empties. The driver would have known something was up if we'd gone to the bathroom every five minutes. I eventually pissed on the floor by accident. We howled like maniacs as the stream flowed under the seats around us.

After guzzling about four Laurentides each, we've got a good buzz going for Megadeth. We piss and pay the tab, then notice we've been there for nearly an hour, leaving not a lot of time to get to the Colisee before the show starts. We run out to the car and see Andre curled up in the back seat like a baby. We rap on the window and he wakes with a start. He's a little grumpy at first, but laughs when he notices how loaded we are. Rich cranks the ghetto blaster up all the way, making Andre wince, but he still manages to guide the car out of the parking lot.

It's a shorter ride than I anticipate, and we find a spot on a side street two blocks from the arena. I say something about getting a ticket but Andre ignores me. He's more concerned about the possibility of someone ripping off our stuff. I think about the drugs we're carrying. Andre obviously can't take the tote bag into the show, so he spends several minutes poking around the interior for a safe place to stash it. He explains that if someone breaks in, they can take anything but the bag, which doesn't exactly sit well with us. Eventually, he raises the hood and quickly stuffs the bag into a small crevice behind the engine block.

With that done, we make our way to the Colisee. Andre seems fully content now and jostles with us after we rib him about his foul mood. The lights of the marquee come into view and scalpers approach from all angles. Guys and girls with obscenely long hair and leather outfits line the streets, some smoking joints right out in the open. Camaros and Trans Ams roar by, stereos competing for airspace. We linger out front for a while, absorbing the atmosphere, but the anticipation forces us inside.

As our tickets are ripped, security guards frisk us from top to bottom. I'm not concerned for myself, so I watch Andre undergo the procedure. His guy is taking his time, which reveals the money belt. I can't hear Andre's explanation, but it evidently suits the guard just fine. We check out the T-shirts and discuss buying one, but ultimately we take a pass in favour of some munchies to feed our buzz. I can't believe how hungry I am, even after the burger.

The floor of the arena doesn't have any chairs. We're too late to get to the front of the stage, but we get to the middle of the crowd, moving carefully so as not to bump into the wrong person. There are plenty to watch out for. Guys as big as Andre's Chevette, wearing leather jackets that must have been made out of a whole cow and adorned with all manner of Satanic symbols, although much of the leather is covered by yards of hair.

We stake out a good spot with a clear view of the stage. Soon after, the opening band comes on and breaks in our ears. We don't recognize them, but they rock, and that's all that really matters in the state we're in. Every head around us is banging and after forty-five minutes, they finish to an enthusiastic response. The lights come on to reveal a fully packed arena and a solid wall of humanity behind us. Andre mumbles about feeling claustrophobic, and it triggers something that makes me want to puke.

I try to force my way through the crowd as quickly as I can. I guess it's a common ploy to fake sickness to get up to the front. This time, however, I'm going in the opposite direction and people instinctively clear a path. I run up the steps of the closest exit and hunt for a bathroom like a rabbit dodging cars on the highway. There is a slow-moving line to my left, which provides an answer. As I approach, someone yells out that a guy is about to puke. Enough people move aside, allowing me to rush by. I nearly spew on a guy just coming out of a stall, but he gets out of the way in time for me to fall forward onto the cold, damp porcelain. After cleaning up and composing myself, the arena comes into complete focus. I'm suddenly sober, moving calmly among the throng of people grabbing quick smokes. I keep thinking I'll eventually bump into someone I know, but everyone looks the same. I don't enjoy living in the city; too many people and too many dangers. Actually, there's usually nothing to fear as long as you don't go looking for trouble. Andre was in the middle of it every day, and nothing ever happened to him. One time he came home with a black eye and some cuts, but he said it was nothing he couldn't handle.

I guess I've just been messed up by all the stuff my parents told me when I was growing up. One day, you reach a certain age and everything becomes a threat. Then you inflict your paranoia on everyone you know. I don't want that. I don't want to get old.

I rejoin Rich and Andre just in time for Megadeth's set. I tell them about puking, and they have a good laugh. The tension around us escalates when Megadeth comes onstage. The noise is deafening — mostly it's the screaming around us — and people start slamming right from the first chord. It feels great, though. This is what it's all about. We notice some guys crowd-surfing in front of us, so Andre motions that we should lift up Rich. He isn't suspecting a thing when we bend down and raise him by the ankles just enough for people around us to lend a hand. We all give him a push forward, and I see him bounce three times on the bed of hands before his body finds a hole and he's sucked under. What a beautiful thing.

We all have several turns on the waves of humanity after that. Psychologists should start setting up mosh pits in group therapy. I can't imagine a way to feel closer to complete strangers. By the end, we're all completely drained and dehydrated. The band's crew has been spraying water over us throughout the show, but we still need to get some inside. Mercifully, the concession stands are prepared and the three of us drink down several paper cups of water like it was champagne on New Year's Eve.

No one is in a big hurry to leave, so we hang out for a bit, just looking around one last time. I recall the hockey games I've seen here and all the excitement that went along with them. Hockey used to be my life, but after a while it seemed pointless. The players are now my age, some even younger, and they've accomplished the one thing they've always wanted to do. I can't relate. I mean, their lives are basically over when they get to that point. They play hockey every day, and will continue for at least the next ten years. Then what? The game didn't make sense when I thought about it like that. They aren't heroes, they're regular guys like me, doing a job. Their world is for little kids, just like rock and roll, I guess. It makes me think that tonight really is some kind of last hurrah, and I get that same weird sensation I had when we left my parents' house.

The crowd has thinned considerably by the time we exit the arena. A cool wind greets us when we hit the street and I feel invincible. We talk about our favourite moments as we get back to the car, but they're already starting to fade. The car is still there, as I expected, and I sense Andre's relief when he gets behind the wheel again. Before we depart, he opens the hatch and Rich and I grab two beers out of the cooler. We drink quickly while Andre retrieves the stash and puts it back under the driver's seat.

The beer goes right through us. Without making a scene, I piss against one of the car's front tires. Rich runs to a nearby hedge and Andre jokingly puts the car in gear, causing Rich to race back, still zipping up his jeans. It doesn't stop him from pleading for a shotgun battle. I win again, rock beats scissors.

"Come on man, there should be a limit to how many times you can win," he complains.

I'm amused and take advantage of the situation. "What do you want, best three out of five? Seven out of ten? It's a simple game, you must really be a loser."

"Whatever. We're switching at the next stop."

"Oh really? We'll see. Don't put any music on, my ears hurt."

"Aw, poor baby! Maybe some Motorhead will fix that."

He's got "Ace of Spades" cued up and it blasts through the back of my head, triggering a sharp pain at the bridge of my nose. The noise gets to Andre, too, and in so many words, he screams at Rich to turn it off. For several minutes, there's silence. Andre stops for gas and then we we're on our way out of town, heading west on the Trans-Canada highway to Montreal. I love the highway at night, being the only car on the massive asphalt lanes, the spooky glow of the overpass lights illuminating the interior with a lulling rhythm.

Eventually, the lights vanish, the road narrows to four lanes, and we're alone in the wilderness. Andre switches on the high beams. From time to time, an 18-wheeler approaches going in the other direction, but we are the only moving thing on the road for the longest time.

"Are you gonna drive all night?" I ask Andre.

"I'm not sure yet. I'm just gonna go until I get tired."

"I'm only thinking about what we're going to do tomorrow. I mean, if we go all night, you'll probably be pretty wrecked."

"We'll be in Montreal by the time the sun comes up. I'll stop when we get there. You can sleep if you want, I'm all right."

I look in the back seat and see Rich in dreamland, so I lean the seat back and let the hum of the engine put me to sleep.

The day is becoming grey and the Chevette is stopped at a gas station. When I wake, my ears are numb from the concert and a dry throat makes it hard to swallow. I try to go back to sleep but there are too many distractions. A half-hour later we're at the outskirts of Montreal, mingling with the first traces of the Monday-morning rush hour circling the massive fuel refineries. It's like something out of a science fiction movie. Huge tanks dot the landscape for miles, smokestacks huff relentlessly.

As I take it in, I remember my dad's opinions about Montreal drivers. Cars blow by us on both sides but Andre seems unfazed. This is still his home turf, and we have a long way to go. He says he isn't going to worry about aggressive drivers until we get to the States. All he's concerned with is finding a place to pull over. By now, Rich is awake too, his face pressed against the back window. I laugh to myself thinking about how he didn't get to switch seats with me. We'll have to have another game to decide the next leg, and I feel good about my chances.

Andre aims the Chevette at the first exit with a restaurant sign. He says to no one in particular that he doesn't want to go downtown just yet. We pull into a nice, family-style place and park at the back behind an 18-wheeler that looks like it's been there all night. We get out and stretch, Andre instructing us to give him about two hours to sleep. We are to sit inside until he comes in. Rich and I are dirty, but not bad enough to be out in public without a shower. Still, it's a little uncomfortable taking a booth in such a clean, wholesome place. We choose one near a window with a view of the car, in case Andre gets into any trouble. We get coffee, then take turns going to the bathroom before ordering food. When I get inside the small room, my smell finally hits me. I decide to keep my flannel shirt on, since it masks some of the stench, despite making me look like a scumbag. I wash my hands and face, and feel awake for the first time today.

We both ask for eggs over easy; I get sausage, Rich gets bacon. We eat slowly and take full advantage of the joint's bottomless cup policy until we have about three or four in us. Rich grabs a discarded Montreal *Gazette* from a nearby table and we kill more time reading. Thankfully, the waitress isn't in any hurry to kick us out. She actually perks up when Andre joins us and orders more coffees. He looks ten times worse than we do. I suggest that he hit the bathroom, which he does, zombie-like. He returns looking a little more alive and begins leafing through the paper.

I can't hold my curiosity any longer and ask him his plans for the rest of the day. Andre squints, takes a deep breath and says calmly, "I guess we're going to have to do some work." It's approaching 10 a.m., and as we pay the bill, Andre politely asks the waitress for simple directions around downtown. Armed with that knowledge, we pull out of the parking lot, and the car weaves toward the centre of the city. There's no way to avoid the fact that Andre's idea of work is dealing drugs.

We turn onto Rue Ste. Catherine and pass in front of the Forum. None of us has seen it before, and its gleaming glass doors invoke visions of Guy Lafleur, his blonde mane flowing as he speeds down the right wing, or Ken Dryden leaning on his stick like a warrior guarding the gates of Valhalla. Andre finds the cheapest parking lot and pulls in. He pays the attendant the fee and gives him an extra five bucks to keep a special eye on our car. Andre's always doing stuff like that. He expects people to do things his way, with only a little persuasion. He might have made a great gangster, but I can't imagine anyone taking him seriously the way he looks, especially today with his greasy blonde hair and torn flannel shirt.

It's obvious Andre has a plan, but he doesn't share it with us. We just follow as he wanders from block to block, scoping out potential buyers. There's a lot of guys who look in need of a score, but obviously don't have any money. An arcade finally catches Andre's attention. Kids are beginning to crowd in for the their lunch break. Rich and I head straight for a couple of machines, knowing Andre is going to start his sales pitch. I try to keep an eye on him as he gravitates toward a throng in matching uniforms huddled around a WWF wrestling game. It doesn't take long before he and a couple of the guys move to the back of the room near the old pinball machines, and I breathe a small sigh of relief knowing that things are off to a good start. In the next half-hour, Andre makes a few more deals — I'm watching for the manager or cops now — and he seems satisfied when he taps us on the back to get out of there.

Back on the street, I ask how he did.

"Not bad, about a hundred bucks. We can still do better. Let's find a pizza joint."

There's one on the corner, crowded again with the same matching uniforms. Our timing seems impeccable. Some of the kids are hanging around outside, eating slices and smoking, and Andre hits on them as Rich and I go inside so things don't seem so obvious. When we head out again with our slices, Andre is laughing and joking with some of the guys in grey slacks and he introduces us to them. Turns out they're soccer players, and Andre's already set up a big deal to go down before their practice at the end of the day. They confirm the meeting place at the playground, and start walking back to school. There's a sense of accomplishment, even though Rich and I didn't do anything, and a whole afternoon to kill.

Rich finally gives in to the urge to ask, "So how much are you getting from them?"

"Should be another $300."

"What do you wanna do until then?"

Andre, used to spending afternoons doing nothing, doesn't answer. After vainly trying to think of anything, I finally say, "Let's grab a few beers."

We wander around the neighbourhood for another ten minutes, settling on a bar that looks like a place people drink in the afternoon. It's small and dark, with a TV silently rerunning sports highlights. There are a couple of skids at the bar, not moving at all, so we grab a table and order a pitcher of 50. Spirits are still high, and as the beer arrives, I grab a *Mirror* from the rack at the front door and scan the live music listings.

"You wanna check out another band tonight?" Rich asks, sensing my interest.

"Yeah, why not? What else is there to do?"

"Fuck man, my ears are still ringing from last night."

"I thought we were gonna have fun on this trip?"

A silence ensues as we both instinctually wait to hear what Andre has to say. He eventually chimes in, "Maybe we should figure out where we're gonna stay tonight."

The thought had crossed my mind off and on all day, and I knew our best option would be my Uncle Pat and Aunt Marie's place. I should have called them earlier, but it was something I didn't want to mention unless we needed a last resort. When I suggest it, no one has a problem, so I make the call at the bar's pay phone. Aunt Marie answers and is naturally shocked to hear my voice. I explain to her what we're doing and apologize for not calling ahead. She doesn't mind. She thinks it's great that three friends are seeing the country together, something she always wanted to do. I get the directions and tell her we won't be too late.

We split another pitcher before Andre straps on the black tote bag and goes to do the deal with the soccer players. We agree to meet back at the car at six. Rich and I start wandering again, stopping in at any comic book or record store we pass, deliberately trying to kill as much time as possible. "So, having fun yet?" Rich asks.

"I don't know. Andre's got to make his bread, so once that's done, it'll get better. We'll do some shit when we get to Toronto."

I guess that answer is satisfactory, because we return to counting the minutes until we can head back to the parking lot. When we get there, Andre is waiting. There's no indication we're late. I assume that means the deal went as planned.

Andre follows the directions to my uncle's place surprisingly well. The house is in a predominately French neighbourhood, though Uncle Pat is descended from Irish immigrants who came to Quebec during the potato famine. Aunt Marie is my mom's sister. They usually come to visit us, because my dad and Pat don't really get along. You have to put a gun to my dad's head to make him come to Montreal. My uncle's a pretty successful businessman, and my dad can only be described as blue collar. That's probably at the heart of it. I actually find them and my cousins pretty boring most of the time, too, but I can put up with the conversation for one night.

The houses on their street all look the same. Andre has to crawl along while I strain to see the numbers on my side. I finally recognize the basketball hoop nailed to the garage and instruct Andre to pull in. A motion-sensor light comes on when we get to the door. I ring the bell and hear the annoying bark of their dog, a Pekinese named Cheri. Aunt Marie greets me with a warm hug and welcomes us in. Uncle Pat is surprised at our appearance, jokes about us being hippies or something. He's lost a lot of hair since I last saw him, and it makes him look like an old man. I guess women really are attracted to money.

We're led to the downstairs den where my cousins Marc and Paul are watching TV. They seem genuinely happy to see me, hitting me with a barrage of questions while Aunt Marie gets Cokes for us all. Rich and Andre are quiet, but politely answer the general inquiries my uncle throws at them. Andre has his stash with him and is starting to get sleepy after sitting in a plush chair for an hour. I feel as if we haven't done the minimum amount of socializing yet, but I let Andre off the hook, saying he's been driving for the past twenty-four hours and really needs to sleep.

He's briskly led away to another room by my aunt, and I can only imagine the fuss she's making over him. Rich recognizes a chance to escape and disappears, too. I'm now alone with people I haven't seen in years and who I would never go out of my way to see except under these circumstances. There's nothing wrong with them I guess, it's just that sometimes you're forced into a closeness with people you don't have anything in common with. We keep talking for several more hours, until Uncle Pat has to pack it in himself. He needs to be up for work, so we say farewell as I set myself up on the couch. I don't feel bad not getting a bed, it's good just to lay my head on a pillow. It might be the last time I ever enjoy the pleasure.

I dream I'm back in Mario's attic with everybody else, like it was before I went away to school. We're getting high, but for some reason I can't get enough of whatever it is we're consuming. I smoke a joint in what seems like a single drag, then turn around and grab a handful of pills I wash down with a half bottle of Canadian Club. Nothing has an effect on me. I'm invincible, while everyone else is collapsing around me. It's one of those dreams that seems to last all night, but when it's over, I sir to nothing but darkness.

I awake again later to the sound of Uncle Pat stumbling around the kitchen as he gets ready for work. The couch has served me well, but I can't fully fall asleep again. After an hour of trying, I turn on the TV, another luxury I'll probably be without from now on. The guys eventually get up — I assume Andre told Aunt Marie to wake them at a certain time — and I head up to the kitchen to meet them. They are already at the table drinking coffee, and my aunt is frying generous portions of eggs and bacon. I tell her she doesn't have to go to the trouble but she shrugs it off. It turns out to be a fine meal, and I thank her for the kindness as we prepare to leave. She says she hopes we have a good trip and tells me to drop in when we get back. I say I will, trying hard to sell the lie.

It's another sunny day and the rest and showers have us energized. I finally lose a shotgun battle, although it's only for the twenty-minute drive back downtown. Rich still rubs it in. The plan is to hit up the same places and try to score a few more bucks before splitting town. There's no trick to it, as I quickly learn by observing Andre. You just have to be cool and know how to ask the right questions. We don't even see any cops walking the beat, just cruisers looking for illegal parking or street people being a little too obvious doing the same thing we are. That's gotta be our angle — don't be obvious. Just three average-looking kids enjoying some time off school.

The day actually flies by. Before we know it, Andre tells us he's got enough cash and wants to get off the street. Rich and I aren't about to complain. We've been looking forward to a few beers after a job well done. In fact, we end up cracking two open from our cooler as soon as we get back to the car. The scarred roof of the Chevette is noticeable from a block away.

Rich hands me one of the Laurentides, and we down them in our seats while Andre counts his money one more time. "Where do you wanna eat?" I ask, feeling thoroughly content.

"I dunno." Andre suddenly sounds annoyed.

"If you wanna stick around here, you guys better not get too wasted tonight. We gotta skip town right after last call, we should be in Ottawa tomorrow. I don't wanna waste any time cleaning up puke in the back seat, either." His last command is levelled in my direction.

"What do you take us for, man? We're on vacation, aren't we? You should loosen up and have a beer. We had a great day today. We should have fun now, 'cause I don't think it's going to get any easier."

"What do you mean?" Andre's defensiveness tells me he doesn't think we know what's going on.

"I mean, after tomorrow we'll have to speak English all the time, we won't know anybody. We won't even know where we are half the time. I say, let's party like it's 1999." Rich grunts his approval.

I hope what I say makes Andre feel better. Usually, he won't tell us anything until he feels confident it's the right move. The fact that Rich and I are no longer in the dark about what lies ahead instantly makes him open up a little more.

"Maybe I will have a beer." Rich pulls out another Laurentide and the sound of escaping air echoes through the parking lot.

We eat in a tiny Italian place off Rue de Champlain. The best advice I ever got was to eat a large meal before a night of heavy drinking. I actually learned that in high school health class, go figure. The little mom and pop restaurants are way better than the chains, too. There are six tables in the place with only one occupied by a young couple that look like they're on a cheap movie date. I never really enjoyed those nights, but I would have given anything for one at that moment. It was so much easier back home, because the only place to see movies was at the youth centre. Of course, nobody came to watch the flicks. It wasn't until I took girls out to real movie theatres in Quebec City that I found out what a rip-off movie dates are. First of all, they require a lot of money. Second, there are so many things to do in the city I was never sure the girl was really having fun. Then there was the question of how to make a move, to which I never found the correct answer, either. I always came home feeling the entire evening was a waste and envying someone like Rich who never had to think about where his next hand-job was coming from. I can't stop dwelling on it until we get to the bar.

Andre knows this place called Le Foufounes Electriques, and we park in a lot around the corner. He tips the attendant again, and we confidently stride to the front door. The streets are starting to feel familiar. The prospect of a few more days here doesn't seem so bad. It's still early. So early, in fact, one of the bands is still carrying their equipment in from a van parked out front. They look a lot like us: guys around twenty with long straight hair, ripped jeans and flannel shirts. Two of them have pointy goatees, something none of us could ever accomplish.

I hold the door open as they carry their amplifiers in. Andre asks what their name is and one of the goateed guys says, "Dead Starz. With a 'z.'" They're the opening band; The Doughboys are already set up inside. Andre keeps up the small talk until the van is empty, then hits them with his proposition. The guys are interested, but say they won't have any money until after they've played their set. Andre understands but, in a very savvy move, offers one of them a free sample of Mario's meth and wishes them a good gig. In return, another of the band members puts us on the guest list, and we're suddenly making the scene like we own the place.

Dead Starz do a quick, haphazard sound check with the effect of the drug clearly visible and soon after, people start showing up. Within an hour, the bar is packed with punks, headbangers, grunge kids and every other label those fuckers have dreamed up for us. Andre, Rich and I watch it all from the bar at the back of the room, where we coolly gulp bottles of 50. When I glance at Andre, I notice his eyes surveying the room for potential scores. Most of the kids don't look old enough to be here.

When he finds a mark, he goes over and states his case. The first forays are unsuccessful, forcing him back to the bar for another look around. "Just like fishing," he says, several times. He eventually snags a big headbanger and is gone for a long time, leaving Rich and me to entertain ourselves. Rich seems content to suck back beers, but I venture out onto the floor when Dead Starz start playing. It feels great to be back in a mosh pit again, even though it's not as intense as the one at the Colisee. The band's music is pretty good; a little unoriginal, but a lot of energy. The singer — one of the goateed guys — rages around the small stage, often colliding with his bandmates, who don't seem to mind. At one point it looks as if he's about to leap right into our modest gathering, but he thinks better of it after making eye contact with the little schoolgirls down front who clearly can't support his weight.

I'm probably more exhilarated than the band after the set. They finish up by swinging their guitars around while the singer bashes the microphone amid a cloud of sonic sickness. For this, they receive mediocre applause. I turn back to the bar and see Rich standing in the same position he was when I left him.

"Having fun now?" he asks with cooler-than-thou smugness.

"Yeah." He doesn't deserve a cordial response with that kind of attitude. I order a beer and ask where Andre is.

"Back and forth. He just went backstage to make the deal with the band." Everything is right with the world: Rich is getting wasted, Andre is making money and I have my choice of all the girls on the floor. Another great thing about mosh pits is the body contact. A hand can casually brush against a breast without anyone being the wiser. It's not that I'm trying to take advantage of somebody. It's just so easy to lose your inhibitions when you're new in town. I'm hoping we stay at least a week in Toronto.

The floor is packed with bodies by the time The Doughboys come on. I work my way to the middle of the mass and I am immediately lifted overhead. The first song starts with me suspended by anonymous hands. It's like the toboggan rides I used to take as a kid; seconds of pleasure, my body at the mercy of the environment. Eventually I'm swallowed and receive a few accidental kicks, but someone pulls me up. It's Andre.

He's made another $500, which he counts one more time in the car as Rich and I have one more for the road. This first stage of the journey is a success, and we're all savouring it. Even Andre. He speaks with true happiness during the walk from the bar to the parking lot. It's as if he's cracked the combination to the lock and now just needs to give a swift kick to open the door. He's also becoming cocky, and his swagger makes me worry a bit. Still, this new Andre will be a lot more fun to travel with. He starts the car as Rich and I engage in the shotgun ritual. I lose again, paper beats rock.

Andre skilfully follows the signs and takes the first exit to the highway heading west. Ottawa is only a few hours away, and we'll be able to get some sleep somewhere on the road. The outskirts of Montreal vanish in a heartbeat and we're back on four lanes heading into darkness. I suddenly wish we were driving during the day. I can't see anything, apart from the occasional illuminated sign hovering above a roadside rest stop. I keep wondering when Andre will pull into one. After an hour, he does. There are a hundred kilometres to go until Hull, and I want to sleep all the way there. Instead, we're parked between two 18-wheelers behind a McDonald's. It takes me several minutes to get used to standing still.

4 Sylvie
Ottawa: May 11, 1994.

It has to be a miracle of nature, that you can wake up in the morning and, for at least a few minutes, not have a clue about what happened the night before. Even the most traumatic events can be forgotten in the first few seconds after you open your eyes. But they always come back, like high tide.

Andre is gone. An idiotic, immature girl bawling her eyes out in a slutty black dress, his last impression of me. The morning after that awful night was the toughest, tougher than the first mornings after he'd moved to the city, when I couldn't stop picturing him dead in an alley.

But it's gradually gotten better. This morning, the reality of studying for finals is actually the first thing in my head. I get through mostly by studying, and not thinking about him and the note he slid under the front door the day he left. It was short; just a few lines apologizing for leaving so abruptly and saying again that he loved me. Somehow seeing those words on paper made them more meaningful than hearing them from his lips, and it's gone a long way to reassure me that things will work themselves out.

All my efforts to suppress my emotions throughout the day are shot to hell as another letter is waiting when I get home. I drop my knapsack and stare at the envelope with my name and address on it for a long time before going up to my room. I should be elated, but I'm hesitant to open it. I can only lie back and prepare myself by recalling for the millionth time how innocently this all started.

When I was in Grade 10, Andre came up to me at a party, put his arm around my shoulder and said it was time the two of us stopped kidding around. I didn't brush him off because, of course, I felt the same way. We'd known each other all our lives, everyone at school did. One day, the guys were snapping my bra strap, the next they were leaving notes in my locker with crude propositions that at least a few other girls had accepted. Guys all became losers, overnight.

Except Andre. I'm sure he had impure thoughts about me before we hooked up, but he managed to keep them to himself. It was always more fun imagining him thinking about me in that way. He could read my thoughts, too. That's what made us so right for each other — we didn't have to talk and talk until the words inevitably drove a wedge between us, as I'd seen happen to so many of my friends. Andre knew I was a virgin and he respected my decision. I knew he dealt drugs and, probably because of his respect for me, I likewise tried not to poke my nose into his business. It was kind of cool being his girlfriend anyway. We had the best of both worlds, until he moved away. He was hanging out with the most interesting people, and if he had problems at home, he could escape at my house.

My parents didn't care what we did as long as my marks stayed high. Both of them are old hippies who teach at the high school. They moved here just before I was born, so they could get back to nature or whatever it was that people were into back then. They probably thought small-town kids would be easier to handle, too. I'm sure they had an easy time until guys like Andre's brother and Mario came along. It was around then that my parents began giving long talks about sex and drugs. They told me up front they'd done both at my age and that I shouldn't do either. They said things like, "When we were young, we didn't listen to anything our parents said and we learned the hard way. We don't want you to go through what we did." You know you've grown up when your parents tell you they were wrong about something.

I suppose they thought Andre and I were a typical high school romance. We probably were, if what I've seen on TV is any comparison. We messed around a little bit and he got me to smoke pot a few times, but he never forced me to do anything I didn't want to do. I guess that's why I fell in love with him. After he quit school, though, it got kind of weird. At first it was fun going to the city without my parents. Those trips to see him were my first real adventures on my own. But by then, the city was changing him. At school, he always talked big. After he left, he hardly talked about himself at all. I didn't know how to get through to him. I'd go home on Sundays and head back to school, worrying constantly about him working the streets.

I guess I could have ended it there. Other guys were asking me out, but I turned them down. If Andre didn't pick me up on Friday, I'd stay home the entire weekend. Everyone else would be at the community centre dance. My parents thought I was crazy. I probably was. During those times I'd get so mad at him I'd actually consider getting on a bus and tracking him down just so I could chew him out and go home again. There was no point talking to him on the phone. He never had anything interesting to say. But when we were face to face I could read his emotions, and all the anger would melt away.

I guess that's another sign you're grown up, you realize the person you love is thoroughly dependent on your support. Some of my friends learned this lesson when they got pregnant. I didn't have a baby, just someone who saw me as his only escape from the trouble he faced every day. At least that's what he told me. It didn't freak me out, even though we didn't really have anything in common anymore. I still think I would have married him if he had asked. I don't know why.

Maybe it was because he wanted me to go to university and make something of myself, and he wasn't jealous at all. We fought about stupid things instead. The distance between us made our imaginations wander. I worried about him getting hurt on the streets and not being considerate enough to let me know every once in a while that he was all right. At times I think he was more comfortable when I was mad at him; he'd become accustomed to a hostile environment. He used to take his anger out on me when we'd get together, but later, when he became more distant, he wouldn't talk about his family or the other stuff at all. In those moments we would never fight, unless I provoked him. I provoked him the night before he left, and now I regret it.

I didn't know what to say when he told me about the trip. It hurt me when he said I wasn't invited, but I was still glad to see him motivated. I didn't buy that shit about looking for a place to settle down, I knew he wanted to get something out of his system. I was just hoping that that something wasn't me. The first note has partially convinced me. At least it's given me enough confidence to finally open this letter.

It starts out talking about how they stayed at Serge's uncle's place and were pretty glad about it . . . slept in a real bed, got to shower and shave . . . having a great time, bumming around the city . . . stopping in at all the cool shops and buying new tapes (they were already sick of the ones they had brought along) . . . looking forward to going to a club the following day, and the Megadeth concert was awesome . . . still feels like home, though . . . looking forward to seeing places that don't have French names, places where he doesn't feel so self-conscious.

I realize that he's finally telling me things he's never had the courage to say. Sure, he can say he loves me, but this is like the first real conversation we've had in a year. I want to be with him right now, no matter how impossible it is.

I read on about how his life has led him to a point where he's finally fulfilling his destiny . . . even though they were only a few days into the trip, he knows it to be true . . . The only way he could be happier is if I was with him.

That's what he wrote.

I fall back on my bed, overwhelmed by exhilaration. All this time we've been together, and I've never had such feelings. I have to do something, but I'm in a stupor. I sit down to write a letter back, but I come to my senses and understand I have nowhere to send it. I think about calling somebody, but then decide to keep it to myself. There's nothing worse than someone who's in love bragging about it to someone who isn't.

I sit back down on my bed and read the letter again, savouring every word, as if Andre was whispering them into my ear.

I wake up a few hours later in the same position, the letter lying beside me like a raft, adrift on the ocean of my comforter. Everything is dark, and I hear the television's faint muttering, which means it can't be that late. I'm wide awake and faced with the proposition of remaining so until morning.

I sit at my desk and write him a letter anyway. I imagine it as a message in a bottle when it's done, that my thoughts will be psychically transmitted to him somehow. I think about the ocean way too much. Maybe I should move to the Maritimes. I've heard Halifax is a pretty cool place. I should have told Andre to go there, instead of going to all these scary places. I wonder how hard it would be to find him. Those courier companies brag about delivering parcels to the ends of the earth. I'll just tell them to deliver the letter to a blue Chevette somewhere on the 401 heading to Toronto.

I read what I've got once more: *Dear Andre, I got your letter and I'm glad to hear everything's going all right so far* [Scratched out]. *Dear Andre, I love you more than you'll ever know. I'll go wherever you want me to go* [Scratched out]. *Dear Andre, I'm so happy you wrote. I didn't want us to part the way we did. I didn't understand what we have until you'd gone. I now see that you had to go on this trip without me in order to find yourself. I've been searching a lot myself and I just want to tell you that whatever you decide to do, I hope you'll want me to be a part of it.*

This time apart has made me want you like I never have before. Don't worry about me going to school; I'll go wherever you want to settle down. Don't worry about my parents, either. They think you're doing the right thing. There's no future here. Just promise me you won't sell drugs anymore. I'm glad you're using the money you made this year to pay for this vacation. There's something very fitting about that. It seems like such an easy thing to do as long as you have the strength to quit while you're ahead. I know you have the strength.

I'm ashamed about the last night we spent at the cemetery. I should have believed you when you said you love me. It was so nice the way you were holding me, though. You hadn't held me like that for a long time. It was so nice that I didn't want anything to disturb it. That was a mistake. I want you to make love to me now. It's idiotic to still be playing games with you after all these years, when you're the one I want to spend the rest of my life with.

Here's what I should have said a week ago: I love you, too.

I can't bring myself to write any more, as I abandon all hope of him ever reading it. I just sit and stare at my words until they become meaningless scribbles. It's easy to write that I love him, but can I really say it to his face like he did to me? That's another sign of being grown-up I guess, knowing that words actually have meanings and knowing the meanings before you use the words.

I spend a long time dissecting what I wrote. There aren't too many different ways to interpret it, though. Any brain-dead moron would get the message loud and clear. Whatever. It's how I really feel, and there's nothing more I can do about it. I try to go back to sleep, but I can still hear the television. It's quiet for a while, then the sound of laughter and applause drifts upstairs. My brother is watching some talk show.

My mind returns to my pathetic situation. Two weeks of studying. I turn the light on again and fish out my Canadian history textbook to resume reading about the Plains of Abraham. The two armies face each other and charge. The battle is over in a matter of minutes. General Wolfe and General Montcalm are both killed. Sounds like a football game.

I fall asleep.

The sun coaxes my eyes open, and the sound of my mother puttering around the kitchen forces me to get up. I throw off my blankets, revealing the same clothes I had on yesterday. My history text is also still beside me, prompting a brief, frantic search for Andre's letter. There it is, on my desk, next to my response.

I read my first few lines again and wince. I feel the disgust of what I imagine the aftermath of a one-night stand must be like. I can't get in the shower fast enough. It's not that I've had a change of heart; it's just that seeing my emotions on paper makes me cringe. Worse, there's the thought of Andre actually reading it.

I don't bother to check the clock and I'm surprised to see it's close to one in the afternoon by the time I've cleaned myself up.

"I was getting worried," my mother says half-jokingly. She has the day off, too, because of exams. It really sucks being on the same schedule as your parents.

"Oh, I was studying all night," I tell her with complete sincerity. I sit down to a bowl of Cap'n Crunch when the mail arrives. My mother meets the carrier at the door and they share some idle chatter. As she shuts the front door, she announces in a mocking tone that I've got another letter. She nonchalantly drops it in front of me and exits, saying something about adults having the right to privacy. I hate it that she knows, but I'm too distracted to play along with her little mind games.

This letter is from Ottawa, postmarked the day after the Montreal letter. There isn't a return address. My emotions go into overdrive. I put aside my half-consumed bowl and run back to my room, where I rip it open like it's a Christmas present. It's a longer letter — single-spaced — in Andre's trademark Grade 5 printing style. I've never been sure if he was kidding around or if he really wrote that way. He was never the world's greatest speller, either.

From what I can make out, he's writing from the lobby of the National Art Gallery. The boys apparently had some time to kill, so Rich suggested checking the place out and seeing that one painting everyone made such a fuss over a few years ago. Andre can't remember the name of it, but I know it's "Voice of Fire." When he saw it, he says it reminded him of colouring books he'd had as a kid. It was always frustrating trying to stay inside the lines and making a consistent field of colour with waxy Crayolas, he writes. The artist impressed him with his ability to do these two things, but Andre still couldn't believe he got $3 million for it.

The only other artists in the gallery that he knew were the Group of Seven, only because we were taught about them in school. Andre appreciated their "no-bullshit" style. "They painted the wilderness as we know it, a place with boundaries that can't be crossed." His words. Anybody can paint a tree, he goes on, but how many people can paint how a tree feels? Trees are planted, they grow and become shaped by the environment, then cut down for the benefit of a greedy society.

Andre has always said stuff like this, but now I wonder whether he's joking or not. Anyway, that's all he wanted to see at the gallery, so as Rich and Serge wandered around on their own, he says he decided to write. This was their second day in Ottawa. They'd arrived the previous morning after crashing overnight at a highway truck stop. His first impression of the city was surprise. It was too small to be the capital of a country. Compared to Montreal, it seemed like a toy village, with clean streets and pre-served buildings.

The drive in from the Trans-Canada was like taking the back-woods route home to La Forest. As they got closer, Andre noticed how everything was spread out in tiny pockets of suburbs where he assumed all the politicians lived. It was a nice enough place in his view, though. No big polluting factories or imposing skyscrapers. He was almost afraid they would get arrested for vagrancy when they stepped out of the car.

They'd had breakfast at a greasy spoon on their way into down-town, which prepared them for a day of sightseeing. However, it turned out to be the first time it rained on their trip. They lingered a long time in the diner, drinking coffee, then made a dash to the car. Andre drove them downtown to the Parliament buildings, the thing they really wanted to see. This was when Andre says he felt out of place. Even so, he had as much of a right to be there as any-body. He says he realized this as soon as he walked through the door for the tour. It wasn't a sense of pride, he writes, but a sense of closure. I pause for a moment to interpret this remark, then get then get distracted in deciphering what the government represents to me. It's always seemed like a secret society, something that exists in another dimension. I've never been to Parliament Hill, but reading Andre's primitive descriptions gives me a sense of its realness. I suddenly feel proud, picturing Andre, in his unkempt state, walking through the hallowed halls and giving the finger to anyone in a suit who looked at him wrong.

The guide led them through the library, the Senate Chamber and the actual Parliamentary Hall, where they sat in the Speaker's Chair and at the Prime Minister's desk. They were shown his office, too; the politicians were, of course, on vacation as well. Andre thought it was funny that tourists were visiting someone's workplace while the workers weren't there.

Then again, we did that all the time as kids. The schools took us on field trips to all kinds of places. The first one I remember was our town mill. We also went to farms to see how cows were milked, or restaurants to see how pizzas were made. It was as if they were telling us, "If you don't stay in school, this is what you'll end up doing."

After the tour was over, they explored other nearby buildings. The Supreme Court was next, and it was there that Rich and Serge started clowning around on the huge statues on top of the giant cement steps. There were other statues on the grounds a person could fit quite comfortably on, and nobody seemed to mind that the gesture could be seen as a slur against our country's great image. Andre took more pleasure in leaning over the majestic cliff that overlooked the Rideau Canal and, picturing that scene, my heart once again swells.

From there he could see Hull; he wanted to hang on to the last remnants of Quebec for as long as he could. When they went out that night, Rich and Serge wanted to go to Hull; mostly to test the nasty reputation we all heard about while growing up. They saw it as a kind of Last Chance Saloon that cowboys find in the movies.

What they did first, instead, was make the rounds in Ottawa's downtown market district. They filled up on beer and burgers, listened to some street musicians, then popped into a live music bar, Barrymore's, where they saw a band called the Bourbon Tabernacle Choir. At first they thought they were corny — all those horns and keyboards — but after a few songs they started getting into it.

The rain had stopped by the time they left the club and followed the rest of the patrons over the bridge spanning the canal to Hull, where the party continued for the rest of the night. A couple of seven-dollar pitchers of Export went with them. Rich was pissing on the closest street, when a couple of Hull cops noticed and jumped all over him. They tossed Rich spread-eagle against their cruiser, while Andre and Serge drunkenly roared from a safe distance. Andre tells the story better:

"Where are your buddies?" one cop goes. "Ne parle pas Anglais," Rich goes. "Ou est son amis?" he asked again. Rich kept looking around for us, but he was too drunk to see straight. The other cop goes, "How are you getting home?" "I'm walking, I live here." That was the smartest thing Rich ever said in his life, because just then a fight broke out half a block down the street from where we were hiding, and the cops took off on foot leaving Rich free to go.

They finally grabbed Rich, and escaped in the opposite direction. It took a long time to find the car. At this point Andre says that he'd only had two beers, because he knows how much I hate him drinking and driving. I don't know why he bothers, I can't do anything about it. For all I know, the whole letter could be one big lie. Anyway, they slept in the car that night, Rich in the back seat, in the parking lot of an Ottawa convenience store. The manager chased them out a few hours later when he came to work, but by then the sun was coming up on a gorgeous spring morning.

But this was when things went wrong. After the shock of the night wore off, Serge said something for the first time to Rich about calling Anne-Marie. It was like the earth stopped moving for a split second. Rich's face turned white, and his eyes bulged like two billiard balls. "Oh my God, what am I going to do? I told her I'd call her every day. It's been almost a week" . . . *"Hey, man, she'll understand. Just tell her we've been having too much fun. That's the truth, isn't it?"* . . . *"Well, yeah, but that's exactly what she won't want to hear"* . . . *"Jesus, man, if that's what you think then you're better off not talking to her ever again"* . . . *"But, I've got to call her"* . . . *"All right, but if she gives you any shit, you're hanging up. I don't need your fucked-up love life spoiling my vacation."*

Why is Andre telling me this?

We stopped at a gas station and Rich made the call. I filled up the tank and Serge bought Cokes. They sucked them back, and Rich was still standing in the phone booth, his back to us except when he turned to insert more quarters. When he ran out of money he slowly walked over, his head hanging like a beaten dog's. "What happened?" . . . *"It's over"* . . . *"What, just like that?"* . . . *"She said if I didn't come home right now, she doesn't want to see me again"* . . . *"Holy shit. I guess it is over 'cause there's no way I'm taking you home now"* . . . *"Andre, you fucking bastard, I could take the bus you know"* . . . *"But you're not going to, are you?" Pause. "No, I'm not."*

I put down the letter, and after a few minutes call Anne-Marie. I don't know her very well, but I can't fight the sudden impulse to find out the truth. As I wait for her to pick up, I can't stop glaring at Andre's plea: *"Syl, try to let Anne-Marie know that everything's cool out here, but that, as you can see, Rich really wants to fix things up when he gets back."*

"Hi, this is Sylvie, Andre's girlfriend. Remember, from math class?"

"Um, yeah, how's it going?"

"I was just curious about something. I got a letter today from Andre and he said that you and Rich broke up. I'm not trying to make anything out of it; I just thought I'd call you in case you wanted to talk to somebody. I know how bad it is when they're far away and won't tell you what's going on."

"Andre told you we broke up?"

"Yeah."

"That means Richard told him we broke up. What a prick! I didn't break up with him. I was really mad that he hadn't called, but I just told him that this whole trip was really stupid and I couldn't see him lasting another day the way he is."

"What do you mean? How is he?"

"He's a wimp." I couldn't believe she said this with such conviction. "I told him before he left he'd come crawling back to me after a few days, but he didn't believe me."

"But you didn't say you'd never see him again if he didn't come right home then?"

"No. Is that what he said? What a fucking asshole!"

"Um, I've got another call. We should talk more at school."

"Yeah, that'd be great. Bye."

I'm thoroughly confused as I hang up, no longer sure how I fit in. Andre is telling me he loves me, and there's no way I can respond, while Rich is lying about breaking up with Anne-Marie. I stare hard at the letter again, realizing there is no way I can truly believe any of it. There's still one page I haven't read.

After Rich's phone call, they went to the art gallery and Andre started writing. But now he says it's later, and that he's writing from a coffee shop while Rich and Serge are taking out their frustrations at a nearby arcade. Andre knew Rich wouldn't go home. There was too much left to see, and because he hadn't complained, there was no reason to suspect he wasn't having a good time. Besides, Rich could never say no to Andre. Andre has a way of making you feel you've wounded him when you tell him no. There were few things that could get his hopes up, and if he was denied them, he'd be fucked up for days.

Except for sex. I could say no about sex because I knew deep in his heart he didn't want it bad enough. Andre wants so little, really. But I know now that he really wanted this trip; that's why I had to let him go.

The end of the letter is more lovey-dovey stuff, but it doesn't get to me as much now, with all these other things on my mind. Still, one part bugs me: *You're probably wondering by now where future letters are going to be coming from, so you can get back to me. I would love to hear from you, obviously, but I can't tell you for sure when we're going to be in certain places. I mean, I'm still kind of playing it by ear, you know? I'll tell you that tomorrow we'll be on the road to Toronto, where we'll be for at least a few days. You can send a letter to the post office there and I'll check every day to see if it shows up. After that, though, it might be a little dicey. There are a lot of things to see in America, and I want to experience as much as I can before we get to Vancouver.*

Vancouver. That's where everybody eventually ends up. They go out there on summer vacation and never come back. They go out there looking for a job and stay, even though they never find one. Why didn't I see this in the beginning? That's the only place Andre could end up. It's the only place in this country a guy like him can be accepted. And you know what? That's where I'll be when he pulls into town.

My plan formulates almost instantly: I'll finish my exams, get great marks and then tell my parents I want to enrol at UBC. I'll have to go out and inspect the campus, right? That's the only logical thing to do. And while I'm there, I might as well make a vacation out of it and invite Lise to go with me. Weren't you guys bumming around when you were my age, Mom and Dad?

My studies are neglected for the rest of the day as I think things through more thoroughly. I can't help wondering if Andre formulated his plan in the same way, which forces those dangerous feelings to surface again. Of course he would appreciate what I was doing, right? What could make him happier than finding me sitting in an outdoor cafe on his first day in Vancouver? Maybe I will enrol at UBC, and we can get a nice little apartment in Gastown, and he can find a job and everything will be all right.

By dinnertime, the only thing left to do is talk to my parents. I wait until after we eat and launch into it when my father casually inquires about my exams. I tell him what he expects to hear —

everything is fine — then he asks if I've received any responses from the universities. It's already assumed that I'll go to Laval, with McGill and Concordia the backups, because I haven't been sure about a major. Like everyone else, my English isn't that great. I tell my father I haven't received any responses yet, then drop the bombshell about UBC.

To my amazement, he doesn't seem that surprised. "You know, it's funny. Your mother wanted to go there when we first met, but I already had work in Montreal so I persuaded her to stay. Have you mentioned this to her yet?" I tell him no. "Ah. She wouldn't have told me about it anyway. I hope you've been thinking about this. There would be a lot more work involved."

"Oh yeah, I know. But I know my marks are good enough."

"You want to get out of here, right?"

"Not away from you guys. I just thought if I worked hard all summer, I'd have enough money to do something different."

My father muses in silence for a long time. "You know we'll have to work on your English?" I nod in the most innocent way I can muster. "I'm not going to say yes or no unless you get accepted."

"Well, I was thinking, at least I could maybe check out the campus with Lise when exams are over. I've got enough for a plane ticket already."

"If you wanted to go on a vacation, all you had to do was ask. But only if you get straight A's."

A cloud seems to lift and I'm gushing. "Thank you, Daddy." I kiss him on the cheek and run to phone Lise. I don't have to do much convincing, she has a cousin out there who we can stay with.

Tomorrow is History, and I have to force myself to study. Andre's descriptions of Ottawa make diving into the books a little easier to bear. Even so, my mind is already heading west. I think of buying the plane tickets as soon as the exam is over, until reading about the Last Spike sparks the idea of taking the train. Regular train service had been cut almost completely in our part of the province, but those TV commercials suddenly flash in my mind, the ones showing discount rates for cross-country journeys. It's perfect. If it all works out right, my trip will last just long enough for Andre to make it out there, too, and at the same time I'll be sharing in his experience.

I know exactly what I'm going to say as I dial Lise's number, not realizing that she's supposed to be studying too. After the sixth ring I consider hanging up, but she answers. "What are you doing calling again? You know my dad will take away my phone privileges if I don't study."

"Oh, sorry, but I just got a wicked idea. Let's take the train."

She sounds sleepy. I can tell she doesn't fully comprehend what I'm saying. "Um, okay. Won't that take a lot longer?"

"Well, yeah, but that's good. We can see the whole country, and it's probably cheaper too."

"How much longer are we gonna be gone?"

"Oh, I don't know, an extra couple of weeks. No big deal. This is our last big summer of freedom. Let's enjoy it!"

"All right, whatever. Talk to me tomorrow." Lise has been my best friend since we were kids. We've never argued over anything, so I have no reservations about springing something like this on her at the last minute. Even during all the time I've spent with Andre, she's never seemed jealous or demanding, and when he's gone, she's always there for me. She's got her own life, though. Her dad runs the town hardware store and she, being the only child, has been forced to help him out. I think her dad knows that her looks attract a lot of business too. It's almost sick the way all the men in town know her by name, but, thankfully, she doesn't want anything to do with them. She plays sports at school and keeps to herself, mostly. Her biggest concern about this trip is leaving her dad in the lurch.

I wake up the next morning without a thought in my head. I try to recall if I'd dreamt anything, but that exercise proves futile. I've slept like a log the night before a final exam; it's the worst thing I could possibly have done. I scramble for my books even before I get dressed and start flipping through the pages of my text as if my life depends on it — and it does in a way. The information slowly starts to surface from somewhere deep inside my brain, and my panic subsides a little. I still have three hours to cram.

The time passes in an instant and the next thing I know, I'm walking to school in a late spring downpour. The town is quiet in the mid-morning rain. Both my parents have to be at school today, too, and I have that strange feeling I get from time to time that the school is actually my home. I guess the principal made some rule that neither of my parents were allowed to have me in their classes, but I still feel their presence every moment I'm there.

I know everyone has waited for me to screw up royally, just to see how my parents would react, but somehow I haven't. They all thought Andre would be my downfall, but even he couldn't lead me astray. I've shown them all. But it's been a hollow victory, because Andre's never seen it from my point of view. "Why are you so concerned with what everyone thinks of you?" he'd always say.

I arrive soaking wet, manage to clean up a bit at my locker, then locate the exam room. The nervous tension is already at a fever pitch when I walk in. I take a seat at the front of the room beside my friend Chantal and engage in a little small talk as other damp stragglers show up. For some reason, I mention Richard and Anne-Marie's "break-up," which drops Chantal's jaw to the floor. I look around to see if anyone else hears me, but practically all the noses are buried in books.

Before Chantal can respond, I hastily add that this is only what Andre told me had happened, that it might not be true. The guys' trip has been big news around school, and this is the first word anyone besides me has received from them. It's not what they were expecting to hear.

The sudden extra pressure of being the guys' messenger throws me off and affects my writing as the exam commences. I almost feel like crying when I leave school two hours later. This one slip of the tongue has undoubtedly cost me my whole summer. I don't go straight home but walk downtown, even though it's still drizzling slightly. I just want to clear my head a little, and I happen to pass the hardware store. I see Lise through the window looking bored as she thumbs through a magazine behind the counter. It's nice to see she's alone, but I would have gone in anyway.

"What are you doing here?" she asks, not entirely surprised to see me.

"I just blew my exam. How's it going with you?"

"Look around. My dad figured it wouldn't be busy, so he stuck me here until six." I end up staying in the store for the rest of the afternoon, talking to Lise about the trip and we both feel a lot better about everything. Only two people come into the store during that time. Both are old men who buy cheap little household gadgets and interrupt our conversation to chat-up Lise while ogling her at length. She says after that these two come in almost every day and it's no big deal, but she's thrilled about getting away from it for a while.

Before the day completely slips by, we decide to buy tickets for the earliest available train. I have two more exams next week, so Lise calls VIA and makes the arrangements. There's no turning back.

It's enough to distract me from worrying about the rest of my finals over the next few days. I write them on auto pilot. Anyway, my fears over my father cancelling the trip turn out to be unfounded after I tell him about the test and he hints that he saw my mark. He even volunteers to drive us to Quebec City to catch the train. We have to wake up really early, but it's worth it to see the beautiful sunrise as we pass through the countryside on our way to the station. There's a hazy glow around us as we stand on the platform and say our goodbyes. The train's headlight is visible from miles out and approaches slowly, like a good omen. This is the way I'd hoped we'd leave.

There aren't many other passengers, so we don't hold back our giddiness. My father just smiles and waves even though I can tell his heart is probably breaking. But, all I can think about is Andre, and holding him in the shade of a giant redwood.

5 Richard
Toronto: May 13, 1994.

"Hey, everybody still awake up there?" The shock of hearing my own voice instead of Alice In Chains is too much, so I crank up the ghetto blaster again. I've been nodding off ever since we got back on the road. Andre and Serge are awake, but they don't answer. There hasn't been much talking since we pulled out of Ottawa a couple of hours ago, after Andre made one last score with some street trash in the market. While Andre was doing the deal, Serge tried to talk to me about what had happened with Anne-Marie and I told him to fuck off. It was the first time I think I'd ever lashed out at him, and I instantly regretted it. I tried to explain later that I was just tired of the two of them nagging me about being whipped, so I said she dumped me, just to get them off my back.

She *was* mad at me though, and that always makes me say stupid things. I can't understand how she can fly into such a rage all the time. I was calling to tell her I was all right, for Christ's sake. Something just snapped.

Even still, I feel like I could follow Andre to the ends of the earth now. I have no reason to worry about the situation; she'll be there when I get back. Everyone knows she's my girl, and after what's happened she hates me so much that there's no way she could seriously go after another guy. I mean, I can't imagine who that poor fuck would be. I've got the rest of my life to be with her. Right now I want to live. Serge will be happy to hear that in the morning. It's better if we sleep this off.

I've lost track of the time, barrelling down the barren 401. We pass Kingston, but I don't notice until Andre points it out. "Hope they have our rooms ready," he says, obviously referring to the penitentiary. I think I catch a glimpse of it but there are only a few lights over the overpass piercing the darkness. I can feel it out

71

there somewhere, though, the sense of hundreds of men and women rotting in small cages as we drive by.

It's similar to the feeling I get when we drive by a graveyard. What purpose do they serve? We don't need to be reminded we'll be gone someday. I don't want to be a reminder to someone else. I don't want some kid to pass me by and think how pathetic it is to live an entire life, only to end up in the ground. But the feeling I have passing by the prison does drive home the point: we're running the risk of having everything we've got taken away if we make even the slightest fuck-up. Andre's drug deals so far have been kids' stuff. Toronto is going to be the big challenge. And I'm not even going to think about crossing the border until we get there.

Andre never tells us what he's got planned until we get somewhere. Mentioning the prison is the first time he's even jokingly said anything in hours. It's funny how I put so much trust in him, when I'm never sure what he's thinking. Still, it's too late to do anything about it.

The little towns are coming at us with greater frequency. Once we pass through Oshawa, there isn't really any countryside left. Identical housing projects begin popping up and the strip malls lining both sides of the highway give me a comforting feeling, even though all the signs are in English. Andre exits and pulls into a gas station to fill up. Serge and I stretch and lean against the back of the Chevette as the gas and oil fumes jar us out of our drowsiness.

"We really hauled ass tonight, eh?" I ask Andre, just trying to break the silence.

"Yeah, I think the sun's starting to come up."

The clock in the window of the kiosk reads close to six. A guy about our age, wearing the service station uniform, barely moves from his chair as Andre pays. When he comes back out to the car, Serge asks the usual question about where we're going to sleep. This has become a pointless exercise, because even though I can't second-guess Andre, I know he's always thinking ahead. One of us just has to draw it out of him, and Serge always gives in to the urge first. Andre assures us there's got to be a youth drop-in shelter downtown, and he figures there should be some beds available now that it's morning. This seems reasonable to me, and I'm too tired to argue anyway.

The traffic starts to get heavier as the four-lane road expands to eight. Eighteen-wheelers blow by us on their morning runs. Andre has a map he bought at the gas station, and Serge is guiding him through the asphalt maze as best he can. We make a quick exit and are suddenly on our way downtown. I have pleasant memories of Toronto, so I'm not really worried. In some ways, it's more familiar than Montreal.

Andre drives like he's playing with a slot-car race track as we dodge streetcars, buses and double-parked delivery vans. Serge is craning his neck left and right, trying to catch glimpses of street signs. All he and I remember is walking up and down Yonge Street during our hockey trips, so we finally decided to take that route.

The sights instantly connect with my memory once we turn onto Yonge and the Eaton Centre casts its shadow across the street. Andre is driving slowly now, as if sniffing out the youth shelter he knows should be around here. And there it is.

We pull into the first parking lot we find, even though it's charging an outrageous fee. Andre performs his usual trick, tipping the attendant to keep an eye on the Chevette, but the Pakistani man in the booth doesn't seem to understand. Andre hands him a twenty and says keep the change in his hilarious English accent, but I don't laugh, knowing I'll be sounding like that too.

We bring along our knapsacks and Andre has a sandwich bag of meth stashed somewhere in his jacket. He tells us to look tired as we enter the shelter, but the advice isn't necessary. We stumble through the glass doors, the interior smelling faintly like a locker room. A young girl behind a desk, obviously just starting her shift by the way she's rummaging through papers and cradling her coffee mug, is the first person to greet us. Before she can ask how she can help, Andre steps forward and spills his guts in his broken English about driving all night and being broke. She immediately gets up and shows us to the large sleeping areas, saying in simple sentences that we can crash if we need to. We thank her using our best French charm and each choose one of the mattresses orderly arranged on the bare floor. The room is fully lit and a constant noise comes from the kitchen, but I pass out almost as soon as I set my knapsack down.

The sleep is surprisingly satisfying, until I feel a hard nudge in my chest. I ignore it the first time, but when I open my eyes I see Serge sitting up beside me on his mattress, his face frozen in shock as a large Indian crouches beside him, carrying on a conversation Serge can't understand. I quickly look for Andre, but he's not around. As I become more cognizant, the Indian appears to be getting frustrated by Serge's unresponsiveness. I don't want to leave Serge at his mercy so I instinctively yell out, expecting some uniformed security to pounce on him. Instead, the Indian faces me, and I get a full view of his wasted state, even at this early hour. His eyes can't look directly at me, and I brace myself for whatever shot he plans to take.

He keeps talking, getting louder with each sentence, occasionally turning back to say something to Serge. From the corner of my eye I see a skinny kid with a ponytail quietly enter the room. He smiles and puts his finger up to his lips, signalling me not to do anything. The Indian continues to babble as Ponytail approaches him from behind. The kid grabs the Indian's right arm, the one that's making constant gestures, and brings it back into a half nelson. At the same time, he puts him into a headlock and raises him to his feet. The Indian is unable to struggle in the state he's in, as the kid roughly ejects him from the room. In the process, a switchblade falls from the Indian's jean jacket and clangs on the tiled floor. Serge picks it up and snaps it open.

"Do you want it?" he asks.

"No. Maybe Andre does."

The kid returns and sits down with us. "You guys all right?"

Serge and I look at each other and nod hesitantly. "You're the French guys who just came in, right?" the kid asks, and we nod again. "My name's Mike. If you guys need anything, talk to me. Don't worry about that fucker, sometimes he thinks this is the Salvation Army shelter down the street."

Serge shows him the switchblade. "He had this on him."

Mike smiles. "Thanks. I'll put it in the lost and found." Serge and I laugh.

We understand Mike a lot better than the Indian. He's jovial, and doesn't seem fazed at all by the incident. As he gets up to leave, he mentions that there's breakfast left if we want any. We thank him but he's already out of the room.

There's still no trace of Andre, and a brief jolt of panic replaces my momentary adrenaline rush. Since there's nothing else to do we decide to get in on the breakfast. We go out the way Mike exited, and are surprised to see him sitting at a table with a freshly showered and shaved Andre, eating fried-egg sandwiches. They're talking like old friends about the city and some of Mike's experiences here. Andre's English is better than I thought.

The two of us join them and start eying the sandwiches. Mike points to a table in the corner where about half a dozen rest on a platter next to a coffee machine and some mugs. I grab my share and return feeling relieved that Andre has made a connection. Mike immediately gets us involved in the conversation, making a crack about us being afraid of the Indian, at which Andre laughs loudly.

I suppose Andre has already told him about the trip, because Mike doesn't inquire much about what our business is, so far from home. He actually speaks a little French. Kids from Quebec often turn up at the shelter, therefore all the staff is required to know phrases like, "Do your parents know you're here?" He tries a few things on us, but stops after we chuckle uncontrollably at his clumsy phrasing.

The pleasant conversation continues while Serge and I finish eating, then Mike unexpectedly asks, "So, you guys selling drugs?"

The two of us reflexively glare at Andre with wide-open eyes, waiting for his response. One that isn't forthcoming.

Andre finally manages to stammer, "You want to buy?"

The entire time, Mike's stony expression hasn't changed but he finally laughs, realizing the fear he's put into us.

"Oh man, you guys are never gonna make it," he says. "I don't give a shit what you do if you're only staying for a few days. Just don't let me catch you doing it in here. As your friends noticed this morning, dangerous situations come with the territory, so conduct your business outside."

I'm catching maybe every other word, but I can see that Andre gets it all. There's an uncomfortable silence until Mike begins suggesting places we should check out. He tries to explain the layout of the city, and we're all dazed after the onslaught of information. The centre is empty for the most part, except for a guy sweeping up, and quiet except for an occasional rattle from the kitchen. Beyond the reception desk, I notice a bunch of kids loitering outside the front doors. In talking about his job, Mike explains how he likes to believe the residents looked for work during the day, but admits that most were out begging for change somewhere in the vicinity. Mike's close to earning a degree in social work, and has worked at the centre for almost a year to receive extra credit. The afternoon is his time off and hearing this makes me conscious of cutting into his sleep cycle. He puts us at ease, though, saying it wasn't that often that he meets kids who are just passing through. Many of his kids had been at the shelter as long as he had.

Just as we expect him to leave, he starts thinking out loud about why these kids are drawn to Toronto. The city doesn't have the magic of Hollywood or the twenty-four hour rush of New York. Toronto is a business town, he says, and kids who come looking for excitement inevitably wind up doing business at its most basic level, drugs and prostitution. I can see Andre's wheels turning during Mike's little speech.

Mike finally concedes that he needs rest, but we don't seem

ready to venture into the street, even after everything he's told us. Yawning, he shows us to a small room past the sleeping area. It's small enough that we hadn't noticed it, but it contains a couple of unplugged arcade games. We rectify that situation right away, and it's an added bonus that we don't need to throw quarters in to play. I'm enjoying the distraction, until people start filtering back to watch the small television chained to a corner of the ceiling. The room also holds a foosball table, a couch and a few matching cushion chairs. After a few hours, Mike pops back to tell us dinner is at six, and we realize we've wasted the entire day.

I'm not bothered in the slightest, but Andre seems to suddenly face reality again, huddling us into a corner to lay out his plan. He wants us to stick to our regular nightclub routine, but Serge wants to revisit some of the places we'd hung at during our previous trips. I know without asking that he wants to go to the strip club that let us in as under-agers. Andre rolls his eyes. He just never was comfortable going to those places. Back in Quebec City, Serge and I would often get the urge to see dancers, but Andre would always turn down the invitation. He never told us why. A confrontation is brewing, before Andre finally concedes that he has enough money to get us across the border, so the desire to have some fun wins out.

No one bothers us in the rec room until an hour before dinner, when two young punk girls take seats on the couch and turn on a talk show as if this was their own basement. I watch them out of the corner of my eye, but they sit silently, glued to the set. The show has something to do with fat people from what I can understand. We go back to the video games until Mike calls us to dinner.

The meal consists of cream of mushroom soup, served from a huge pot, and bologna sandwiches. The way everyone's eyes are fixed upon us, I get the impression that this is the usual crew. We don't talk, but try to decipher the conversations going on around us. Most of the chatter concerns getting hassled by cops, or the rudeness of people on the street. At that moment, it strikes me that we don't look like anyone else here. They all have long hair, or none at all. Many are wearing grimy Goodwill corduroys. Almost all have their bodies pierced in places besides their ears. Our hair barely falls to our shoulders, and I know I have at least a few unsoiled clothes stowed in my knapsack.

Andre is sitting across from me, and I recognize him sizing up the room for possible scores. It amazes me how his mind stores everything. We eat slowly in order to let others leave the table before us. Some head to the game room and some go out for cigarettes. Without saying anything, Andre leads us out the doors to scope out the situation, even though none of us smoke. After a few minutes, Andre speaks up.

"Parlez-vous francais?"

The crowd looks at us as if we were from another planet. It was worth a shot, I guess. Andre tries again, this time in English.

"Anyone looking for some speed?" This different approach doesn't alter many expressions. Some smile at each other, and some politely shake their heads.

One guy extinguishes his butt and moves closer. He's a head taller than Andre and bends down to speak into his ear. "Whatcha want for it?" Andre whispers the price through the guy's long hair. The guy answers with a nod and motions to go back inside. Andre quickly balks at this, saying they'll have to go to the Chevette parked across the street. The guy agrees and they start walking. Serge and I remain at the door until Andre looks back with a piercing glance and waves us along. I catch his drift that he wants a show of strength if he's going to be sleeping under the same roof as this guy.

Andre and the guy make the deal in the front seats while Serge and I pretend to root around in the back for something. "If this stuff's good, I'll be wanting more," the guy says as I watch him slip a $100 bill into Andre's hand.

We slam down the back hatch as the two emerge from the side doors, Andre unable to conceal a smile. There's a different attendant in the kiosk, so Andre again waves a $20 bill in his face in exchange for watching the blue Chevette. This man understands perfectly, and the evening is off to a good start. Andre's customer returns to the centre and lights up another cigarette while we stick to the other side of the street, with the intention of stopping at the first bar we come across. The whole time, I have a nagging feeling Mike will jump from the shadows and beat us for what we just did. Suddenly I don't want to be involved.

The first bar turns out to be the Hard Rock Café. We order a pitcher of 50 and bask in the rock memorabilia hanging on the walls. It's kind of like being back in Mario's attic. Influenced by the atmosphere, I ask Andre why he didn't try to get another band together. "We were complete shit, that's why," he answers. I disagree, to which he responds, "Don't kiss my ass, man, it doesn't suit you. You know as well as I do that nothing was going to happen. Kurt said it all better than I ever could." As if by magic, a few minutes later "Smells Like Teen Spirit" comes blasting through the stereo as we toss back our mugs of beer.

After another round, it's still early, so we start asking our waitress about other things to do. She's pretty hot, and I like how she laughs at our accents. I can't help wondering if all English girls are as easy as she seems. We down a third pitcher and the place begins to fill up. It's one thing to be in a crowded bar with a band playing, but it's another to be in one with nothing to do but drink.

There are still traces of sunlight visible when we hit the street again, meaning it's still too early to go to the strip club. I mean, we don't want to look like perverts. Instead we unknowingly embark on our traditional crawl along Yonge. It's so easy to lose your inhibitions among all the crap available in the shops. We go into every discount T-shirt place and feel temporarily amused just flipping through the poster racks. Kurt's face follows us everywhere. Andre says something about the T-shirt makers being pimps, and he's visibly distressed. However, he does pick up a Nirvana cassette we've never seen before. It has a cheap, black-and-white cover, and on the back it says it was recorded for $600. At that moment, Andre has more than that on him.

The tape is stashed in Andre's flannel jacket after it's paid for, and we continue our aimless wandering. We pass several pornography shops. The first is a video store, and we laugh openly at the tasteless titles displayed in the window, all of us undoubtedly looking like total hicks. The next is a magazine store and we go in. There are a few men milling near the back who we stay away from, and the old man behind the counter can't drag his attention away from a lesbian scene on the television above him.

I recall how, just a few years ago, porn was really exciting, but any remnants of those feelings are gone. There's nothing fun about it at all. It isn't a question of morality; I'm just thinking about Anne-Marie and missing the great sex we'd had. We'd explore each other for hours, building up the tension until we'd explode. We were both teases with great self-control. She often wouldn't even start taking off clothes until I begged her. Sometimes this satisfied me enough that fucking was a letdown. Looking at the men in the back of the store, I can tell they've never experienced anything like that. It makes me even more sad for myself that I'm here with them when the real thing is back home.

It's completely dark as we leave the store, but the numerous streetlights and signs make the city feel like an entirely different place. We get our bearings and head for the strip club that's haunted our imaginations. We take a few wrong turns, believing it's closer than it is, but backtracking to Jarvis Street brings us there.

This time, there's no anxiety about entering. We walk past the doorman and that's it. Our eyes are immediately drawn to a slim girl in a G-string on the stage in the middle of the room. She's dancing to some nondescript hip-hop and fondling her rather small breasts as if dreaming they were a lot bigger. We take a table near the bar and a waitress in a bikini brings us the first of several pitchers. The girl onstage eventually removes the G-string and accepts donations from the throng of men at her feet.

There isn't really much to talk about. We're in serious drinking mode now, no time for distractions. A few more girls do their acts, and we watch men around us getting lap dances.

As I watch a stripper grind away on some fat fuck, the more intrigued I become with getting my own lap dance. I finally say to Andre, "Gimme twenty bucks." It's the first time I think either Serge or I have asked him for money. He gives me a predictable look of disdain and slowly reaches into his petty-cash pocket. I'm thinking he's just curious to see what I'll do with it. Running my fingers over the bill's coarse texture gives me confidence, and I purposely swivel my head around in search of the nearest half-naked woman. One finally approaches, and I wave the twenty in her face like some coy 1920s debutante waving a handkerchief. She has long, dark hair and is painfully thin, but she breaks into a wide smile when she starts grinding in front of me.

She asks my name as she removes her bra, and I'm overwhelmed hearing her French accent. I begin to ramble on uncontrollably in my native tongue and she laughs so hard she has to briefly stop her gyrations. I feel an instant bond between us, although I don't tell her to stop. A carnal urge to take her right there rises inside me, but just as I feel like I might burst out of my jeans, she gets up, puts her bikini back on, smiles and says, "Nice to meet you." She disappears to the other end of the bar and I can't stop myself from pursuing her. Andre yells out when he sees bouncers swooping in on me. All I can do is call out to her to come back for a drink. She turns her head, says she'll think about it, and the bouncers escort me back to the table.

I don't look at Andre or Serge as I refill my glass. "I think she liked you," one of them says, and they both laugh. They just can't lay off. More dancers come and go, and I drink in silence until Serge taps me on the shoulder and says, "She's coming over." I jerk my head up and try to open my eyes. She's wearing a T-shirt and jeans and holding a tall glass of brown liquor.

"We're closing up now, so I thought I'd take you up on your offer," she says in a surprisingly perky tone. "My name's Monique,

I'm from Montreal. You guys just visiting?"

The guys wisely let me answer. "Yeah, we'll be here for a few days. Business trip."

"Yeah? What kind of business might three hip young men like you be in? Oh, wait, ching-ching!" She toasts my glass and my heart melts.

Andre bursts in, sensing an opportunity. "We're carrying some hot shit, pure meth, you interested?" She turns away from me and I feel invisible.

"You shouldn't say that too loud in here, undercover cops are in all the time." Monique looks around the room and then at me. "Did you have fun tonight?" My spirit instantly lifts again and I nod stupidly.

"You know, it's nice when I meet some honest French boys. Are you staying in a hotel? No? Well I wouldn't be much of a French girl if I didn't invite you back to my place, would I?" Fear grips my throat, and the others must feel the same as no one answers right away. "Come on, it's only a few blocks away."

With that, we awkwardly get up from the table and leave. Visions of an orgy come into my head. The night is still warm and the streets are calm, with only scattered pedestrians shuffling past the hookers and cabs on Jarvis. I stumble once or twice but keep my eyes squarely focused, using Monique's onion-shaped ass as a guiding beacon. A hooker in red stretch pants and four-inch heels says something like, "Want me to take one of them off your hands honey?" and Monique laughs loud and long.

"They're all mine."

From a safe distance, Serge tries to yell, "What's your student rate?" but it comes out horribly mangled in translation. Monique lives on the second floor of a duplex, and the pungent aroma of marijuana hits us when she opens the door. We're all paralyzed by the sight of the prone frame of the longhaired guy Andre had made the deal with a few hours earlier. Apparently, we've woken him.

Panic sets in, and Andre is already backing down the stairs when the guy gives us a warm greeting. "All right! I was wondering what was taking you so long. I saw you at the club, so I told Monique here to show you a good time. Did she?" We're too stunned to respond. I nod, feeling like I've just admitted to cheating on an exam.

Monique sits beside him on the couch as he rolls a joint on the coffee table. "Do you live here, too?" I meekly ask him.

"Whenever I have to. See, me and Monique — my name's Boo by the way — me and Monique look out for each other. She's got a lot of friends and I got a lot of friends. Between us we know a lot of people." I don't grasp what he means. He lights the joint, takes a long pull and passes it to Monique before continuing. "It seems with the shit you guys have, you know some people too. I want you to know, as long as you want to be my friend, I'll be your friend."

Oddly enough, Boo's cordial attitude is making us more uncomfortable. We all take short hits and wait for Andre to say something. Boo doesn't give him a chance.

"I need more of that stuff. That's some killer shit, man. I could have kept it all for myself. Where'd it come from?"

After a pause, Andre says, "Back home."

"Where's that, Paris?" He and Monique can't hold back a dopey giggle.

"Quebec City."

"Hmm. I don't get up there that often. What would you want to go back there and tell your people to mix me up some more and then bring it back? Ten grand?"

Andre doesn't hesitate this time. "I got more."

"Yeah, it must be powering that little shit box you're driving."

"I'll give you the rest for ten grand." We look at Andre in disbelief. He's as cool as a movie drug lord.

"All right! Buddy's a high roller. How much you got?"

"Half a pound."

"I like this guy!"

"Let's do the deal later. I don't know where I am."

Boo laughs loudly. "Yeah, one day in town and you hit the jackpot.

You're lucky I'm such a nice guy, but I gotta get my shit together tomorrow, you dig? So we'll do it on Thursday, *ca va?*"

Traces of a smile show on Andre's face, and we're all more at ease now. We all understand it's just a matter of not saying something that will fuck things up. The only problem is getting out of here as discreetly as possible. I keep eying Monique though, without trying to be too obvious. She and Boo don't appear to be lovers; they barely acknowledge each other. I can't stop picturing her in nothing but a G-string, grinding her pelvis into mine. We'd practically fucked.

Eventually, she steps into another room and Boo quietly says to me, "You like her, eh? It's all right man, I've been in your shoes. You're a long way from home trying to cash in on the first pussy that comes on to you. Don't feel bad. She ain't for sale, though. You gotta work for it."

I think this over until she returns and Andre tells us we're leaving. He and Boo go over the deal once more, and I start to worry about finding our way back to the shelter. Boo alleviates my concern. "You're not going back to the shelter are you? It's closed at this time of night."

Panic strikes again, then Monique says the words I've been dying to hear all night: "You can stay here if you want." Andre and Serge don't seem too eager, but I immediately settle into my spot in the chair. There's some commotion as the guys stake out some room on the badly-stained rug. The last thing I remember is seeing her emerge from her room, a blanket in each hand, striking a magician's assistant pose, arms spread wide, as Boo lights up another joint. I'm asleep before it comes around.

Sometime later, I realize the chair is killing me. The room is a hazy grey in the early sunlight, and my bowels are screaming. I don't know where the bathroom is and I have to carefully step over Andre and Serge to look for it. The only sign of Boo is a full ashtray, a pack of Zig-Zag rolling papers, and a few empty beer bottles. I start by trying doors. The first is an empty linen closet. The next is Monique's room. I quickly close the door and find the bathroom by the process of elimination. On the way back I'm compelled to take another look in her room. Monique is facing away from me, her bare back partly covered by her hair. I expect to see Boo there with her but she's alone. Her figure draws my fingers like a magnet. After a minute, she turns onto her back and her breasts point to the ceiling. They look beautifully natural here, not like in the bar, where they are required to work. She exhales heavily and I quickly back away.

I'm almost content stretching out on the couch, although I can't sleep. My thoughts drift to how I can manage to spend time with Monique — lunch, anything. She'll appreciate that. How many guys here have taken her on a real date? At least it might get Andre and Serge off my back. Eventually, they begin stirring. "Where's the can?" Serge asks, barely able to stand.

"Last room at the end of the hall." Andre follows him and afterward, we get together on the floor and try to map out the day. I stay quiet, waiting to hear what they have in mind. The consensus is to head back to the shelter first to get some breakfast, then go sightseeing. At some point, Andre has to call Mario and tell him about the big score. That's it.

"I think I want to hang here for a bit," I say.

"What? Are you nuts? This is Boo's pad, too, and if you think you'll get anywhere with her . . ." Andre's voice trails off into early morning brain-lock.

"Well, we shouldn't leave until she gets up." They reluctantly agree to this courtesy, and we retreat into our own worlds since the only amusements around are drug paraphernalia and some old fashion magazines. Monique gets up about an hour later, surprised to see our faces gawking at her when she appears wearing nothing but a T-shirt and panties.

"Do you guys . . . want anything?"

Andre replies, "No, we were just leaving. Thanks for letting us crash."

The guys make a move for the door and I'm still on the couch.

I struggle to say, "Um, I was wondering, if you're not doing anything today, if I could take you to lunch or something."

She smiles. Her tits look even sexier sprouting under the T-shirt. "Sure, I know a place. Just me and you?"

I glance at Andre and he shakes his head.

"Meet us back at the shelter for dinner. We'll be cruising around today."

They leave and I'm suddenly filled with a mix of triumph and terror. Monique makes a pot of coffee and we pass the morning talking about Toronto and Montreal. She'd left two years ago after getting some high-paying gigs here. She just ended up staying. She didn't say anything about drugs, but I imagine that was part of the reason, too. I ask about Boo but all she says is he's all right as long as she did things his way. Looking at her in full daylight, I can see numerous scabs and bruises she'd hidden with makeup. It's troubling, but not enough to change the way I feel about her.

I persuade her, after the coffee's gone, to take me somewhere where we can get some fresh air. It's another hot day and we walk aimlessly through identical blocks of shops until she pulls me onto a streetcar that takes us to a place she calls High Park. I think that's pretty funny, but it turns out to be the actual name. Without warning, she sits down in the middle of a maple grove and stretches her arms and legs out wide, embracing the sun. "Are you working at the club tonight?" I ask.

"Yeah, actually in a few hours. We make some of our best dough when guys come in after work."

"I really think you're beautiful."

"Is that why you dragged me out here? You want to do it in the park?"

"No. I just have never met anyone like you before. I think I love you."

She laughs. "Ah, that's sweet. Did you buy me a ring? You didn't have to go that far for a fuck, I know you're just passing through town. I probably owe you anyway for making Boo so happy."

I don't know what to say. I feel empty. She leans over and kisses me on the lips.

"I'm sorry. I didn't mean it like that. I think you're cute, but listen to what you're saying. You don't belong here. I don't belong here either, but I'm stuck. Now if you want something to remember me by, we can do that." She puts one hand behind my neck and the other on my cock. I'm getting what I want but it's all terribly wrong somehow. I'm almost on the verge of being sick.

I pull away and politely ask her how to get back to the shelter. She looks puzzled, then tries to sort out the directions. As I leave her, she says "Merci" and her voice breaks on a high note that rings in my head all the way back. The blocks start adding up, and so do the questions. Why was Monique "stuck" here? Why was I in love with her? Why couldn't I stay? What force was preventing this from happening? Something Andre said before we left crosses my mind, about people not seeing all the shit in the world until someone rubs their face in it. I don't want to admit this to myself as much as hope someone should do it to Monique. I become so engrossed in these thoughts that I briefly lose my way. The store signs are an indecipherable blur, and the number of homeless people make me even more depressed. Some are lost in madness. A guy with no arms and legs begs for change. Some are my age.

I end up hailing a cab and try my best to explain where the shelter is. There, I purposely avoid eye contact with the people standing out front. I head straight to the games room, where the same two girls are watching the same talk show. I play a video game until the screen becomes blurry. It's weirdly soothing every time my Street Fighter gets killed. It looks awfully painful, but he always comes back for more.

Mike gives the dinner call and I'm not surprised to see Andre and Serge already wolfing down the soup and chicken-salad sandwiches. It's actually a relief to hear about their day. They'd visited the CN Tower, checked out some guitars and stood outside of

MuchMusic hoping they'd get on TV. I tell them Monique is a whore and I got what I wanted, and we silently decide to leave it at that.

After the meal we hang around a bit with Mike, and he tells us to go to Lee's Palace and check out this band called Treble Charger. On the way, Andre calls Mario from a phone booth. I genuinely don't care what they discuss, but Andre seems satisfied when it's over. "The package is on the way to the border," is all he says.

The band lifts my spirits a little, but I make sure we leave in time to get back before the shelter closes. Mike is waiting for us at the reception desk. "Just trying to be a good host," he says. He's saved us beds and I spend the night hoping the Indian will cut my throat. I want to go home.

All kinds of noises keep me awake and I'm a wreck when Mike rouses us for breakfast. We shower and Andre begins a vigil for Boo. Apparently, he didn't say when he'd show up. Things are tense all day. Serge and I even help Mike clean up to get our minds off the situation. Late in the afternoon, Andre spots Boo out front having a smoke. He's wearing a long leather coat, which only means he came prepared, since it's another abnormally hot day.

Andre persuades us to back him up again but I refuse. This is your game, I want to say; I'm just along for the ride from now on. He curses me and Serge walks out with him, eyes wide with trepidation.

They return shortly, looking flushed from the excitement. Andre happily shows me the money, which now bulges from his belt. I try hard to feel happy for him. Mike convinces us to stay for dinner and gives us a curiously emotional send-off afterward, saying, "You guys shouldn't be doing this, you aren't cut out for it, but be careful anyway. I don't want to see you back here again."

Crossing the busy intersection, I couldn't agree more. I wonder how I'll learn to cope with it. All I have left is my faith in Andre.

The Chevette starts with a cough and Andre lets it idle before we pull out. We could have left later, but Toronto doesn't have anything else to offer now. We'll hit the border at midnight if we don't stop, but Andre eventually realizes that it won't do us any good. He agrees to splurge on a motel.

We get caught in rush hour traffic and it takes a long time before we fade into the wilderness again, far away from Boo and Monique — and all the people who are getting high on Andre's meth.

6 Andre
Detroit: May 15, 1994.

Dear Sylvie,

I went to the downtown post office in Toronto hoping I'd get a letter from you. I know it was probably a long shot but I've been feeling lucky lately. Did you even write? I don't blame you if you haven't. I thought it would take me a lot longer to admit what I said in my last letter. I hope you took it the right way. Anyway, T.O. was a blast but I wouldn't want us to live there. We'd need a lot of money. I hope you don't mind me saying "we." I figure that's the way it should be from now on. At least it will make me feel better if I can think of us that way. We saw the CN Tower and the Eaton Centre and Maple Leaf Gardens. There were some really cool record stores, and you would love shopping on Queen Street. I think we even got on MuchMusic. Steve Anthony was on the street when Serge and I walked by. We hung back because we didn't want him to ask us any questions, but I think the camera was on us the whole time. Did you see us? We ended up not staying as long as we planned just because there wasn't much to do besides the regular tourist stuff. It's a full-time job surviving there. There's no way we could have lasted two weeks without one of us dying of boredom. How are your exams going? I don't mean to nag, but you've got to do well if you and I are going to get anywhere. You've got the brains. Don't ever forget that. I'm writing from a motel room outside of London, I think. All these towns on the 401 are beginning to run together. They're so evenly spaced, too. I don't even have to think about stopping for gas, a service station is always there. I just have to work on my own timing. We've been arriving at places in the middle of the night, which isn't the most convenient time to look for shelter. I think the manager of this place thought we were escaped cons. Why else would three greasy guys with French accents be on the road so late? My timing's been pretty bad with you, too. I wish I could have talked to you like this when we were together. I'll take the blame for that. It may be too late for you to write me, 'cuz we're going to be moving a little faster now. I should call you but, like I said, I don't think I can communicate my feelings that way, especially not without seeing your beautiful face. I'd really love to hear your voice, though. So I will call. Soon. Until then, know that I love you and I always will.

Andre

I let the guys take the beds. I don't feel like sleeping. I had to write Sylvie after I didn't get a letter in Toronto. I feel better. Maybe I will sleep. This is a mistake. We should have kept going. Mario said it's easier getting over the border early in the morning. The guards pulling the graveyard shift ask fewer questions. That reminds me, what am I going to tell them? The truth. Yeah, the truth. Canton, Ohio, the NFL Hall of Fame. That's right sir, we're all huge fans of Terry Bradshaw. We want to see his sweaty jersey in person. Or was it the Baseball Hall of Fame? No, you say that when you cross at Buffalo.

Just to be an asshole, I wake the guys yelling, "Fire! Fire!" I'm not surprised that they expect something better than this half-hearted gag. I told them to get their shit together as I go to the office to check out. The same guy who checked me in is dozing and seems truly scared, opening his eyes to find me staring him down. I'm polite while handing him the money, but can't resist saying, in French, "If you tell anyone we were here, I'll kill you," as I leave. I don't get to witness his reaction, but the thought keeps me chuckling all the way back to the room. Serge and Rich are already asleep in the car when I pull back out onto the nearly empty 401. We pass through London without seeing many other vehicles. The terrain is flat, and the first rays of dawn bring the tobacco farms into view. The border is two hours away, and for the first time I feel myself nodding off behind the wheel. It's terrifying, but I can't force myself to pull over.

I'm driving like an autopilot — no music — and there is nothing along the road to keep me amused. The desolate stretch goes on forever, and I start counting the kilometres to stay awake. That's when I see the fuel light come on. Suddenly, all those service stations are miles behind us and the Chevette soon persuades me to pull over by emitting a few coughs. It dies on the shoulder just ahead of the "Welcome to Windsor" sign.

The guys wake up expecting the worst, but lay back after I tell them we've run out of gas. I feel useless standing at the side of the road, so I yell at them to get out and join me. The only thing to do is flag someone down to take us to the Husky station just over the hill. We shiver for a few minutes, actually enjoying the novelty of real hitchhiking, until the first pair of headlights approach. As the car nears, I can make out that it's a souped-up, early '70s hunk of shit, which I assume is being driven by some greasy loner who won't hesitate to put a bullet in each of our skulls and haul our stuff across the border.

I tell the guys to start walking, but the driver has spotted us and pulls over a few yards ahead. Without hesitation, Rich walks up to the driver's side and explains the problem. Serge and I stand well back until Rich waves us forward with a wide grin. "We just need to get to the nearest gas station," I say, not trusting Rich's English.

"No problem. You guys are lucky, I just finished my shift. I'm an OPP officer." He adds with a laugh, "Ten minutes ago I'd have to haul your butts in for this."

Rich laughs out loud as the cop moves the passenger seat forward to allow him and Serge in the back. "Nice car," I say, trying not to dwell on the irony of the situation.

"Yeah, not as many toys as a cruiser, but it puts out just as much." He gives a brief demonstration before we hit the exit for the gas station. I buy a gas can off the attendant while Rich and Serge make friendly chatter with the officer. I maintain a stony silence, mentally preparing myself for what it'll be like if we get busted. This whole situation has got to be a bad omen.

The cop drops us off back at the Chevette and squeals his tires for us as he departs. A couple of minutes later, I pull back into the station to fill up for real. The guys are wide awake and in a good mood now, so I take the opportunity to refresh their memories on border crossing etiquette — have the birth certificates ready, speak only when you're spoken to, we all say the same thing. At that moment, I'm inspired. We'll tell the border guards we're going to visit relatives in Louisiana. It makes more sense with all the stuff we're carrying.

I have to do some banking, too. I'd deposited the ten grand Boo paid me in Mario's bank account before we left Toronto and kept the rest I'd made to get us through our first days in Detroit. I change this amount to American funds at the duty free shop. I hand Rich and Serge a small share of the identical American greenbacks each, and we spend a few minutes carefully examining them as if they were pages in an ancient book. That pyramid with the eye in it freaks me out. Mario told me to watch what we say around the border, because there are hidden microphones and cameras all over. I guess the unblinking eye is a good symbol for America.

The bridge across the Detroit River feels endless. I can't tell how nervous the guys are, but I'm resisting the urge to pull a 180 and head north. There's a lot of lumberjacks around Thunder Bay who might be willing to pay good money for this shit. It's early dawn and there isn't much traffic yet, so I roll up to the first available kiosk and brace myself for the questions.

"Citizenship?"

"Canadian."

"Destination?"

"Baton Rouge, Louisiana."

"What's the purpose of this trip?"

I put on my best Pepe le Pew accent. "We go to veezeet rela-teeves."

There's a tense lull as the guard runs my license through the computer. He tells me to pull over. Rich and Serge start nattering, but I tell them to be cool — we haven't got anything on us, remember? The agents command us to empty the car, and they search through our stuff while we're led to the office for further inquiries. We're told to empty our pockets and asked a few questions to test our story. We come through with flying colours. The next thing I know, we're loading up the car again.

The agents confiscate the beers we had in the cooler, but they're skunky anyway. They let us go with a stern warning. Getting through this ordeal brings out unrestrained laughter when we finally pull away, now fully embraced by the open arms of America. It actually wasn't that hard. I could have had two bricks of hash taped to my gut and they wouldn't have noticed.

But the good feelings pass quickly, as we soon find ourselves deep in the bowels of Detroit. I've made a wrong turn already, leading us up a deserted street lined with boarded-up brick buildings undoubtedly housing scores of crackheads waiting for my car to stall so they can strip it down. Welcome to the jungle. Maybe I'm overreacting, but I turn around in the nearest parking lot and backtrack to the freeway. I can tell Serge and Rich are shitting themselves the whole time.

My attention is soon diverted by the abundance of potholes. Normally, I wouldn't worry, but these motherfuckers could snap an axle in half if I hit them squarely. The Chevette swings onto the freeway, at which point the engine coughs for a split second, forcing me to gun it in order to blend in with fast-moving Motor City traffic. We're passed on all sides; even an old rusty pick-up truck filled with Mexican-looking labourers in the back blows by us with little regard for its human cargo.

I get into the flow gradually and find an opportunity to look around a bit. The big sight is the Ford factory. It looms, monolithic, and my thoughts drift to the thousands of men who have toiled there over the years so we might have the freedom to come all the way from Quebec to see it. Serge is in the back and has cleverly inserted *KISS Alive* into the ghetto blaster. "Detroit Rock City" is now blaring. I lose my train of thought as the two of them bang their heads to the song's stupid chorus.

My attention gets back to the road as I anticipate the cut-off to Royal Oak. I'm hardly surprised. Suburbs in the States are the same as suburbs in Canada. We cruise the main strip looking for the post office, where Mario's package is supposed to be waiting for us. Not finding it right away allows Rich to talk me into stopping at a McDonald's for breakfast. Serge suggests having a Denny's Grand Slam, but Rich wins out, arguing that he wants to try a Breakfast Burrito: "You can't get them in Canada." I sip a coffee while they eat. It all looks disgusting.

We move on past more strip malls until a giant eagle marks our destination. I get our story straight one more time. We're on vacation and expecting a care package from my parents. No problem. The building is new and sterile-smelling. There are no other customers, only a few employees mingling behind the counter. I take a deep breath and approach the clerk, who greets me with a beginning-of-the-day smile.

"My name is Andre Bouchard. I'm expecting a package from La Forest, Quebec."

The clerk disappears briefly and returns with a large, heavily taped cardboard box, which he drops tantalizingly in front of me. It actually made it. Mario's a genius. "I need to see your ID sir." I'm shocked back to reality at this request and clumsily reach for my wallet. "It's COD. That'll be eighteen dollars. Sign here."

Just as we're leaving, flushed with success, I remember the letter to Sylvie in my pocket.

"Oh, I need a stamp for zis. We have to let our parents know how we're doing, no?"

The package is loose and small things rattle inside. Large stickers on the outside announce it to be fragile. Rich holds it like a trophy in the passenger seat as I search for a safe place to inspect the contents. I settle on the parking lot of a huge mall, where the Chevette is an anonymous drop in an ocean of vehicles. I carefully open the box, the guys hovering over it like vultures. Reaching inside, it's filled with cassettes and small pieces of paper. I extract the first unusual thing I touch, which turns out to be a note from Mario: *If you're reading this, keep up the good work. If not, we're all fucked. See you soon either way!*

We have a good laugh over this before I pull out one of the cassette cases and discover it contains a small plastic bag containing a gram of meth. The little pieces of paper are perfume samples from magazines, dozens of them. They fooled the drug-sniffing dogs, but it takes several hours to get the stench out of the car once the full blast of odour escapes the box. The upside seems to be that we won't have to shower today.

I methodically sort through every cassette case and collect the little bundles of rocks in my gym bag. The weight of selling this shit starts to creep up on me again. The guys, as usual, have other plans.

"Man, I'm dyin'," Rich says. "Let's get some beers and a hotel room or something. We're set up now."

Serge adds, "Yeah, we need to figure out a plan anyway, and you should get some sleep." I can't argue with him. I aim the Chevette back onto Royal Oak's main drag and stop at the first Motel 6 I see. I take care of checking in, and after the guys go to explore the motel's grimy pool, I pick up a couple of six packs from the nearest convenience store. Miller High Life. It certainly is.

Laying back on one of the beds, I crack open a can and surf the TV. This is the first time I've watched television in over a week and I barely understand a word. The watery beers go down fast. After a while, the guys return drenched and refreshed and finish off the few that are left. We have nothing to do and it feels great. It's almost like old times, sitting in our apartment getting drunk.

Nearly every channel is broadcasting a talk show or soap opera. From time to time, a newscaster appears with a brief update, which today involves a murder scene somewhere downtown. Throughout the afternoon, I see the image of a covered body lying in the street so often that paranoia once again begins hampering my thinking. What I'm actually seeing is a picture of my own covered body. I don't want to be on the news, with some moronic reporter speculating on what we were doing.

One guy kills another guy. One's a murderer and the other's a victim. Is that all there is to it? They might have been best friends until something went wrong — a drug deal, a woman, who knows? There's more to peoples' lives than the moment when somebody pulls the trigger. It's good to recognize this now. I need to get the whole story right. Sylvie deserves that much.

The beer is gone by five and we're hungry. Serge says he noticed a Ponderosa nearby and suggests we eat there before going into the city. He remembers eating at one once as a kid, so he wants to see if it's still the same. He's a little tanked. So am I. But I don't realize it until we're in the car. The familiar glow of an early-summer-afternoon beer buzz has settled on my brain, and for a split second I think about just chilling out for a few hours. But Serge is still gung-ho about going, so I drive.

It's the same stretch of road — with a large centre turning lane — we've been down several times already today, and I'm quickly starting to hate it. I hope the rest of America isn't this boring. The restaurant is not busy. Four identical black waitresses lounge around the register, probably exchanging gossip. We take a booth and one slowly approaches us with menus. We forget some English due to our drunkenness, and she seems offended, as if we were making fun of her. She tersely points out the specials and the salad bar. We can't control our laughter as we nod our approval and she walks away in a huff.

The meal is one of the worst I've ever had. Even Serge reluctantly admits his childhood memories of Ponderosa are permanently tarnished. The food does defuse some of the alcohol in my system, but the unfamiliar freeway soon has me mesmerized. We're attempting to conquer it at the height of Detroit's rush hour. Auto plant workers on their way home after another killing day on the assembly line. It's bumper to bumper as far as the eye can see.

The constant stop and go eventually becomes soothing, and Rich and Serge start making fun of things they observe, like the immense factories and neighbourhoods they imagine are actual ghettos, where black kids wear baseball caps sideways. I remind them that saying that stuff outside the car will get us killed, and they shut up.

The jam begins to thin out and I start to enjoy a little space when Rich catches a glimpse of Tiger Stadium. I'm momentarily taken by the gloriously rundown structure, so much so that I almost don't hear Serge yelling. A long second later, both of my feet are on the brake, and we're eye to eye with a "Baby On Board" sticker on the back of a mini-van.

As we're catching our breath, I resolve never to lose control like this again. The last thing we need is to lose time and money with a car accident, especially since I'd be thrown in jail for DWI, — never mind the meth. More importantly, the highway is no place to die. I've already established that. Our bodies will return home in the same form they were in when we left.

I keep driving, and eventually the shock of our close call fades. The large overhead signs tempt us with Canada, but I ignore them. Detroit is a marked change from Toronto. Obviously a blue-collar town. This gives me a slight sense of comfort, even though I've never seen so many black people before. We'd grown up learning racism was wrong, even though many of our parents didn't think twice about telling racial jokes or dropping words like "nigger" into conversations. Back home, the only people who looked different were Indians, and our parents shaped our opinions of them at an early age. Even in Quebec City it was rare to see black people. I don't feel any animosity toward them, but it's still strange to feel this weird guardedness as we scope out the downtown core.

None of us know what to look for. The sun is going down, and the same nervous tension at the border crossing has returned. I don't want any more beer, but finding a bar seems like our only option. We'll kill time and maybe make a contact. The youth shelters here are probably a hundred times rougher than the one in Toronto.

As we crawl down Hastings Street, Serge is hanging out the passenger side window, gazing in awe at the fancy hotels. The Hilton and the Sheraton are easily recognizable, and there are several others with names we can't pronounce. Serge finally asks, "Hey, we've got some cash, why don't we stay at one of these places tonight?"

"I didn't check us out of the motel. We're there until tomorrow."

"Fuck that. That place is a dump. Why've we been jerking around at all these shit dives when we should be living like high rollers? Mario's got his money now, we've got a new stash, let's be players, not some fucking losers who deal hash on the weekend."

He makes a good argument. Paying back Mario was my biggest concern, and the reason I had to watch our spending in Canada. Now he'd probably be happy getting back half of what he deserves just because it means he won't be going to jail. I wonder if he called the post office to see if I picked up the package? He must be shitting bricks since I called him last. I haven't even thought of calling him to say everything is all right. Fucking long distance, it can be traced. But who cares? I could call Sylvie too.

"Pick one out, we're getting a room," I declare. The guys are clearly down with the decision, so happy in fact that we get into an argument trying to choose which hotel to pull into. Serge wants one with valet parking so he can see the guy's look when the Chevette rolls up. I don't like that idea.

I glance around and realize we should have cleaned ourselves up a little. We'll never make it through the front door of most of these places, so I pull into the Best Western thinking it looks less intimidating than the others. It has underground parking, which is good, and the doorman even offers to carry our knapsacks for us. He must think we're rock stars or something. The desk clerk is a kind-looking woman, but something about her says don't fuck with me you little punks.

I smile and work my accent. "Do you have any available suites?"

"You don't have a reservation, I presume?"

"No, my friends and I are on our way to Louisiana, and zis is our first time in America. We've been driving a long time but we want to see Detroit, Chicago and, um, St. Louis."

"Oh! Where are you from?"

"Quebec."

"Oh, it's beautiful there isn't it?"

"Yes."

"And how long do you plan to stay?"

"Um, better make it three days. Your city looks very exciting."

"Oh yes. Do you like baseball? The Tigers are playing the Angels all weekend."

"Sounds great."

"You can sign here . . . and here's your key. Enjoy your stay!"

I don't know what it is, the accents maybe, but people just keep buying everything I sell them.

The suite is the most amazing room I've ever been in — we're clearly not worthy of it in the state we're in. We take turns showering and shaving and realize we're down to our last clean clothes. We'll have to hit a laundromat while we're here. Rich and Serge can't help dredging up their past fancy-hotel experiences, when they'd go to Toronto for hockey tournaments. They'd fill up bathtubs with ice and beer, try to hit cars with stuff thrown from the balcony and play tag through the halls while everyone else tried to sleep. The one story I don't mind hearing again is about getting one of the guys to pass out, then stripping him, tying him up and sending him up and down on the elevator.

We all shave, but Serge leaves a goatee. He says he needs to look meaner. I say it will take a lot more than that. I'm starting to feel so good about this new setting, I don't bother to devise a plan for the evening, and the guys don't remember to ask as we head down to the lobby. I'm feeling self-conscious, though, wearing my heavy flannel jacket, in order to keep the stash in the inside pocket. The sooner I can dump this shit, the better. Still, I can't resist giving a wink to the desk clerk as we pass, and she smiles back. Maybe she isn't really a bitch.

In the artificial glow of evening, walking down Hastings Street in search of a point of entry, it's obvious this isn't a tourist town. The bars are for drinking, not socializing. Our choices quickly narrow. On the opposite side of the street, a neon sign announces "Cold Beer" alongside a giant illuminated martini glass straight out of some old black-and-white movie. I'm drawn to it like a magnet, so I get the guys to cross the street and gingerly squeeze between two El Dorados parked outside the front door. After another quick look at the exterior, I have trouble believing the place is even real.

I scan the interior. It's well lit, with a small bar at the far end and old, framed rhythm and blues concert posters on the walls. The clientele does a quick scan of us, too. The eyes of a middle-aged black couple at one table are fixed on us, as are those of a group of younger black men across the room in a corner booth, who start laughing purposefully. I try to ignore them and lead the guys to the bar where a surprisingly jovial black man takes our orders after checking our IDs.

"Well well, got some Canucks looking for action."

His voice booms within the small space and I'm poised like a rabbit to bolt out of there. I miss the chance when one of the young homies from the corner booth approaches.

"Yo, we got us some tourists here?" He's wearing a Detroit Pistons jacket and high-top Nikes. "Y'all lookin' for the real thing by comin' here? Where y'all from?"

I suppress my fear by trying to get a read on him, to see if he's a player.

"Quebec."

"Kay-beck? Shit, that ain't far. I thought you might have been some real frogs from Paris or something." He directs this statement to his friends and laughter fills the room again. I'm hoping this exchange will be the end of it, but he moves in closer and changes to a friendlier tone.

"Well, let me just imagine what might bring three boys like you to a place like this. Y'all are record producers lookin' for the next

Ice-T right? No? Maybe you're some big-ass clockers lookin' to bust up my crew?"

I'm barely understanding him, but his stare sends a shiver through me. A response is in order, but I can't come up with one. His face changes expression again.

"Maybe you just lookin' to score?" I can't hold back a smile. I glance at the bartender to see if he poses any threat to a deal. His back is turned.

I refocus on the homie and say quietly, "I'm selling." He gives out a surprised laugh and goes back to tell this to his friends. They laugh in the same way, but I sense this time it's not meant to deprecate us. They're interested. One of them waves me over to the table. Rich and Serge make no move from the barstools to follow me.

"What can I call you?" the largest in the group asks as I sit down. Before I can answer he says, "Fuck it, I'll call you Frenchie, all right?" I nod as I glance at the black faces surrounding me. They're beautiful and terrifying at the same time. I feel the same as I did the first time my father put a gun in my hands to go hunting with him. It's an instant bond. I want to take one of these guys back home and just walk down the street with him. Everybody would be freaked out.

"You can call me Skeeto, if you have to. You don't speak English that well, huh?" This obviously being a point in my favour, I say no.

Skeeto then says slowly, "Watchoo got?"

I lean into the huddle and say, "Crystal meth, three ounces."

"Lemme see some." I pull out one of the little bags and pop the seal. Skeeto dips his bulging black finger in, then touches it to his tongue without a reaction.

"Three ounces, huh?"

I nod, hesitantly reaching into my jacket and showing the rest of the stash. Skeeto waves his hand for me to bring it out, and each baggie is snatched up by the crew surrounding the table. Satisfied, Skeeto says in a low tone, "Chill, give my boy here a five-spot."

I can't believe this deal goes down so quickly, and in the middle of a public place. A kid with a sideways baseball cap reaches down the front of his baggy jeans and slaps a roll of hundreds in my hand. I stare at it for a second, dumbfounded, until he gives me a stiff nudge to put it out of sight.

"Yo, man, you earned that green, know what I'm sayin'? Don't start getting stupid now."

Skeeto says this as he rises from the booth, immediately followed by the rest. "If you got any more, drop by here again. It was nice doing business witchoo."

The air is sucked out of the room as soon as they leave. I look for the older couple and they've somehow vanished, too. There's only the bartender and a group of four scruffy white guys like us in an adjacent booth who I hadn't been concerned with. It feels like the right time to split, but they invite us to their table to have a beer, and I can't reject their obvious generosity in my stunned condition. Rich, Serge and I pull up three chairs and introduce ourselves. "Looks like you just won the lottery," says the guy who made the invitation, who calls himself JT. He does most of the talking, explaining that we just met the big players in the neighbourhood. His friends seem on the verge of cracking up with laughter, as if what just went down was something they'd been watching on TV.

Their attitude rubs me the wrong way a little, and after the bartender brings our round, I can't hold back asking what they're doing hanging out on Skeeto's turf.

"Oh, we get along fine. He's always there to help us out."

I catch JT's drift, and the conversation begins to loosen up. It sinks in that these guys are impressed by how we handled ourselves. We start sharing a little — JT and his friends are from Grosse Point, a suburb, but they're always where the action is downtown. He says it's fine if you know the right people, and Skeeto is one of the good guys to know. When the inevitable topic of music comes up, we talk about Kurt and express our sorrow over his death. I'm enthralled to hear someone else's opinion, and JT seems moved as well, hearing how much Kurt meant to me. At times, I have trouble expressing myself in English, but JT and the others are patient, and help me search for words when I stumble. At other times, I can't believe I'm being so open with total strangers. Rich and Serge talk about seeing Nirvana in Toronto, but I don't let that stop me from making it clear that I'm the bigger fan.

We have another round and talk more, before one of JT 's buddies, Tyler, suggests we go to another dude's place nearby to get high. I give a quick glance at Rich and Serge, already knowing what they'll say, and politely decline the offer. But, seeing that the night has gone so well, I extend my own invitation for them to come to our hotel room tomorrow night for a party. They gladly accept, and even cover our tab as we head our separate ways.

We find ourselves back at the hotel sooner than expected. It's still early, not even midnight. None of us is actually tired, but there's no desire to do anything apart from bask in the opulent surroundings, knowing that we won't have to do any more deals. No one speaks of it, though, and I break the general silence by ordering a pizza. While I'm on the phone, Serge and Rich begin channel surfing. They quickly discover the pay-per-views and settle on watching Jim Carrey goof off in *Ace Ventura*. The pizza is thin and greasy, nothing like back home, but it tastes good after the disastrous Ponderosa experience.

By the time the pie is gone, the parade of pornography has started, and it holds our attention until we pass out one by one. After seeing all the drilling on TV, I allow myself to dream about having sex with Sylvie. We're in the middle of a field of tall grass with nothing around for miles. Despite this, I hold her as if something is nearby that could take her from me. Her tiny, naked body glows in the bright sun, and each touch warms me until euphoria lifts us into the sky. It's the best dream I've ever had.

I awake feeling a lingering afterglow, which quickly develops into a blinding impulse to call her. I've slept all night on the couch while the guys had moved to the bedrooms. I have trouble recalling what day it is as I dial. Friday? Saturday? No, it's Sunday. Her parents are at church. Perfect. It rings eight times, then the machine picks up. Fuck, I can't leave a message. All hope vanishes and I don't bother calling Mario. I know he's all right.

A storm had passed overnight, leaving everything outside grey and damp-smelling. We've got nothing but time on our hands today anyway, until JT and his friends show up. I wonder if it will feel like this when we get to Vancouver? There'll be nowhere else to go and nothing to do but wait. I try to comfort myself by thinking that killing time is what I've been doing every day of my life. By the time we get to Vancouver, I'll have achieved the goal and it will be easy. I'll be in control.

The guys awake and we head down to the lounge for breakfast. It's overpriced and the portions are tiny. We talk a little about what to get for the party, so I suggest making a day of it and going to the baseball game like the front-desk girl recommended. The sun returns as we find the stadium, and it's surprisingly easy to get caught up in the experience. We buy bleacher tickets from a scalper and settle in, each taking turns buying the beer. I'm happy I thought of this, especially as Cecil Fielder crushes one out a few sections over from us. But by the late innings, the Tigers have the game won and the feeling of comfort turns to restlessness. My thoughts drift back to the party, and the tantalizing possibility that we'll wreck the suite just like real rock stars.

On the way back, we stop at a Subway for dinner. We all need something healthy. The hotel lobby is more crowded than usual with men in suits, probably just arrived for a convention. I leave the boys at the elevator and go to the corner store to pick up a twelve-pack, a twenty-sixer of Southern Comfort, and another large bottle of vodka. So much for my vow not to drink too much on this trip. I return to find Rich and Serge trying to laugh at Jim Carrey yet one more time. Fuck it, if we're going to wreck this place, the cable bill isn't going to matter.

We've already had a couple of drinks when JT and the guys show up, just before ten. I welcome them in, and direct them to the kitchen area to start pouring their own drinks. Eventually everyone congregates around the TV, where the porn is back on, and we return to the familiar conversation topics.

"You guys should've got some whores to come up here tonight," JT says.

"I guess, but that's not really our thing," I reply.

"What, you guys got pussy back home?"

I look at Rich and Serge, both clearly uncomfortable with this subject, before answering, "I guess you could say that."

Another of JT 's friends, Jimmy, rolls a couple of fat joints on the coffee table, and soon the air is thick with smoke. We all take hits from it, but I'm careful just to inhale enough to be polite. When these are done and everyone is sufficiently sedated, JT gets us talking about our trip again.

"Man, you guys have really got it made. I mean, life on the road is where's it's at. I got a little brother who's following around the Dead, but you guys are doing your own thing, and that's way cooler."

"Well, you guys could do it, too," I say, rising out of my seat to mix a fresh drink. "All you need is a car."

"Yeah, we got wheels. We just need a little cash."

JT 's face instantly hardens as he says this and he raises his eyebrows to signal the others. Two of them who are sitting on the couch pull out handguns and point them at Rich and Serge. JT leaps from his chair and lays into me with a flurry of punches and kicks. I fall over a stool, and he and Jimmy are both on top of me, showing no mercy. Voices yell out, "Where's the fucking money Frenchie? Give us your fucking money!" All I hear out of Rich and Serge are cries of pain, making my own beating somehow twice as bad. JT finally gets off me and orders the others to stop.

"Let's hear what they got to say now."

My body is in complete shock, and my first instinct is to see how Rich and Serge are. The guys are still being held down by the two with guns, but I can't move toward them anyway with what feels like a few broken ribs. JT attempts to regain my attention, yelling to make his point this time.

"Frenchie, I'm fucking talking to you! Now, we can end this all right here if you just give us your money. That fucking simple enough? Then you can be on your way. If that ain't good enough for you, well, me and my friends are willing to negotiate for as long as it takes."

I try to catch my breath, summoning the courage to voice my only recourse.

"You can have it . . . just leave us some money to get back on the road."

JT smiles the smile of someone who knows he holds another's destiny in his hands as I feebly point to the closet where I put the tote bag containing Skeeto's money. Jimmy rushes to retrieve it, dropping it in JT 's lap. They begin mulling over my proposition. Jimmy whispers something to JT, prompting him to yell out again, "Take that motherfucking money belt off too bitch, or it's going around your fucking neck!"

I slowly move to undo it, but Jimmy takes one end in his hand and jerks me upward, causing shudders throughout my body. He takes his time pulling out the bills, then takes several more minutes counting them on the table in front of the couch, while JT counts the bills from the tote bag. They form two virtually even stacks, then lock eyes with me again.

"Like I said Frenchie, you're lucky you ran into such a generous man like Skeeto. But we're just as generous in our own way. We're gonna leave you enough to get your asses back home, instead of capping you right here in this room. I hope you've learned never to fuck with shit that's out of your league."

I don't need to respond. JT and Jimmy stuff the piles of cash into the tote bag and the gunmen follow them out the door. For a moment, I stare at the cash they've left us, then turn to Rich and Serge. Both are still breathing heavily and their faces are already beginning to swell up from the shots they took. No one seems to know what to say. I try to get to my feet, but remain doubled over in pain. Rich moves to help me, and once on my feet I take the money and put it back in the belt. It takes a deep breath just to say, "Let's get the fuck out of here."

I swallow the last dregs of the Southern Comfort before we drag our bags down to the lobby, not fully conscious of how we must appear. A middle-aged man is behind the front desk and his reaction gives me a clear idea. He doesn't give in and ask about it though.

"Checking out sir? I trust there was no damage to the room?"

"No, no. We have a long drive tomorrow. Going to Louisiana," I say as coherently as I can. Out of courtesy he tries to smile as my trembling hand signs the bill. Rich and Serge are also shaking. Some of the pain subsides as I fall into the driver's seat, gingerly pull the car out of the underground garage and drive as smoothly as I can back to the Royal Oak Motel 6, wondering what it's going to take to get to sleep tonight.

7 Richard
Chicago: May 17, 1994.

I still feel like shit. The headache is gone — we split a bottle of Tylenol 3s when we got back to the motel — but the bruises make it hard to move. We haven't spoken about what happened, and a cloud of utter defeat hangs over us. The thought of splitting and finding the next bus home momentarily crossed my mind as I stared at the ceiling, unable to sleep. Then I wondered what the point would be, leaving in such a cowardly way. I think we all understand we have to keep going, for a little while longer at least.

We have to check out early, which isn't a problem since none of us really slept. When I did begin to doze, I was jarred awake by Andre's moans and shifting on the other mattress.

We get ready to go with automatic efficiency, Serge and I doing the majority of the heavy lifting while Andre settles the bill. He's moving like an old man, and the damage to his face is plain in the light of a brand new American day.

We don't utter a word the entire time, and none of us are concerned where Andre is directing the Chevette. Once we're on the westbound interstate, Serge, riding shotgun, finally asks Andre what he has in mind.

"I don't know," he answers with a laboured sigh. "Where do you want to go?" More silence ensues as our attention returns to the scenery, endless miles of industrial wasteland.

"How much money do you have left?" I'm eventually forced to ask Andre.

He takes another strained breath and replies, "We'll be all right. No more fancy hotels though." I actually pick up a tinge of amusement in this comment, and the mood seems to lighten. I settle back into my seat and can't conceal a smile.

Whatever the humour, it goes over Serge's head.

"But it was our drugs," he chimes in, sounding testy. He doesn't look or sound like he took as bad a beating as we did. "What if the hotel gets suspicious and calls the cops, or those guys rat on us? We gotta get back over the border while we can." Andre lets the question hang in the air, trying to maintain his steady breathing.

"Don't worry about it," he finally blurts out. "Nobody knows who we are or where we are. I've been using a fake name at all the hotels. Let's go to Chicago and get a plan together there."

As usual, I'm impressed by Andre's foresight, and I can't resist asking, "What name did you use?"

"Burt Cobain."

With peace temporarily restored, I start recycling through the tapes to break up the monotony. After a half-hour of Jim Morrison's voice and a screeching organ, I can see Serge fidgeting. I fixate on what Andre said about nobody knowing who or where we were. Of course, we're hardly alone. Small towns and rest stops rush by at an alarming rate. Still, an overwhelming feeling of isolation descends upon me. We aren't a part of anything anymore. Our families and friends are somewhere else. Anne-Marie is fading from my mind. Even Monique's daily routine of dancing and getting stoned seems halfway around the world.

After two weeks I'm finally scared. Not just because we were nearly killed — I've lost touch with myself. I'm not learning anything on this trip that I didn't know before. I'm not growing as a person. Instead, I've fucked things up with Anne-Marie beyond repair, and Andre is leading me to hell in a piece-of-shit Chevette. Still, I have no reason to fight him anymore. The headache returns.

"Can we stop for some more Tylenol? My head's fucking exploding."

The pills knock me out for a time, so I miss much of the ride into Chicago. I imagine it's more of the same suburban blight, marked by signs I can no longer decipher. The road has become one never-ending billboard where good-looking men and women, larger than life, frolic. I'm roused just as skyscrapers are coming into view, and the sight sends a rush through my limbs. I've always felt more comfortable sleeping in a moving car. There's something about waking up disoriented that's appealing. My aches and pains have subsided a bit, and I begin looking forward to a fresh start in a new location.

This is the biggest city we've been to, but its size doesn't overwhelm me. I understand now that we only have to worry about the inhabitants. It's mid-afternoon and we haven't eaten, so I reach behind me and dig into the cooler buried under our knapsacks. I grab the last warm Miller High Life and take a tentative gulp. Andre hears the cap come off and shouts, "What the fuck do you think you're doing?"

"I was thirsty. I should have gotten a Coke with the Tylenol."

"If you don't recall, it's illegal to have open alcohol in a car."

"Yeah, so is keeping a half-pound of meth under your seat. I think you can handle a little bitty ticket for an open beer."

Andre chooses not to respond for some time, before coming back sarcastically, "Yeah, what the fuck. Drink all you want man, now's the time to do it." I sit back and try to enjoy the beer. It's a hollow victory. I have to learn how to pick my battles with Andre.

We're almost in Chicago now, on a freeway that's branched out into several lanes and complicated interchanges. I'm glad I'm not driving. I think about throwing my empty bottle out the window, just to see it shatter on the asphalt, but remember that everyone around here probably carries a gun. They'd love the opportunity to unload on us. It's funny how you can watch the news a few times and instantly believe American cities are dark jungles with bodies piled up on street corners. I was almost one of them; I guess I understand now how people accept the fear. What's the use in being scared anyway? I've just faced up to something I never imagined I would, and it doesn't seem like a big deal. Once you do that, anything is possible. Kurt knew that.

I think I'm also beginning to understand what Andre used to say about him. What good is dying if you can't change the world by doing it? God knows guys like us can never change the world while we're alive. Once you get past the fear, it begins to make sense: dying should serve some sort of purpose. That's what soldiers are taught, right?

We pass O'Hare just as a jumbo lands. We're almost parallel to the runway so Andre hits the gas and pretends to race it. It's the first time we've all felt good today. Serge has been the most quiet. I know this has hit him hard. I mean, he hasn't gone through a traumatic experience on this trip up until this point, not like me anyway. There is a gulf forming between us. I've decided I'm on this trip until the bitter end, but I can't guess what he's thinking. We've been best friends for a long time, and have always gone the same way. Even when I started seeing Anne-Marie, we stuck together — to go to university and whatever. But he's never had a girlfriend, and now I'm wondering if he really knows what I'm going through.

Andre can see it and I'm getting more comfortable opening up to him. I'm no longer worried about where he wants to take us. But I'm starting to worry that Serge has become excess baggage.

That's another fear I have to face; losing faith in something I've trusted all my life — Serge's friendship. He's a million miles away most of the time. I can't let these thoughts hurt me as much as the things Anne-Marie or Monique said. If I do, then there really won't be any hope. Maybe I'm completely wrong. Maybe Serge is just trying to get out of his own state of confusion. I bring all my troubles down on myself, and maybe he does, too.

I wish I saw the world like Andre. He's found a place for himself and he doesn't need us hanging around. He could have done this trip alone. Maybe he's starting to think both of us are expendable. I wish we would talk more. All this thinking is driving me insane.

I turn my attention to the city, but the congested gridlock of the downtown core soon loses its excitement. The same cabs jockey for position, the same newsstands dot the corners, the same cops with thick moustaches badger the same homeless people.

"How about having a cold beer for a change?" Andre suddenly asks.

"Sure," I reply, my voice cracking after the long stretch of silence. This time Andre doesn't bother tipping the parking-lot attendant, and we shuffle into an Irish pub situated at the base of an office tower, all of us now wearing our baseball caps and sunglasses, trying to conceal the marks on our faces. The place is full of suits, some as young as us, recovering from a hard day upstairs. Many eye us with curiosity, although now we're fully aware of our appearance, the worn-out clothes aside.

We grab a table out of the general view and a waitress in a short uniform promptly serves us. We order three Molson's and she grins upon hearing our accents. These people are morons. When the beer arrives, I decide to prove it. I haven't tried being rude in French right to somebody's face, so I dare Andre to tell the waitress to take her clothes off when she comes back. Before he has a chance, she starts in with the usual routine questions about where we're from and where we're going. After our routine answers, she walks right into our trap by saying she's never had anyone speak French to her before. Andre cheekily reminds her it's the language of love and asks what she wants to hear.

Without hesitation, she tells him to say, "I love you, I can't live without you." He responds with, "I want to slip my sausage into your bearded clam," and we have to restrain each other from laughing.

She continues to smile innocently, oblivious to our horrible trick.

"You guys are so sweet," she says unexpectedly, causing Serge to spew out a fine mist of beer once she heads to another table. When she's out of earshot, we unleash a stream of laughter that, despite the pain I know it causes in each of us, puts a large dent in the tension of the past 48 hours. We toast Andre and feel like friends again.

The beers keep coming from our happy waitress, and we eventually forget what we're doing here. The buzz blindsides me. Andre, with his alcohol-retarded accent, ends up asking the waitress if she knows any cool places to go.

"What, this place isn't good enough for you?"

We laugh nervously, not fully comprehending her humour, as she turns to the ceiling in deep thought.

"Have you been to Buddy Guy's place?" We stare back blankly, the name meaning nothing to us. She continues, "There's that, and there's the Fireside Bowling Alley. A lot of kids have been going there lately."

Bowling? None of us can even lift a ball at this moment, but when she goes on to mention that bands play there, we ask her for directions. She draws a detailed map on a napkin, stressing that we shouldn't talk to anyone on the street. Her warning doesn't register with me, though. Like I said, that fear is gone.

On the street, Andre has trouble following the map in the growing darkness. We have to stop at every corner and carefully examine its sign. We're led into a rundown neighbourhood, but the building is plain to see from the small gathering of kids loitering out front. We nod hello and I detect a few snickers as we enter. Not much bowling is going on, but there are many more kids standing around drinking Cokes and smoking while a band sets up in the corner. The scene reminds me of the old youth centre back home and the gigs Andre's band played there. I ask him if he feels it too.

"A little," he admits, intently eyeing the band's equipment. Nostalgia, I suppose.

I can't remember the last time I saw Andre play his guitar, but it's obvious from his unwavering stare that playing in a band is still a hidden dream. At times, he motions as if he's about to approach the guitar player and ask him about his instrument or his amp. Instead, he stands beside us in silence, refusing to be distracted by kids going about the teenage rituals we'd be indulging too, if we were home.

These aren't street kids, like in Toronto. They wear shitty old clothes on purpose, not out of necessity. We're beginning to cross that line though, beginning to take on the appearance of true losers. We have that experience now, and most of these kids probably don't. That's what makes me feel comfortable around them. Too bad there isn't any booze in this place.

The band starts playing some loud, indecipherable songs, which I try to get into. The kids almost instantly started pogo-ing and slamming. We stay back — none of us need any physical contact — but it doesn't matter because the band really sucks. Still, it feels good being among the kids, making the day not seem like a complete waste.

The band takes a break after 45 minutes and people actually start bowling. It looks bizarre, longhaired kids in corduroy pants doing something I've only seen middle-aged men do. We have no desire to make any more friends. It's pointless. The girls are really young, too. *Really* young. Nothing makes me feel me age more than watching really young girls.

There's nothing perverted about it. They're the same girls I fell in love with in Grade 9, it's just that I'm a little bit older now. I look the same and act the same, I just have more confidence in what I would do with them if I had the opportunity. I can say to a girl that age that I love her, and she would be at my heel for the rest of my life. I'd done that with Anne-Marie and I now know it was a mistake. Yet, I could say it to any of these girls and leave her broken-hearted tomorrow. That would be sweet.

I think about calling Anne-Marie and telling her it's over, telling her I'd met a great girl in Chicago who wants to hear me speak French to her all the time. A girl from the suburbs who hangs out downtown and likes to drink and fuck like every good American girl. Yeah, that's right, there were other guys going after her, but she wants me. I'm thinking about it, but we're having such a blast travelling it's a sure bet there will be many more just like her somewhere else down the line. Yeah, that's what I'd tell Anne-Marie. She wouldn't believe me, but she'd have no choice. With no one to contradict me, she'd go out of her mind imagining the stuff I was doing. Then maybe she'd understand.

There's a lot to be said for the fantasies I've created for myself lately. I don't know who I am anymore, so why bother being anyone? My eye catches three girls standing in front of the stage, all about sixteen. For no apparent reason, I walk over and pull an ignorant tourist act to see how far I can get, and maybe even prove my theory right.

"This place is really cool," I say to none of them in particular. "I'm from out of town."

"You must be, you talk funny," a petite blonde with bobbed hair replies, eliciting giggles from her friends.

"I'm French, from Paris. My colleagues and I are looking around America for new bands to tour Europe. How do you like these guys?"

"They're all right. You should check out Veruca Salt, they're the best." I don't understand what she says, still I nod politely as if I do.

The conversation grinds to a halt. The only move left is to grab the one giving the answers and take her right there on the stage. That's what this whole night has been building up to. But I back off, give them a half-hearted "Adieu," and slink back to the other end of the room, fully expecting Andre and Serge to reprise their old ribbing of my sexual frustrations. They haven't seen anything, though. Serge is talking to Andre about where we're going to stay tonight.

"I don't fucking care," Andre says. "We can keep on driving, I'm wide awake." For the first time in a while, he actually looks wasted.

"I thought we stopped here to get a plan together. I don't want to be stuck in downtown Chicago in the middle of the night." Serge is real edgy. I guess he hasn't worked through his fear yet.

"Look man, I stopped here to have some fun. Just chill out and we'll get back on the road after we get out of here." I'm impressed again, watching Andre hold his temper in check. He could have easily told Serge to be on his way right then. I would have.

The band starts another set, and I'm shocked to see Andre move up to the front of the stage through the swirling pool of kids. I can't imagine the pain he's in, but at that moment he's transformed. The dark cloud hanging over him is temporarily lifted. I don't join him, but I feel better seeing him crash and weave among the crowd, an unmistakable smile alternating with an occasional grimace.

"Are you freaked out by all of this?" I ask Serge.

"Yeah. I'm scared man. Andre doesn't know what he's thinking anymore. I mean, look at him over there. He won't be able to walk tomorrow."

"Ah, man, let him go. He's obviously not in as bad shape as we thought. We should be out there, too. We've got to put all this shit behind us and get back to having some fun."

"Don't give me that. The cops are gonna find us. The hotel is gonna think a drug deal went down, they'll nail those assholes and someone will rat us out."

He's close to raving, and I sense a scene building.

"They'll never find us man. You heard Andre. As long as we keep moving and get back over the border, we'll be fine. Don't worry." The band stops a song just as I say this, and my voice rises above everyone else's chatter. I nervously look around, but nobody seems to care that there's a Frenchman in attendance.

The next song restores the comforting din. Serge ignores me, sipping a Coke while blankly gazing into the faceless mosh pit. Andre emerges triumphant after the last song and, without hesitation, we make our way back to the parking lot where the car is in perpetual readiness. The streets are still alive as the after-hours crowd makes its way home. We don't bother with the map, relying on instinct.

We pass a twenty-four-hour laundromat/café and immediately agree to take on the nagging chore of washing our clothes. Within minutes we're standing under a fluorescent glow in front of an attentive line of washing machines. Only the sound of a single machine can be heard. It's at the back where a guy our age sits flipping through a newspaper.

Andre gets two handfuls of change from the dozing clerk, along with a few tiny detergent packets, and we drift to the back near the other customer. After a brief, awkward time figuring out the machine, we toss in our raunchy clothes and the detergent. A rush of water signals success and we take seats to observe the action through the machine's window.

After the guy hears us speak to each other, he turns around and starts acting friendly. There's nothing else to do but play along. He's smaller than us, with short hair and a slightly feminine face. But his clothes are ragged and baggy, giving the impression he shares our predicament.

"You guys travelling through?" he asks, in a deliberately non-threatening manner.

"Yeah," Andre replies, trying to get a read on him by the tone of his voice.

"Where you headed?"

"Oh, we're not sure yet. West. Seattle, Vancouver maybe."

"Would you be interested in giving me a ride?"

"How far?"

"As far as you want to go. I've got money and I won't bother you."

Andre talks to us in French, sure that the guy can't understand.

"What do you guys think? He looks harmless. If he gets to be a problem I don't think it would be hard to dump him."

"It's pretty tight in the back seat," I say. "He'd better not have a lot of stuff."

Andre turns to the stranger and asks what he's carrying. He pulls out a backpack about the same size as ours from under the row of identically moulded plastic chairs.

"This is it."

We look at each other and silently consent to take him in, not fully knowing why.

His name is Joe, and he's from a small town near Boston. He says he's been on the road a few days after getting away from his abusive family. He's only needed two rides to get to Chicago; both came from truckers who didn't ask any questions. His first impression of us was that we'd be a lot friendlier travelling companions.

"Who else but drifters would be in a laundromat at three in the morning?" he says, breaking the ice. His conversation turns out to be pleasant, and we share our stories through wash cycles.

He's hoping to get to anywhere on the west coast so he can start a new life. I immediately interpret this as going to Hollywood to be a movie star, but soon realize that's the furthest thing from Joe's mind. He talks about San Francisco and Seattle as if they were the last places on Earth untouched by greed and viciousness. I can tell by Andre's smirk he doesn't buy the theory.

After a while, Andre finally takes off his baseball cap to reveal his bruises, and admits to Joe that there is a possibility of hassles up ahead.

"I'm just warning you. But we're not criminals. We didn't do anything wrong."

Joe seems unfazed. "Thanks, I'll take my chances. I've had my share of that shit, too." His face takes on a hardness as he says it but nothing about him makes me feel uneasy. I convince myself I can take him if need be.

All of us are close to passing out now. The manager of the place is asleep behind his counter, so we decide it won't do any harm to lie back in our chairs until someone kicks us out. Joe says he'll stand guard.

I awake to the noise of more people coming in to use the machines. The sun shines brightly through the front door and Andre and Joe are gone. I nudge Serge, feeling a bit frantic, and we hastily gather up our clothes.

Luckily, instead of rushing into the street, I happen to glance through the glass door separating the washing machines from the café. The pair calmly sip coffee. Serge and I collect our wits and gratefully join them with our own steaming mugs.

"You ready to go?" Andre asks as we sit down.

"Can we drink these first?" Joe lets out a short laugh after I say this. It seems Andre has been entertaining him well. Both are in great moods, despite a lack of sleep.

"I told Joe I want to start heading north, maybe cross the border in Alberta." I grunt approval and take a deep gulp. The hot fluid slides slowly down my scratchy throat, causing me to wince. My body still aches, but I can feel my strength returning.

It does trouble me a bit, seeing Andre and Joe becomming so close. Andre should know better. This guy wouldn't be dumb enough to be travelling alone cross-country without some kind of weapon. If Andre flashes any of the cash we've got left, we're as good as dead.

"What have you guys been talking about?" I abruptly ask him in French.

"Just making chit-chat. Don't worry, everything's cool."

"How far are we taking him?"

"I don't know, just trust me. And stop speaking French, it's rude."

I give Serge a nonchalant shrug and get back to drinking my coffee. I have trouble getting over our surreal night as we walk to the car. This will be my memory of Chicago, along with some really young girls in a bowling alley and a gullible waitress in an Irish pub. What a fucked-up world.

The air is already humid in the early morning. I beg Serge to let me ride shotgun and he reluctantly agrees. He isn't too keen to sit beside Joe. Neither am I. Before we started out on this trip, I assumed we'd be faced with the choice of picking up a hitchhiker, but it seemed clear by Andre's attitude that he'd want nothing to do with a stranger invading our space. Now Andre's talking to Joe more than he's ever talked to us.

The first order of business is hitting a gas station. The closest Mobil isn't busy, so Andre takes some extra time to check the Chevette's vital fluids, leaving the three of us looking on idly like city workers standing around a manhole. Finally, I give in to the urge to piss, and head around the side of the gas station to the bathroom. Turning the corner, I'm nearly bowled over by a skinny black kid coming the other way. I want to yell something at him as he takes off down the street, but then remember where I am. After pissing, I'm washing up at the bathroom's rusted-out sink, when I notice a gym bag left in the corner. My curiosity peaks, and I discover more small clear plastic bags of white powder. My rational mind is screaming "Drop it and walk out!" but something else tells me Andre would want to see this. I leave the bathroom not fully cognizant of what I'm doing. Serge and Joe immediately notice the bag as I approach.

"Qu'est que c'est?" Joe says, attempting to be funny. I show them.

"Holy shit," they whisper in unison.

"I think a kid just left it in the bathroom. He almost ran over me as I was going in," I say, more just to break the uneasy silence. It suddenly hits me that whoever is supposed to be picking up the bag might be in the vicinity, and my head starts moving around like a rabbit's. Just then, Andre slams the hood down and moves over to see what's keeping us occupied.

He doesn't react when he sees the bag, but he looks straight into my eyes and says quietly, "Okay, here's what we're going to do. We're gonna take this to the police. We'll be the good guys this time." The tempo instantly increases.

"What? That's the fucking dumbest thing I've ever heard."

"Is it?" The gleam in Andre's eye is a bit too maniacal. I glance at Joe and he seems thoroughly shaken.

"Okay, but what do we tell the cops?"

"We tell them the truth, right? We found a fuckin' pound of cocaine so we decided to turn it in, end of story. We'll be fucking heroes. Besides, it's gotta be good karma."

"All right, whatever. Let's just get to a police station and get this over with."

"I'll ask the guy where it is when I pay."

Andre strides as confidently as he can into the variety store, leaving me holding the bag. Serge and Joe haven't moved from the gas pumps, and I'm about to join them when a decaying red Cadillac pulls up to the adjacent pump. I freeze like a deer in headlights. I instinctively know this is the guy coming to make the pickup. My feeling is confirmed when his eyes lock on me after spotting the bag in my hands.

My brain again tells me to drop the bag and run but, remembering Andre's plan, I hold onto it like a life preserver. As the pickup man is manoeuvring his large frame out of the car, I bolt into the variety store, hoping the clerk will summon the cops before the guy starts shooting. Serge and Joe have already hidden behind a dumpster when I burst in and give Andre the urgent news in French. He immediately yells at the clerk, "Is there a back door?"

The stunned clerk doesn't move until he spots the huge black man heading inside, his right hand already reaching inside the jacket of his tracksuit. Andre and I take off in the opposite direction.

As we bust open the back door, I hear a booming voice demand, "Who the fuck are those guys?" I don't turn around to see who said it. Instead, I locate Serge and Joe and the four of us dash to the car. As Andre turns the key, I can see the Cadillac moving again as the Chevette barrels blindly into the street.

Traffic is denser in this section of the city, and Andre struggles to zigzag through it without running red lights, all the while begging, "Find a cop! Find a cop!"

The Cadillac has caught up to us, causing Andre to be even more reckless. At the height of our panic, Joe yells out, "Turn right here! I think there's a station on this street." The guy in the Cadillac must have known that, too, because he doesn't follow us. Andre slams the Chevette to a halt behind a cruiser parked in front of the building, and we climb the cement steps, me still clutching the bag like it was a small child.

A female officer behind the reception desk is the first to notice us in the room filled with blue uniforms. It strikes me: I've never been in a police station before.

"Can I help you?" We wait for Andre to speak up but he stands silent, staring at the bag in my hands.

I have to step up, stumbling with my English in all the chaos.

"Um, we find drugs at gas station and we turn them in, yes?" I open the bag and almost shove it in her face.

After giving me a confused look, she tells me to step back and grabs the bag herself, examining the packages of coke, each tagged with unusual felt tip marker symbols. "You guys found this? And it's not yours?"

I almost laugh when she says this, and I'm sure I make an isn't-this-ridiculous kind of gesture. To my relief, Joe takes over the story.

"Yeah, I know it's unbelievable but the guy who wants it saw us with it and was chasing us until we got here. It was at a Mobil over on Maxwell."

We direct her as best we can to the gas station and describe the guy and his car. She makes a quick call, and then runs after a passing officer.

"Don't you guys move, I'll be right back. You better not be bull-shitting me," she says over her shoulder as she passes out of sight.

Andre nudges me. "Let's get the fuck out of here." I'm paralyzed again.

"But, but, you heard what she said. They'll come after us," I stammer.

"Not if we go now. Come on." Joe has already gotten the message and is out the door. Andre is pulling at my sleeve, but I don't move until Serge gives me a shove. The bag of dope rests on the reception desk.

Once through the doors, we run down the steps and pile into the Chevette. I fully expect a squad of police cruisers to be on us right away, but Andre turns down every side street he sees until we're completely lost. After several minutes, it's clear we're going in circles. I want to grab the wheel from Andre, as it's obvious Joe's directions are getting us nowhere. We finally find an underpass and Andre screams to Joe, "Should I take it?"

After an eternity Joe says, "Yeah, what the fuck." Andre instantly swings into the right-hand lane and gets on the ramp at the last second. The Chevette hums up to speed and we're on the freeway heading God knows where. It turns out to be north, which suits our immediate purposes, and we breathe a collective sigh of relief. All I can think about now is what made Andre want to get out of the police station so quickly? Maybe Joe is running from the cops, too, and Andre is protecting him.

Serge finally asks Andre in French, "What do we do now?"

"Speak English, damn it! They'll find that guy, he'll rat on the guy who dropped the bag and we'll be long gone. We did our good deed for the day."

A few more minutes pass silently as I contemplate this. All I wanted to do was see the country. We're only halfway and I feel like I've seen too much already. I glance over at Serge sitting beside me in the back seat and his face is turned away, looking out the window. I can't bring myself to watch it all go by anymore. I can't even talk to him. There's nothing out there that holds any interest for me and I close my eyes. There is nothing but the void. No sound of the engine, no passing cars, no unreadable signs. No Serge, no Joe, no Andre, no Monique, no Anne-Marie. Just nothing. Darkness. And it feels great.

Then it passes. Andre and Serge are fighting in French over directions. The car swerves dangerously every time Andre turns his head to yell into the back seat.

"What if we get pulled over for something?" Serge asks. "Maybe they've told the state troopers to look for a car with Quebec plates?"

"It won't matter. We'll be out of Illinois in a few hours. You guys keep forgetting, we haven't done anything wrong."

"We've been lying all along. What do we say now? I think it's time we finally decide what the fuck we're doing."

Andre pauses while he aims the car at an exit Joe has pointed out. Serge is getting impatient. "Well, are we going to Vegas or New Orleans or what?"

"No, we're going to Seattle." Then, a minute later: "Always tell the cops the truth when you haven't done anything wrong."

I'm still getting my bearings and can't hear Andre that well. I ask Serge what he said. He tells me our destination, and my spirits lift slightly knowing that we have a goal. It puts me in a talkative mood.

"Maybe we should go back to Canada until the heat dies down," I tell Andre.

"Yeah, we'll go back eventually. I think we should go to Seattle now, while we can."

"Is that where he wants to go?" I ask in French, in reference to Joe.

Andre gives me a disdainful look, one I've never seen before.

"What difference does it make, we all want to go there, right?"

I sit back, stung.

8 Serge
Montana: May 20, 1994.

We get kicked out of the first campground we stop at. I guess saying that they won't let us in is more accurate. We don't have reservations, we look like dopeheads and we talk funny. So I guess I understand the reasoning. It's some state park in Wisconsin or South Dakota or somewhere. I don't even know where we are anymore. We've driven all day from Chicago, and we've only passed through a handful of cities since.

Joe came up with the campground idea, but it's well after dark before we stumble upon this one. The guy at the gate is a fat, unsympathetic redneck who obviously enjoys wearing a uniform. He doesn't even ask where we're from, something everyone we've met so far has done.

I don't know why Andre agreed to Joe's idea. We don't have a tent. Joe said it was a great night to sleep outside, and doing it at a campground would be a lot safer than at the side of the road. In the end, we have to make our way back to the interstate.

As we proceed, I notice a small but intimidating clutch of tepees, like giant shadows of men, looming near the park entrance. They must be there for show. There's no way the government would allow Indians to live like that now. The ones back home might as well be in prison. It's hard to believe there's even fewer prospects for them than for us.

It makes me think of my uncle, who used to have a friend at the rez north of town. He showed him the best secret trout streams. One day we all went fishing. My uncle and I picked up the Indian early in the morning, and the reservation seemed deserted. We fished all day and had a great time. I hooked a rainbow that was too much for my spindly arms, but my uncle came behind me, covered my hands with his and helped me jerk the rod while I clumsily reeled in the line. I'll always remember the broad, toothless grin on the Indian's face when he pulled the trout out of the net, but I couldn't recall his name, even if one of those thugs put a gun to my head again.

There were people milling around the reservation when we dropped him off, and my uncle told me to duck as we pulled out on the long dirt road that led back to the paved highway. I asked him why, and he said I'd see soon. After his pickup was safely away from the rundown shacks, my uncle floored the gas pedal and put his right hand on my head, resting near the gearshift. In a few seconds, I heard short pops over the roar of the engine, which kept revving higher and higher. Finally, my uncle gently patted me, a signal that I could sit up again.

"What was going on?" I asked.

"They were shooting at us," he said.

"Who was shooting at us?" I asked.

"The Indians," he said.

"Why?"

"Because they don't want us here."

This is the first time I've recalled that day, and when I see the tepees I feel like someone is going to start shooting at us. Andre revs the Chevette out to the interstate. We drive for about a half-hour before Joe notices a roadside rest area. There are a few other cars in the gravel parking lot, but no humans in sight. My thoughts drift to those silent, lonesome cars I've always noticed on the side of the road. Why were they left there? How long would they sit before someone picked them up? Where were the drivers? What were they doing now, without their car?

"You still want to sleep outside?" Andre asks Joe. A few lights on the bathroom building make the scene more scary than complete darkness. Light makes shadows and shadows frighten me more than anything. Just like movies from the 1920s scare me, even when they're telling happy stories.

"I think we'd better stay in the car," I say.

"Why don't we just keep driving?" Rich asks. "There's gotta be a motel or something up ahead."

Andre glances at Joe, whose eyes are cast down sleepily.

"I thought it would be cool to sleep outside," he says.

"Let's do it then," Andre says, getting out of the driver's seat. He goes around back, opens the hatch and grabs his sleeping bag. He moves confidently to the front of the car, spreads out the sleeping bag on the hood and climbs on. The sudden transferral of his weight, and the stress on the car's suspension, jolts us awake. Joe opens his door and does the same thing, leaving Rich and me to ponder our next move.

There isn't much to do but get comfortable. I lay myself out on the back seat and Rich reclines the front seat as far back as it can go. We await the Midwest dawn, occasionally startled by an unexpected shift from the pair on the hood. They talk for a while, but not loud enough for us to hear. I don't want to know what's going on anyway.

Their bond has me confused and unnerved, feeling like the victim of a conspiracy. Rich has been trying to reassure me, but paranoia is setting in. I'm not myself anymore and I don't know how to recover, apart from leaving them here and now. If I had any balls, I'd slip out to the interstate and flag down a semi headed for home. But I don't have balls. That's Andre's department. Now he's found someone who can appreciate his neuroses, Rich and I are no longer necessary.

I'm freezing in the back seat. I imagine Andre and Joe are even colder on the hood. I'm so cold I can't fall asleep. The best I can manage is a semi-conscious daze, like the kind that comes with a fever. It's the kind of state where streams of thought become real, but you can't enjoy it because you're tormented by the uneasiness of your body's unending restlessness.

I think about girls I want, and the fact that I haven't masturbated since the trip began. Now is no time to start. The car constantly shifts from the movement of the others. There are noises outside, too, but I can't tell if they come from animals or Andre and Joe, so I don't allow them to get to me. I resign myself to not caring if I sleep at all; I just want the sun to come up so we can return to civilization. Human beings belong in cities.

With the sun up, I'm relieved enough to actually sleep. But by then, the traffic on the highway spoils everything. Someone opens the back and roots around, waking me for good. After it's slammed shut, I look out my window and see Andre fiddling with the Coleman stove in an attempt to make coffee. Joe is sitting against the left front tire having a cigarette. This is actually what I'd hoped the whole trip would be like.

Rich gets out before me and walks around the rest area, stretching and yawning. It looks like a fine day in the making, so I try to muster some optimism. I warmly greet Andre and Joe, who both return the courtesy.

"I'm getting coffee on, where's your cup?" Andre asks.

"I'm all right. I can wait till we get to a town," I respond. "Where are we anyway?"

"I think we're just leaving South Dakota," Joe says. "So that must mean we're coming into Montana."

"What's there?" I ask him.

"Not much, but it's close to the mountains."

"It's close to Alberta, too," Andre says. I'm glad to hear him say this and hope it means he has his sights set on the border. I'm satisfied with my time in America.

The coffee tastes horrible and Andre laughs it off. Today is a day where we can afford to laugh. The warm sun beats down hard in contrast to the frigid darkness of the car. A vast desert of jagged hills and wild scrub-bush lies before us, the highway cutting through it like a vein. Rich has pulled the ghetto blaster out of the trunk and is fooling around with the radio stations out of boredom. Most of what he gets is crap, and we laugh some more at the hysterical voices incessantly booming out of the speakers, saying things we don't understand. Joe explains what the voices are talking about — American politics — but it's useless. Eventually, he just sits back and grins, contented, as he sips from his mug.

At that moment, I notice Joe in a different light. His face hasn't grown any stubble since we met him. That isn't unusual, I guess. Some guys can't grow it, I think, as I stroke my own goatee, which is now getting thicker by the day. Joe also looks a lot smaller wearing just a baggy T-shirt and jeans. His exposed arms showing small, round tattoos just below the inside crooks of his elbows.

After the coffee is gone, Rich and I head for the rest area's bathroom and clean up as best we can while Andre and Joe ready the car. We hear it explode to life from inside the can, and I can't help saying something jokingly to Rich about how much farther it'll be able to take us.

"Don't talk like that," he says with a tinge of fear. "It'll break down now for sure."

The Chevette is purring calmly when we return to find Andre, anxious in the driver's seat, with Joe beside him, smiling.

"You snooze, you lose," Andre says clumsily in English, causing Joe to burst into laughter. As long as Andre is happy, we accept the back seat. The driving gets boring almost immediately. I try to imagine where we are on a map. I wonder if this is how Manitoba and Saskatchewan look. The highway is busy, but we cruise along smoothly and soon reach a point where states converge, judging by the increased number of cars whipping by with different license plates.

I'm drifting off when Joe directs our attention to a large *Welcome To Montana's Big Sky Country* sign. I immediately adjust myself to a new, unique part of the country, even though it's still the same road and the same scenery. Somehow, though, it always feels different passing from state to state. I know Canada prides itself on cultural diversity, but in America, the diversity is multiplied by a thousand. No wonder their patriotism is ingrained — how else could they keep this country together? I hated Americans for that, but now I think it's essential to the stability of the planet.

It's growing hotter by the minute when Andre stops in a tiny crossroads town for gas. The place has two pumps and a garage where someone is working on the underside of a pickup truck. This person emerges after Andre starts filling up, a middle-aged man covered in grime from head to foot. He politely makes small talk, but all Andre bothers to ask him is how long it will take to get to the border. When the man says about six hours, it feels like a huge weight is lifted off my chest. So close.

Andre gives the man two ten-dollar bills for the gas and the man gives him a friendly farewell.

"Are we really going back to Canada?" I can't help asking when we're back on the highway

"Yeah, what the fuck. We can always see Seattle once we get to Vancouver," Andre says.

I start counting the miles to the border, a frustrating task given American distances are a lot longer. That's one good thing about the metric system: it doesn't take as long to get where you're going.

Towns continue to pass by and the Rockies loom in the distance, unmoving. We're in the foothills now, and the car begins bobbing and weaving like a drunken sailor. Andre is enjoying himself behind the wheel, but showing little regard for our safety. We're off the interstate and onto some two-lane blacktop heading north — according to Joe's reading of the map — to what is probably a seldom-used border crossing.

Andre has to rev the Chevette high going up hills, giving our stomachs that queasy, roller-coaster feeling. It's fun at first, but soon I've had enough.

"Hey, take it easy man. You're gonna get nailed for speeding."

"The faster we go, the sooner we get home," Andre says. I can't argue with him over the roar of the engine, so I hope Joe will say something to make him stop.

More miles click by with Andre still pushing the pedal to the floor, until we descend into a wide valley, which allows the car to coast for a while. Then Andre spots the hill on the other side.

"Check out the size of this one. This is gonna be sweet." He floors the Chevette again and starts the climb.

I expect the tiny, worn engine to give out at any moment, but the car keeps scaling the hill at a surprising speed. My back is suctioned to the seat and my eyes grow wide when I finally see the crest of the hill. Then, nothing. We've caught air, and the momentary silence resulting from the steel-belted tires no longer rubbing the asphalt freezes the few seconds of terror in us all. Another wide valley lies below and the unconcerned mountains loom on the left. All four wheels reconnect with the road, and an instant later we're blinded by the car's hood violently slapping the windshield. Someone lets out a scream as Andre frantically gets the car under control and pulls off to the right-hand shoulder.

All he says is, "Fuck!" as we pitch to a stop, the last sound the rat-a-tat of small stones hitting the car's guts.

We sit in silence and our isolation hits me like a train. Andre gets out to inspect the damage while worst-case scenarios run through my head. The car is dead and we'll be eaten by mountain lions; or maybe the cops will finally catch up with us and we'll be thrown in some hillbilly jail. This whole trip is beginning to feel like a film, and this breakdown is the perfect opportunity for the cops to nab the bad guys. I've seen enough movies to get that impression, but I believe Andre when he says we're not bad guys. Maybe all this time those guys in the movies weren't bad either. I recall what Andre used to say before we left, about movies and the news giving us false impressions of the world. It's funny it would hit me here in the middle of nowhere, with the end so near. I watch Andre puzzling over the situation, wondering if he still thinks about such things.

Suddenly, I'm struck by a more rational fear — that we might have to shell out the rest of our money for a new vehicle just to get home. Being broke for the rest of the trip isn't a tempting proposition. People say money creates more problems than it solves, but I've come to learn in the past week that the ability to live without thinking about money is the greatest thing of all. Even all the violence I've experienced hasn't affected me as it could have, knowing we could buy our way out if we had to. Our car was always our biggest enemy, and now it's finally the one holding the gun to our heads.

Andre comes back with a damage report. "The engine is all right. It's just the latch that's busted. I guess we warped it, sleeping on the hood last night — and it snapped when we caught air. I can tie it down with some wire until we get to the next town. That is, if we have any wire."

The search begins for something to tie down the hood. As we scour the car, Andre can't resist saying, "That was pretty cool, huh?" to no one in particular. I silently agree with him, but now isn't the time to applaud recklessness. We have to keep moving. Just these few minutes of standing still makes the panic rise in me once again. I expect a state trooper to come over the hill at any moment and get a little too curious about our situation.

To speed up the process, I suggest using string from either the knapsacks or the sleeping bags, but Andre quickly decides it won't hold. Andre then remembers he has a coat hanger stashed under the driver's seat. He contorts it into a pliable hook that might fasten the hood to the grill.

We all watch as he confidently ties the metal together in dramatic twists, then tests its strength by pulling on the hood. Satisfied, we get back in the car and start off again, this time at a sensible speed. A few drivers pass us, but Andre's usual surliness is kept in check by the realistic possibility of another breakdown. The Chevette now struggles up the hills and Andre applies the brakes on the downslopes fearing a sudden rush of air will snap the wire.

They say driving is a reflection of your personality. If this is true, Andre has become someone I don't know. He's suddenly cautious, almost too careful. The car has just shown a sign of mortality, and Andre respects it. The Chevette lunges as he methodically shifts gears. I begin praying for any semblance of civilization, anything besides the incomprehensible road signs. My English has gotten a lot better, speaking it constantly, but I still can't read it.

Another crossroads town appears and Andre pulls into a carbon copy of the last gas station. It truly feels like déja vu when another middle-aged man covered in filth comes to help us out. Andre explains the situation as best he can, and Joe helps out when needed. The mechanic compliments Andre's makeshift repair, but in that understated way mechanics have that creates instant feelings of inferiority. He gives Andre an estimate, saying he'll have to replace the latch with one from one of the old wrecks behind the garage. It'll be ready in a few hours. He suggests we go down the street to the town's roadhouse, or to the drugstore where they serve ice cream sodas, just like in the '50s.

The sun is beginning to set behind the mountains and it's hard to decide. For some reason Andre and Joe find the prospect of ice cream tantalizing. Rich wants a beer.

We split up. I join Rich at the bar. The place is just as I pictured it: bare-bones wooden decor with neon beer logos and bucks' heads adorning the walls. It's surprisingly full for late afternoon on a weekday. Almost every customer is a bearded, lumberjack type. It reminds of a beer commercial in which two skinny punks not unlike ourselves walk into a bar not unlike this one, and are promptly belittled and thrown out. I take notice of possible threats, but apart from the standard quizzical looks, the lumberjacks seem too loaded to care.

For the first time on the trip I feel like I'm home. The bar is like the Lion Rouge when the mill closes down for the day. Though I was never old enough to go in, it was common knowledge that the Lion Rouge was the place to find anybody between four and six.

All the barstools are taken so we sit at a small two-chair table in the corner. A rough-looking but friendly waitress arrives promptly and we each order Molsons.

"You guys must be from Canada," she says. We nod politely, not looking to tell our story to yet another waitress.

There isn't really much reason for Rich and I to talk to each other. We sit for a long time, soaking up the atmosphere of the room and observing the many other conversations going on.

"We're almost back in Canada," I finally say.

"Yeah, it's gonna be nice." Rich takes a pull off the bottle. "Do you feel better?" The question catches me off guard.

"Yeah, I guess so. I haven't really thought about it."

"Come on, you were getting out there for a while."

"I didn't want to bring you guys down. You and Andre were getting along pretty good. I just needed to get my head together."

"Were you thinking about going home?"

"No. You guys would never have forgiven me, would you?"

"Probably not. But we're still friends, I hope you know that."

It's great to hear him say this, and I let the words ring in my head as I take several long swallows.

"You know, Andre's been a lot cooler lately," I say, not knowing exactly what I mean by it.

"Yeah, I'm glad you're finally seeing he's doing the right thing."

I don't understand this either, but I let it go and finish the beer with a long gulp. It's a good opportunity to take a leak and I get up to search for the bathroom.

When I'm finished and washing my hands, one of the lumberjacks emerges from a stall and stands beside me at a sink. I'm trying to be invisible, but he says, "Nice goatee fuckface. Your boyfriend give you that shiner?" I'm at a loss, but I know enough not to make eye contact.

I decide to calmly turn the tap off and walk out without responding.

"Yeah that's right, go back to your fag buddy. Next time use the ladies room," he says as I leave. I'm shaking when I get back to Rich.

"Some asshole just tried to pick a fight with me. I think we'd better get outta here."

"I just ordered a burger and nachos. Come on, we haven't eaten." There is no way to get him to leave now, so I pray this guy won't be waiting for us outside. As Rich eats his burger, a half-pound of dead cow with all manner of slop oozing over the side, I nibble at the plate of nachos and absorb the ever-present glare of the lumberjacks. I can't decide which one's the guy from the bathroom, they all look the same.

I begin psychically urging Rich to pound down the food, but he takes his time savouring his first nourishment of the day. He even orders another round when the waitress pops by again.

"What'd you do that for? We gotta split," I tell him.

"Calm down. Nothing's gonna happen in here. See, you're getting paranoid again."

"Fuck you, these are bad dudes and they think we're fags. I can't stay here any longer."

I fumble in my pocket before dropping a five-dollar bill on the empty nacho plate, and walk out without looking back. It doesn't hit me until I'm outside that I've just abandoned my best friend and that this will surely have repercussions, especially if a fight breaks out. I try to put it out of my head as I walk the town's main street back to the garage. I'm alone for the first time in a while and it feels great. The sun is almost fully set and there's a magical glow on the mountaintops. The main drag is beginning to shut down for the night. My anxiety passes.

I soon come upon the drug store with the soda fountain. It's still open, there are a few cars and pickup trucks parked in the angled spots out front. I enter hoping to find Andre and Joe but they aren't there. Watching Rich pig out at the roadhouse has fired my appetite, so I can't resist the temptation of a double-scoop cone.

I sit on a stool at the counter while a grandfatherly white-haired man serves me. When he brings back the cone he says, "You sound like that other pair what was just in here." In between licks I nod and confirm his notion.

"I was just at the bar for a beer. Those two don't drink." He laughs good-naturedly,

"You young folks ain't into liquor anymore, eh? Good thing you still like ice cream or else I'd be out of business." He laughs again at his own logic and leaves to tend to other customers.

The butterscotch ripple tastes like mother's milk. I haven't had anything this good in years. I let every mouthful slide down my throat slowly until I get to the cone itself and have to use my tongue to push the remaining ice cream to the bottom. I forget about Andre and Joe in these sweet, short minutes. But when the cone is gone I know I have to find them, if only to get rid of the insane idea that they might have taken off without us.

In the growing twilight I start back up the street toward the garage. I'm keeping my eyes open, and soon after I spy two figures sitting on a bench at the town's baseball diamond. They have their backs to me but I recognize their voices. I'm about to call out when I see the two shadowy heads slowly come together in what can only be a kiss.

I stand unblinking, 25 feet away, in shock, but withholding judgment. As their bodies press together, I question my sanity. Andre has lost his, clearly. And Rich is probably getting the shit kicked out of him. Where am I?

Several long minutes pass as I watch them grope and pet, oblivious to anything else. After the initial shock wears off, I start thinking of how I'm going to explain this to Rich. But my mind is quickly overwhelmed trying to explain Andre's sudden homosexuality. I'm not surprised Joe has revealed himself, but Andre has never even hinted at an interest in men as long as I've known him. He's been with Sylvie so long it seems impossible.

They keep making out, and I decide the longer I stare, the more I risk an embarrassing scene. I start back toward the roadhouse, a slight wave of nausea creeping into my gut. As I pass the drug store, I'm relieved to see Rich approaching in the opposite direction, unharmed. He greets me with a "What's happening?" which leaves me at a loss.

"I thought those rednecks would've worked you over," I finally say, still somewhat dazed.

"Nah, they're just good ole boys, not meanin' no harm, just like the Dukes of Hazzard." We laugh, but I feel the heat of the moment. I have to tell him what I saw. "Is the car ready yet?" he asks.

"Um, I don't know."

"Is Andre at the garage?"

"Um, no. Listen man, I've got to tell you something that you're probably not going to believe." He looks at me as if expecting to hear that someone is dead. "I just saw Andre and Joe, um, kissing."

He gets the same puzzled look I imagine I had when I saw them.

"You mean, like, making out?"

"Yeah. They're probably still at it if you don't believe me." Rich just stares at the sidewalk and shakes his head.

"I don't want to see." He looks like a pathetic lost child and I suddenly have great sympathy for him. He's already dealing with this new twist. I'm still in disbelief.

"C'mon, it's almost dark. Maybe they're at the garage now. I'm sure Andre will tell us about it when the time comes. He can't hide something like this forever. Just let him do it himself. He might never talk to us again if we embarrass him." Rich doesn't respond. We start walking slowly toward the park.

I dread seeing them again, for Rich's sake, but the diamond is deserted. We walk a little while longer in silence until we see the lights of the garage. The Chevette sits out front, eager to go, and I can see Andre and the mechanic settling the bill in the office. We stand with Joe by the car and don't speak. He's avoiding our gaze, as if there's something big either he or Andre are keeping from us.

We don't challenge him over the passenger seat. Neither of us wants to sit beside him.

"Seventy-five bucks just to fix a little fucking hood latch?" Andre bitches as he gets behind the wheel.

"He probably doesn't get much business out here. He's gotta make it count," I say, trying to break the tension.

"It's fucking robbery."

We're back on the road and Andre defuses the tension once and for all by rolling down his window and yelling, "Montana, you can suck my cock!" after we're safely away from the town. It's a hollow act of revenge, but it makes me feel a little better.

I glance at Rich, but his eyes are glued to Andre and Joe, searching for signs of a romantic bond. I feel tired all of a sudden and don't want to pay attention. The last thing I want my life to resemble is a soap opera, and I think that's something Andre is trying to avoid as well. That's why he's never told us anything. All any of us wants is for everyone to mind their own business.

I think about all the freaks I'd seen on talk shows over the years, and imagine us on one when this is all over. We'll tell our story, then the audience will freak out when Joe puts his arm around Andre and explains how they "discovered" each other. Maybe it'll be fun. I've never been into shocking people. We're just regular kids doing what we do, but nobody seems to accept that anymore. Andre is right when he talks about the media pushing the image of a perfect kid on housewives around the country. We obviously don't fit the mould, but what was wrong with us? So Andre was gay, big deal. We'd never be able to get that idea across on television, I decide as I fall asleep.

I wake up as the engine shuts off. We're bathed in the neon light of a motel. "We're almost at the border. Let's get a good night's sleep and we'll be back in Canada tomorrow." Andre sounds like a mother — just not mine. We all stretch while Andre gets a room. I have momentarily forgotten the recent development, but it all comes rushing back when I see Joe leaning against the building, head cast down to the pavement. He looks completely helpless. I wonder what will happen if Andre tries to dump him now.

We walk in the room and are immediately presented with the problem of the sleeping arrangements. Andre quickly grabs one bed and Rich and I wait to see what Joe will do. He goes straight for the bathroom.

I don't care anymore. I lay down on the other bed fully intending to sleep in my clothes. There is little novelty left in hotels. They're now just places to sleep. There's no more room service or playing tag in the halls. We show up, sleep and leave, that's all. I don't even open my eyes as everyone gets settled in. A body falls beside me and I assume it's Rich. I really don't care.

I sleep the entire night, and awake in the morning to the sound of heavy rain. I open the curtain to see it's the kind that makes me feel like everything will be wet forever. No one else is up, so I lay down again. For some reason, I don't want to cross the border in the rain. I don't want it to be raining in Canada.

The others slowly rise. We all slept in our clothes on top of the blankets. The beds don't even have to be made. We share a sense of purpose that's been missing since we left. This time it comes from expectation rather than fear. Even Joe is livelier than usual. He's under Andre's sway, now, like I once was. Then again, Joe might love Andre in a way I never could.

We pack up quickly in an effort to keep our stuff dry while Andre checks us out. I wonder if he's still signing his name Burt Cobain. He's soaking wet when he gets behind the wheel.

"Everything cool?" he asks. No response.

"Good, because today is going to be a good day." Normally I would have questioned this statement, but it's obvious Andre is in love in a weird kind of way.

Andre sets the wipers on high, but I can't see much as the car revs to get back on the border road. I can tell we're nearing the crossing when the landscape begins resembling a place that is neither Canada nor the U.S., but a nondescript zone peddling crap to dumb people with no money who think they're scoring one against the government by buying duty free. It's almost identical to the area around Windsor, except that cowboy crap is prevalent. Thoughts of the roadhouse return and my anger momentarily spikes.

We finally stop at a Denny's. Joe suggests it before crossing the border. It's probable we won't return to the States so we don't hesitate to order the Grand Slam, for $3.99. The plates are full, but the food itself isn't exciting. I long for a Montreal bagel or some of my mother's pancakes, with syrup straight from my uncle's farm. I don't think Americans really know what a good breakfast is.

It's a short ride to the duty-free shop, where we all have our money changed to Canadian bills. Joe carefully examines the coloured paper and seems bemused. Andre pulls all he has out of the money belt — substantially less than what Mario's expecting. Andre hasn't talked to him since Toronto. He must be even more stressed than we are.

There is no long bridge to cross, only a harmless little checkpoint. Andre breathlessly reminds us of protocol but he needn't have bothered. We have our birth certificates ready, and I'm a lot calmer than before. We're going home, after all. Our turn comes and Andre stops in front of the guard. We answer the expected questions about citizenship and how long we've been in America. The guard gathers our ID's and runs them through the computer. I try not to show my fear that our names are on the FBI's most-wanted list by gazing at the dull surroundings.

The guard tells us to pull over.

This is it, we're dead. But they don't care about the car this time; they only want us in immigration. We're led into a small, grey office and told to empty our pockets onto the desk. Seeing nothing incriminating, the guard tells us to have a seat. We're left alone for several minutes, and I expect cops to bust in at any second to haul us away. Instead, another border guard enters with a handful of computer printouts and takes a seat behind the desk.

"I'm sure you know why you're in here," he says. I can't look him in the face and fight the urge to cry.

"Would the three of you from Quebec please stand up?" We obey.

"You're all okay, but where did you meet Joanne?"

I glance at the others and see that Rich has the same puzzled look. Andre is looking at the floor. He quietly says, "We picked her up in Chicago. She needed a ride." The border guard jots down a note.

"I should tell you that Joanne's parents have the authorities all around the country looking for her, and I want to make sure you weren't intentionally transporting her into Canada."

I don't understand what's going on. After a pause, a voice from behind us says, "No, they don't know anything about it." I turn and stare in disbelief at Joe. I can see now she is a woman, but hiding it thoroughly. Every instinct I have tells me to run, and somehow purge every judgment from my head.

I gaze at Andre, who's trying desperately to show no emotion. He's in love for sure. I forget about myself. I want to grab him and let him know that I'm a true friend, but I can't. We're all in shock.

"The three of you are free to go. Joanne, you'll remain in custody until we can arrange transportation back to Boston."

The three of us gather our belongings from the desk, and Rich and I make a move for the door. I don't want to look back, but can't resist watching Andre giving a quick goodbye. He has his back to the guard, which allows him to mouth, "I love you" to Joe who is now sobbing uncontrollably. After a pathetic wave, Andre joins us.

We're still in shock when we get back in the car. The scene has completely changed. America is gone and so is Joe. The Canadian Rockies lie before us, along with a lot more unknown territory, but it is still good to be home. The road is smoother, the stores less gaudy and the general atmosphere is cleaner. Just to break the silence, I start singing "O Canada," hoping the others will join in. They don't, but they don't stop me either.

I wonder if Andre will ever speak again.

9 Sylvie
Jasper: May 20, 1994.

This is definitely the best decision I've ever made. I thought there would be a lot of sitting, but the stopovers allow us to explore a little. Montreal wasn't a big deal, but we get to check out Toronto while waiting to change trains. Lise and I only have a couple of hours to bum around, so we just walk up Yonge Street and hang out, pretending to be real mallrats. The clothing stores are really cool and the kids look like kids on TV. We see two girls dressed like vampires, which prompts us to buy black eyeliner and lipstick, just to see what we'd look like. I'd always wanted to try that, but nobody dared to look that weird back home. Even when Andre was into death metal, he never really changed apart from growing his hair. I wanted to dress like people in videos but he wouldn't let me. The way I dressed always bugged him. We never fought about it, but it was easy to tell when he disapproved of my clothes. He'd get all quiet and distant like we weren't really together.

I tell Lise about this, as we're briefly transforming ourselves, and she says I should really shock him by getting a tattoo or some part of my body pierced by the time we got to the coast. She says she'll do it if I do it first.

It's dark and we're tempted to sample a bit of nightlife, but we're afraid of missing the train. Union Station sucks. The place is too small to accommodate the herds of impatient people. We get some junk food and peruse the newsstand but everything is written in English. We each end up buying a fashion magazine and kill the time by making fun of the freaks on each glossy page. We're not like the girls back home who idolized Christy Turlington. Lise is just as beautiful, without trying half as hard. I don't even consider myself to be in her league but I'm satisfied with my looks. The first thing I notice when I go somewhere are the ugly people. It's not a question of being mean, it's just a fact. The fashion magazines are meant for ugly people, and it's up to people like Lise and me to make fun of the models who, after all, probably don't give a shit about themselves, either.

Our new train is going north. The terrain returns to the trees and crappy small towns we've grown accustomed to seeing, so Lise and I slip into the kind of aimless conversation two people create at the end of a long day together.

"Can you believe we're doing this?" I begin. There aren't a lot of people on this train, so we feel comfortable speaking freely. Those who are around can't understand us anyway.

"I wish we could have stayed in Toronto longer. Andre was there for a while." I do my best 90210 lovestruck voice. "It's something we share now."

"Look, I know the whole point of this trip is to find Andre so you two can live happily ever after, but I came along to have fun. You don't have to talk about him all the time."

"Sorry. You don't have to get bitchy." I know she's partly kidding, but the truth still hurts. I *have* been talking about him the whole time. There isn't really any reason for it, so I give in. There are a lot of miles still separating us, and I decide not to mention him again. I won't even think about him. Lise and I are the ones on the road now; it's up to him to worry about me.

"What's the next stop?" I finally ask.

Lise pulls out her ticket and studies it under the tiny lights over our seats. A few others dimly illuminate the rest of the car. It feels spooky, but what makes me uneasier is that I won't be sleeping in my bed tonight. In the morning, I'll be waking up on a moving train taking me further and further from my home.

"I don't know what it is," Lise answers. "There's a lot of small towns here but I don't think it's gonna stop until Sudbury. After that is Sault Ste. Marie, Thunder Bay and Winnipeg. That's our next change."

"Jesus, that's a long time."

"Yeah."

The news overwhelms me with fatigue. Thankfully, the porter comes by and explains the sleeping arrangements. We follow him to the sleeping car and settle in gratefully. As I lay down, it seems the shifting of the train will keep me awake. But the hum has the opposite effect; I fall asleep right away.

The train isn't moving when I wake up. Lise is in the bunk below me and it sounds like summer outside.

"You up?"

"Yeah."

"What do we do?"

"I dunno. Get dressed and have breakfast?"

We do just that, and immediately notice we're at the station in Thunder Bay. It's early, a beautiful-looking day that lifts the spirits of the new passengers as they get on board. There are many who look just like us, kids who could be setting off to see boyfriends or girlfriends in the west. Everyone must go there eventually.

There's a buffet in the dining car, and Lise and I pig out on scrambled eggs and pancakes. We're beginning to recognize our fellow travellers and we all start exchanging polite smiles. The porter recognizes us, too, and gives us a friendly morning greeting. When he hears our accents, he tries his French — but it's a dismal failure. I never know how to react when an English person speaks French to me. I mean, you can't have a normal conversation with them, so all you can do is agree with what they're saying, compliment them on their effort, then try to get rid of them as painlessly as possible. Fortunately, I don't have to do that with the porter — he has to get back to work.

The train starts rolling just after we eat. It's great to have some food in us but it also makes us restless. Lise pulls out a deck of cards, but that doesn't hold our attention. The porter brings a Scrabble board and that keeps us busy until the Manitoba border.

We arrive in Winnipeg in the afternoon, overjoyed to hear we have four hours until the next train leaves for Regina. The city is nice — kind of like back home, only a lot bigger. It's nothing like

Toronto. There aren't as many freaks walking around, but no cool clothes stores either. We stroll down Portage Avenue, ending up at a place called the Forks. There's a big mall, but nothing too exciting. Winnipeg quickly becomes a bust.

As we're having lunch in the food court, I start wondering how kids can spend so much time in malls. I understand wanting to get out of the house but there's nothing to do at a mall aside from looking at other kids. It's like high school without the classes. As we leave the food court, I have an urge to go up to a table of girls, all still wearing their boyfriends' hockey jackets in the summer, and tell them to do something — anything — besides sitting here. It wouldn't have done any good though, since Lise and I are basically in the same position.

"Let's do something," I say.

"Good thinking. You're the one who wanted to go to a mall."

"I know. Maybe we should have a drink somewhere." I don't know why I think of this. None of my friends drink much, not as much as the guys do, anyway. But I break my vow of not thinking about Andre and figure this is something he would have done. I feel his presence guiding me, ordering me to let go a little. I give Lise a mischievous look and almost pull her arm out of its socket as I drag her from the mall. I'm on a mission now, to find a café or any place where we can kick back with a martini like the girls on *Melrose Place*.

I lead Lise back to Portage, trying to keep my general bearings. We can always take a cab back if we get lost, I reason. This is what life in the city is all about.

Finally, the café I've been imagining appears. I'm like a dog salivating in front of an empty food dish as we sit at one of the outdoor tables covered by a large umbrella. Business is slow.

"What should we get? A Manhattan? A Long Island? A zombie?" I'm reading the cocktail list and marvelling at the sounds passing over my lips; words I have never spoken but which feel so natural. Lise ignores me and reads in silence. With great confidence she orders a banana daiquiri when the waitress finally comes to serve us. I end up getting a glass of Beaujolais, because it's just so French. After all, we are ambassadors for our culture, and that means acting snobby.

Another round comes and the alcohol starts taking hold. We talk loudly in French to attract attention, but apparently there is a large Francophone population in Winnipeg so it doesn't work. We resort to scoping out guys. Lise is better at it than I am, since she's never had a serious relationship. Being drop-dead gorgeous doesn't hurt either. Most guys check her out as they pass. She's aware of this, so she waits until they get their eyeful before she rates their asses.

All the guys back home are too intimidated to ask Lise out. Of course, she's had dates for all the major social outings, but she was the one who had to ask. The problem is, she comes from a strong family that's taught her not to take shit. Consequently, she doesn't feel the need to flirt. Many guys, after getting to know her, actually find her kind of boring. Needless to say, she's held on to her virginity like a life preserver.

We end up having four drinks each before the urge to go becomes too strong. The bill is a big shock, too.

"We better not do this too often," I say, laying down a twenty.

"Yeah, I hope they let us back on the train." Lise allows herself an outburst of loud, drunken laughter and I can't hold back either. This finally gets some attention. I don't really give a shit about the money. There's nothing my parents can't, or won't, give me, and this trip is part of it. I know some of my friends resent me for this, but I can't do anything about it. I enjoy making my parents happy, and they always return the favour. Being with Andre was the exception. But as long as I kept goals in mind, it seemed they got a vicarious thrill out of watching me live my life. And if I threw them a bone every once in a while, like going to university, then things remained cool. It could only go sour if I ran out of dreams. That's their problem with Andre, and that's why I had to watch myself when we were together.

Lise wants to try walking back to the station, but I gallantly hail a cab. It turns out we're only five minutes away. The cabbie tries to explain this to us, but we're not listening. Standing on the platform with the other passengers, I realize I'd given him an outrageous tip, but we're still feeling giddy and several people who recognize us come over and say obviously funny things I don't understand. We just smile like we always do.

The train pulls out and dinner is served soon after. Neither of us feel like eating though, and the porter asks if we're sick.

"No, we had a big dinner in the city," I charmingly reply. Still, I can't hide the train-sickness that's creeping up as the engine roars to prairie-cruising speed.

I warn Lise about the potential ugliness, to which she can only offer, "Keep drinking, it'll pass." I assume she's joking, but she doesn't offer any more advice and orders two screwdrivers from the beverage cart. I cautiously sip from the plastic cup, thinking it will set off a bomb in my stomach. In fact, it makes me invincible. Lise and I toast each other and spend the rest of the night over the Scrabble board.

We arrive in Regina sometime in the middle of the night. We're both safely stowed away in our sleeping compartments by then, so we don't see any of the city. Lise and I awake in the morning with the train standing in a station once again. That suits me fine, actually. My head is pounding, and the sound of new passengers boarding is worse than the humming of the rails. The same breakfast buffet as the previous morning is set out in the dining car. I wolf down the food, trying to fill the hole in my gut. My outward appearance reflects the situation. Without the luxury of a shower, both of us are looking grubby, much less attractive than when we took Winnipeg by storm.

Fortunately for Lise, there aren't any good-looking guys in our section, just a couple of older men who look as if they've spent their last dime on a train ticket. They keep to themselves. The rest are young couples seeking adventure. Some even resemble the pictures

I've seen of my parents when they were my age: all joyful optimism, long hair and baggy clothes. These people frighten me a little. One of the flower children tries starting a conversation with me after I've freshened up. She comes on like she's my sister; she might have even called me that. I'm not in the mood to make friends, so I say a few complicated French phrases to scare her away. I've discovered this is a pretty good way of dealing with over-friendly English. I don't mind so much, but I think some of them truly believe we're all on this trip for the same reason. It's the girls who are with their boyfriends who are truly annoying. It makes me wish Andre was here. They spend the day resting their heads on their guy's shoulder, watching the scenery roll by. I have only Lise — who is about as affectionate as a nun, even with me.

It's ridiculous, but as the day wears on I wonder if she might be a lesbian. The thought has never occurred to me before, since so many guys have wanted her. She's never seemed interested in other girls but that isn't a shock either, considering her family's morals. The ride is getting long and boring — endless seas of wheat fields — so I ponder coming right out and asking her which side of the fence she's on. I chicken out at the last second.

"Where do we stop today?" I finally ask.

"Um, Jasper. It says we've got a six-hour layover there."

"Awesome. We can hit a real bar." I wait for a reaction, but she doesn't reveal anything, as usual. I dig deeper. "I'm sorry again for bugging you with Andre. Maybe we can both pick up some guys tonight just for the hell of it, huh?"

"Yeah, that would be pretty funny. Guys out here would probably go nuts for a couple of French tarts." We laugh at this, but I can sense her cynicism.

"Have you seen Alain since the formal?" I ask.

"No, he was all over me that night, so I told him he would get more pleasure out of fucking himself. It's too bad his dick isn't long enough."

That's how she'd left high school, giving one last stiff middle finger to the male population of St. Mary's. At least she'd had a date for the formal. Everyone was too scared to ask me out because of Andre. Of course, he wouldn't take me. He'd already vowed he'd never have anything to do with our high school again. After that fight, I almost told him I didn't want to see him again. It was the most selfish thing he'd ever done. His trip almost sealed things for good, but he talked his way back to me, somehow, before he left. Remembering the formal brings back a lot of pain. I'd actually showed up that night with my parents, who were on the organizing committee. I spent the night dancing with any geek who asked, like I was some cheap whore. My dress was wet from sweaty palms rubbing my back. I was used to Andre's sweat, but this almost made me gag. By the end, nearly all the guys were drunk or stoned after sneaking away to secret places. Other girls besides Lise were getting groped, but it seemed most of them were enjoying it. I was helping my parents and the other teachers clean up. I vowed that Andre would pay for it someday.

Trying to forget about my problems, I get back to Lise's.

"Alain's not such a bad guy. They were all pigs that night."

"They're pigs all the time. You see how they treat me," she says.

"Yeah, but they don't know any better. You should feel lucky that you can intimidate them."

"Did you know someone started spreading a rumour that I was a lesbian?"

"No, I didn't. Why didn't you tell me?"

"I was too embarrassed. When Alain was feeling me up, he said he wanted to find out if it was true or not."

"Fuck. I'm sorry."

"It doesn't matter. It'll be behind me soon enough." That was the great thing about Lise, she never got overly excited about anything, but she never let the bad stuff bring her down, either. She's a rock. That's why she's my best friend. The news of the rumour partially relieves me. I sense an opportunity to open up.

"You know, I don't think being a lesbian would be that bad."

"Is that supposed to make me feel better?"

"No, I'm serious. Don't you think it would be a lot easier living with a woman than a man?"

"You mean, kind of like the way we are now? What about the sex part?"

"Well, I guess you could learn to like it. It doesn't seem as disgusting as what a guy does to you. You could technically still be a virgin, too." As I listen to myself, I realize Lise might interpret this as a proposition. I am making a pretty convincing argument. The prospect briefly crosses my mind as I observe her perfectly shaped breasts. I imagine kissing her right there, just to see what it would be like, but the feeling quickly passes.

"Don't start getting weird on me Syl." She's right. I could never touch a girl, and I saw at that moment that she couldn't either. It will be hard for her to find the right man and that's all that's left to say about it.

By late afternoon the train approaches the foothills of Alberta, and I start getting excited thinking about the layover in Jasper. I'm fully recovered from the previous day's binge, and I want to do it all over again. Andre would be proud of me. The first thing I'll do when I see him again is take him to the nearest bar and order double gin-and-tonics for both of us. Then we'll make out right there in the bar, after we've pounded back the drinks and smashed the glasses.

Dinner isn't being served, the porter tells us, because we'll be arriving in Jasper around seven. He calls out the names of some restaurants we might want to try instead. We leap off the train as soon as it stops. For some reason, Lise is much more jovial after our little lesbian discussion. Her dry sense of humour kicks into overdrive as she constantly asks me what I think of girls we pass on the street. I play along and it turns into a fun game.

Jasper is obviously a tourist trap, and we fall right in. There are tons of souvenirs to buy — all of them crap — but we reason that we're on vacation and that's what people like us do. The mountains cast a long shadow over the main street, giving it an eerie aura, the perfect backdrop for getting hammered. We stop at the only outdoor café we see. They're so much more interesting than the dark, dreary bars the guys enjoy so much. We can at least pretend we're in Paris. That's going to be my next trip; maybe even my honeymoon.

We drink Long Islands until the sun goes down and talk about what Paris might be like. It's funny how my mind is always preoccupied with everything except what's going on right that second. Here we are, in the middle of one of the most beautiful places on earth, and we're talking about a place we'll probably never get to for many years, especially the way we burn money. After about the fifth round, we're loosened up enough to ask the waiter if he knows where the real action is. Both Lise and I are flirting with him and it feels great. I've never really done it before. It's true that there's something about a well-groomed young man in a uniform, especially a guy you can order around.

The waiter tells us about his favourite nightclub in town. He says it's the place where all the pilots from the air-force base hang out, prompting me to look him over thoroughly, to see if he might be gay. It does sound great; more men in uniform. We stumble out of the café and work at getting our bearings under the streetlights while still maintaining the requisite French attitude. That's something Andre always told me: no matter how wasted you get, always look like it isn't affecting you. Most people can't, so you'll impress everyone if you can. It takes a lot of willpower but I think I pull it off.

As we make our way down the street, I take long looks at people we pass and try to read their minds. We must look really cool, because we're really drunk yet somehow keeping it together. A hippie-looking guy with a long, bushy beard passes and sees right through me. He doesn't speak but his eyes clearly say, "Enjoy the ride."

I suddenly forget where we're supposed to go, so I turn and grab the guy. I stumble with my English but he manages to get the gist. "I was going there myself . . . eventually. Might as well go now." We giggle and follow him down the street.

The place turns out to be more of a ski lodge than a nightclub. The interior is all wood and the fireplace looks completely wrong for the room, which is already filled with people hanging around the bar. Somehow they don't strike me as a typical nightclub crowd, though. Band equipment is set up in one corner and weird music is blasting from the PA. I guess it isn't really weird music, I'm just used to hearing Andre play Nirvana all the time and most people back home only played heavy metal. I'm still surprised we all suffered through Mariah Carey at the formal.

The hippie guy vanishes, leaving us to order drinks on our own. I was hoping I'd be able to weasel at least one out of him. To make things easier, we settle for the beer everyone else is drinking, something called Grasshopper, which is actually all right. With a bottle safely in hand, I finally have a chance to survey the crowd. The air force boys are slowing coming in, just as we'd been told. They stand at the bar like a pack of wolves surveying easy prey. When I catch them looking squarely at us, my defenses automatically go up.

Before any of them have a chance to make a move, the music stops and the band picks up their gear. I've never seen a live band before, aside from the times Andre played at school or at the youth centre. I'd felt like a queen those nights, the envy of all my friends. There had probably been other bands in town before, but Andre's band was ours. Still, no one danced when they played and that made him mad. The thing was, we were all staring in awe at them. They probably did sound like shit, but Andre looked beautiful on stage. A couple of girls even told me that, too. It made me happy. I didn't have to worry about my status after that. I always had to be there, though. Andre got really nervous playing in front of our friends, so I had to calm him down by acting lovey-dovey. He didn't like it but I knew it was what he really wanted. It was a small price to pay for what I got in return, although I came to understand the concept of a loveless marriage after that.

Almost every time Andre's band played I had to get him home, too. He always got really wasted. He wanted to feel like Kurt, he'd tell me. One night I helped him back to his house — he could barely walk. We were all alone and I couldn't leave him. I dragged him up to his room, all the while telling him to keep quiet so he wouldn't wake his parents. I remembered from health class how to prop up a drunk person so they won't choke on their vomit. I had to carry his guitar case, too.

I'd stayed there for a long time watching him sleep. I couldn't leave. I had visions of him rolling on his back and desperately gasping for air. In the end I couldn't keep my eyes open either. I started crying after I snuck out of his house. Needless to say, I caught major hell from my parents for coming home at sunrise. I let them vent. I couldn't tell them the truth. They grounded me for weeks afterward, but I didn't care. I did what I had to do.

I have to stop thinking about Andre when the band starts playing because I soon recognize they're something quite different. The lead guy looks similar — small, hair dyed blonde — but he's a real guitar player. They look like they're having fun, too. Their music is a kind I've never experienced before. It makes me want to dance, not just bob my head. The rhythms are jerky and the guitars sound crisp and clean. Lise is actually getting into it more than me. I momentarily lose her in the excitement of the moment, then locate her in the throng closest to the band, which shakes and contorts like a single-celled organism. I chug the rest of my beer and join in, becoming a part of this mass which only minutes before had simply been a roomful of people too cool to interact with each other.

I start paying closer attention to the band. They're also the first with relatively short hair I've ever enjoyed. I guess they're what university guys must be like. The main one, the singer and lead guitar player, jokes continually between songs and improvises brief snippets of stupid songs we all know, much to everyone's delight. The whole feeling becomes one of being at a basement party; suddenly the wood and the fireplace make sense.

Then the main guy starts playing a song on his own. It's beautifully simple, and I hang on every word trying to figure out what he's singing. I eventually get the chorus, which he sings several times: "What a fantastic place to be." These words sting my ears with a clarity that almost makes me faint. I'm close to screaming, "Yes! It is a fantastic place!" But everyone is held in rapt silence until the rest of the band unexpectedly jumps in for the final verse.

I join everyone in bouncing up and down and yelling at the top of my lungs, the sound immediately swallowed by the music. My life feels right. I'm not thinking about Andre. I'm alive at this moment and that's all that matters.

The song ends. I look over to where I last saw Lise, but she's not there anymore. The band plays one more song before stopping for the night. I'm now torn between finding Lise and rushing to the singer to thank him in my own awkward way. I go to her, my eyes darting around the room in search of her distinctive model's frame. There will undoubtedly be a gathering of men around her, like ants around their queen.

I'm right. She's at one end of the bar with a group of pilots. As I approach, I notice their uniforms are different. Some bear a Maple Leaf, but some have British markings and even an obvious American flag. My brief elation is replaced by a sense of dread.

There are six of them, more than both of us could handle even if we were sober. They all take a good look at me when I stand beside Lise.

"Oh, you have a friend," one of the Brits says, not doing a good job hiding his carnal thoughts. Lise is pretending not to understand them; but I know she can. I'm surprised to see her coyly smiling and nodding at them. She's drunker than I've ever seen her before. In a situation like this she would typically get aggressive then walk away. Here, she's appreciating the attention and perhaps even goading them on.

Although she seems to be in control, the British pilot who greeted me keeps trying to drag her onto the floor, which is again populated by people dancing to taped music. She toys with him but finally relents, leaving me to fend for myself.

The guys are actually quite polite. I can see how Lise was so easily swayed. They're all handsome, in a sanitary kind of way. The uniforms give them a bit of an edge but I don't let it get to me. All it proves is that they have a lot more discipline than the average guy. I'm not anticipating a problem until one of the Americans grabs me by the arm and pulls me toward the floor, notwithstanding my feeble resistance. Another one gets him to back off and buys me a drink. I don't even bother to look at the glass as I knock it back. The liquor burns all the way down, making me catch my breath. The pilots start laughing at me. I feel the urge to run but don't know where to go. My only solace is the bathroom.

"Wait, you didn't finish your drink. It won't be here when you get back!"

The harsh fluorescent light is a shock as I stumble in. Some girls are touching up their makeup and approach to help me. I manage to gather myself and enter an empty stall. I want to barricade myself there for the rest of the night. I keep silently asking myself how everything could go bad so quickly, until a picture of Lise flashes in my mind and makes me ashamed for not being there for her. I can't recall seeing any bouncers in the place.

I get back on my feet, determined to grab my friend and leave. It's time to go anyway, I suspect — although I have no idea what time it actually is. We're a couple of Cinderellas, and I feel midnight coming.

She's still dancing and apparently having fun. The other pilots once again surround her, and cheer my return. I head straight for Lise and pull her away by the arm.

"We gotta go. Now!"

One of the guys is already interfering. "What's the matter? You French girls too good for us?" I ignore him and fight through my alcoholic fog.

"Lise, we really have to get back. The train's leaving soon."

"But we've got pilots here. They can fly us wherever we want to go," she slurs. "Where are we going again?" She puts her arms around the British guy's neck and falls back into the dancing mob.

I'm really worried now. The room is spinning, like we're being sucked down a drain. The last thing I want is to be forced to spend the night with these scumbags. They haven't come here for the music, they've come for us.

At that moment I have a brilliant idea. I see the band nearly finished packing its equipment so I grab Lise one more time. "Come with me, I want to meet the band."

"What?"

"I want to meet the band. Don't you want to?"

"No, they really weren't that good. I like this a lot better."

"I don't care, come on." In an instant we're out the back door and standing beside a van where the drummer is stowing the last piece of his kit. He looks at us and smiles. I walk over and notice the others leaning against the far side of the van, passing around a joint. I focus squarely on the main guy and manage to stammer, "You guys were great." He turns his attention back to the gear and mutters something about the show not being one of their best.

"Oh, I thought you were great," I repeat like an idiot. Lise is silent and starting to show signs of fatigue, so I get to the point of telling him of our trip.

"That's cool," he replies. "We're playing in Vancouver in three days, I think. It's too bad there's not enough room to take you." The offer's tempting, but I remain adamant.

"Actually, my friend and I have to catch a train now. Maybe you're passing by the station on your way out?"

He smiles at my attempt at charm and tells the others, "I guess it's just a couple blocks away. I'll drop them off and pick you guys up in ten minutes. I think two beautiful girls deserve at least that much."

On any other occassion I probably would have spent the night with him, but there was only time to throw my arms around his neck and sneak a peck on the cheek. Lise groans as I haul her into the van. We're at the station in a few minutes. The train is there, steaming, as if it was waiting for us to show.

"Well, here you are," he says, throwing the van into park. I don't want to leave him. He's everything I need at this moment.

Seconds become eternities as we're locked in each other's gaze. I can't believe I'm falling in love with him. At least that's what I imagine is happening. I can't tell anymore. Every guy has to be measured against Andre, but this is something different. He's what Andre could have been.

"Make sure you come see us in Vancouver. We'll be at the Town Pump," he says, obviously urging me to leave.

"Okay, I'll try."

"You'd better go." He opens the van's sliding side door and helps me extract Lise from between two amplifiers. She wakes up and manages a weak wave as the van pulls away. I haven't asked him his name. I don't even know the name of the band.

Harsh reality sets in. I punch Lise in the shoulder and drag her to the train. Luckily, our tickets are still in our shoulder bags. I fumble for a few seconds to find Lise's for her, but the porter is patient.

"You girls have fun tonight?"

"Um, yeah. We're really tired. We'll just go to bed."

"Okay, there's a couple bunks left, I think. We'll be in Vancouver in the morning."

I tuck Lise in and get myself settled. It's a hard thing to do. The night has been traumatic in many ways. Events run through my head like an instant replay. The pilots are probably still there trying to get laid, and the band is probably on its way through the Rockies toward its next gig. All I know is I have to see that singer again. Maybe I'll find Andre at the same time and they'll become friends.

Or maybe not. I always feel bad telling a cool guy that I have a boyfriend. It always seems to turn him into something else, something I don't like anymore. I can't see whatever-his-name-is being that way; he probably has a million girls after him. Still, I don't want to take the chance. The night has been perfect in a lot of ways, too. I decide not to tell Andre about him. He'd just be jealous that I fell for another musician.

I awake to the sound of the train hurtling through the BC wilderness. I peer out the window and see nothing but trees. Not trees like back home, but trees with hidden tops, trees that have seen the entire history of the country. I've slept through the mountains, which pisses me off, until I realize I'll see them on the way back.

The porter walks through the sleeping car to announce our imminent arrival. I hear Lise groan again.

"Whatsa matter? Can't handle yer booze?" I whisper from my bunk above her.

"Fuck off," she whispers back.

We get dressed but don't have time to wash. The train has already slowed to a crawl by the time we get our shit together.

"Thank you all for being such pleasant riders. Enjoy Vancouver and maybe I'll see you on the way back." The porter's voice is completely unsentimental. I've grown to admire that in him. I hope I *will* see him on the way back.

We get off the train in the pure sunlight of early morning. The Vancouver station is bright and welcoming, like the the rest of the city, we discover. But I feel something different. We're at our destination, and suddenly there are no time limits. We have a lot of our parents' money left, and I still have some big ideas. Andre, surprisingly, is now only in the back of my mind.

"I hate to ask, but what do you want to do?" Lise says, more normal now as she sips a coffee in the station's diner, fighting off her hangover. I don't think before I answer.

"Let's go to the ocean!" Her reaction tells me she was expecting something worse.

"I'm gonna call my cousin and tell her we're here. Then I guess we gotta do the regular tourist thing."

I take advantage of her weakness. "Maybe there'll be some sailors there for you."

"I'm not gonna tell you to fuck off again."

"I hope that wasn't the real you I saw last night."

"You know it wasn't. I don't know what happened. Being so far from home must do that to you." There's nothing more to be said. I feel exactly the same way.

We manage to get ourselves stuck on a bus tour of the Expo grounds filled with horrible tourists from every corner of the earth, cameras snapping as fast as humanly possible. We escape and wander for miles along the waterfront until we find an open stretch of beach. I could spend the whole day here, wading into the water up to my knees and getting tanned. Lise seems afraid to go in the ocean.

But the sun eventually gets too hot, as it always does. I suggest moving on, so I can begin my silent search for Andre. He'll be in a coffee shop or a record store, I just know. I press Lise to stay in a youth hostel tonight. She understands why, and doesn't object. It will all seem like a big coincidence when I see him again. We snag a bus and hope it will take us downtown.

10 Andre
Calgary: May 22, 1994.

She didn't have to say anything. I should have hid her in the trunk. I should have stayed with her. Anything but what we did.

She told me her story that night in the laundromat. She sensed I was harmless and opened up right away. I didn't know what to say. Serge and Rich would never have understood. They would have felt betrayed, for sure. Nothing on this trip would have mattered if I had gone with her. Now everything matters more. I've lost Joanne as well as Sylvie. Too many times I've considered turning the car around and crossing the border again, but she's probably on a bus heading back to Boston right now; back to a place she hates, a place that's killing her. A place where she is scorned by her family as a freak of nature, where they abuse her for no reason apart from contempt for her mere existence. She'll run away again.

Rich has adopted a small rat he found at the last gas station we stopped at. It seems clean and friendly, but I had my fill of rats back in Quebec City. I'm hoping he'll lose it before we get to Vancouver. The idea of it crawling around in the car makes me sick.

We're on Highway 2, heading into Calgary for no other reason than to take another break, I guess. We should be on our way to Vancouver. I'm starting to feel the pressure of what has to happen there. I have to keep driving until I convince myself it really will. Joanne made me forget temporarily. That's the problem when you have too much freedom, your mind imagines things that could never be and you forget about living in the moment.

Joanne made me believe I had a life. We could have lived together, travelling around the States, eventually maybe even settling down. But on the other hand, I sensed the cops were onto us, that Canada was our only escape. But that was fucking stupid, now that I look back. I should have dumped Rich and Serge in a motel room in Butte or Billings and left forever. A ghost. That's how it should have been.

The guys are happy to be back on home soil, though. I don't think they've gotten over the shock of Joanne yet, but they know enough not to push my buttons. Rich has gotten close to this rat way too quickly. He's talking to it already, and has named it Itchy. He really doesn't have much of an imagination.

The road is calm as the sun sinks on this terrible day. But I don't even know what day it is — they fly by so fast when you're driving. I used to think time dragged when I was back home. There was nothing to do but hustle. I did make a lot of money, though. I probably would have been a great stockbroker. But the days would sometimes go by with nothing to show in the end. Rich and Serge became a nice diversion. They made me laugh when I couldn't laugh with Sylvie anymore. But that's ancient history; I've got to stop thinking about it. All that matters is what's happening now and what's going to happen in the next few days.

What's happening is the road, my foot on the gas and my hands on the wheel. There are no passengers, no rats. The engine is humming, like Kurt's guitar solo on "Lithium." It hasn't been out of fourth gear for hours. The engine is the only thing I trust now. I'm sure it trusts me, too. It won't quit on me.

Rich has the ghetto blaster going again in the back seat. He's put on some old Black Sabbath I haven't heard in about a week. As I sing along in my head, it suddenly occurs to me that I've learned much of my English from these songs. Usually when a song became popular, the lyrics would turn into secret passwords among us. When "Sweet Leaf" comes on, Rich starts bugging me to pick up some pot in Calgary. I assume he's joking, but after a while I feel the craving too. The taste never goes away, no matter how long you've been straight.

I try to recall the last time I've gotten high. It definitely was a long time ago. It must have been the night of Sylvie's graduation formal. I couldn't go back to that school. At the time, I figured I was doing the right thing, but I wasn't thinking of her. I didn't even go out that night. Rich and Serge wanted to go drinking but I just stayed on the couch, doing whatever drugs I had lying around, anything that would take my mind off Sylvie. After the guys came back, they told me I was in my bed with every blanket in the apartment covering me. They tried to get me up and coherent, but I screamed every time one of them touched me. Of course, I don't remember any of this. What I do remember is swearing the next day never to get high again, and pleading with Sylvie on the phone for several hours not to break up with me. I was sincere, and she accepted it. I never did drugs after that night. But at this moment I feel like I never want to be sober again.

The music continues to make my mind drift. I remember how I used to have to blast the radio in this car to keep myself awake on trips home after seeing Sylvie. She didn't want her parents knowing that we were going out, so I'd have to meet her at the youth centre dances. She'd cook up a story about sleeping over at someone's house, then I'd take her somewhere out in the woods. I'd never get much sleep those weekends, we'd just be holding each other and talking about the future, like the night I left for good. A QPP would have put me away for sure if he'd stopped me, but I've always taken pride in my driving abilities. Stopping to rest never seemed right. I would rest in the ground, I told myself.

Now Rich has put his copy of *In Utero* on. "Heart-Shaped Box" is playing, and I picture the video for it. I'd really liked it. It reminded me of where I was, a dark wasteland populated by freaks. I think about the little girl in the video. She is the one who will take me away. The experience will be calm and gentle. The child is happy and playful, so you go along. What will happen after that, I can't say. But I know that dying will not be painful. How can it be? Did God, whatever, put billions upon billions of living things on this planet as a cruel joke, with a punch line of eternal pain and suffering? Things have to get better when we go.

Kurt keeps on singing. He's telling me he knows what I'm talking about. It hits me that I don't need to get high after all. Thinking about death and the universe is enough to alter the brain's chemistry. I begin picturing the car as a spaceship, then wish that Canada had an electric chair. I'd volunteer to test it and pretend it was a time machine. For all anyone knows it could be; maybe we have the power to do whatever we want in the afterlife. Maybe I'll get sent to haunt someone in the Middle Ages, or even in the future. Or maybe that reincarnation stuff is true. I've heard that people who take their own lives always get sent back until they figure out how to live right. Kurt might be a newborn baby at this moment, tucked away with a happy family. There has to be something to explain why some people are born into good families, while others have to live in the gutters of Brazil. The three of us are somewhere in between. We still have at least a few more turns to go.

I know most people won't understand our reasons, just like they don't understand Kurt's. These guys had everything going for them, they'll say. What did they have to complain about? Nothing. Our parents dreamed great things for us, but we couldn't even come close. I don't want to work for minimum wage. I don't want to be a drug addict or a useless asshole sucking off the system. I picture my brother, getting high all day at Mario's and pushing his junk at the reservation. That was my future, no matter how much I denied it, and I couldn't bring that upon Sylvie. Twenty years from now, she'll be successful at whatever she wants to do and there I'd be, sitting in this car across from her house, waiting for her to get home. Eventually, I'd knock and she'd be standing in front of me, but I wouldn't know what to say.

I feel tears welling up and I struggle to hold them in. The scenario will never play out. She'll wake up in a couple of days, possibly to a phone call. Her mother will answer, or maybe she will herself. The voice on the other end will tell her the three of us are dead. It's hard to imagine how someone you love will react to that news. Sylvie will cry, immediately. She's always been over-emotional.

Maybe after an hour or so she'll start calling everyone to see if they've heard. Actually, many will have called her by then, but she will be too distraught to talk.

There'll be a big memorial, too, I guess. Everyone back home goes to funerals, even it they didn't know the person that well. I hope the kids do their own thing for us, like have a big bush party or something. I'd like to see that. I just hope Sylvie has enough sense to know this isn't her fault. I'm doing it out of love and respect for her. She deserves to have a long, good life. I'm just part of her youth, and she should move on.

The sky gets dark and the lights of Calgary get brighter. Passing objects distract me. My brain switches back to city mode.

All the streets in Calgary are numbered instead of named, which makes it easy to get around. It's still fairly early, so we decide to go through the old ritual of getting loaded at the closest bar. This is a cowboy town, and it makes me more uncomfortable than any other place we've been. It isn't much different than Montana, although there, at least I had Joanne.

There is no one who resembles us, no one I can reason with if there's trouble. On the way into the city, Serge brings me back to reality by relating the trouble they'd had at the roadhouse in Montana, and I can't stop mulling over what I'd do if that situation came up here. I'm certainly not in the mood to fight. I'm so depressed, actually, I probably wouldn't feel the pain if a redneck did start pummelling me.

My paranoia has also returned. I don't want any more screw-ups. It's my wariness that has gotten us this far, and I can't let my guard down again. The guys are anxious to drink, but I balk at the first two bars they suggest. They're seedy country-and-western dives, probably with line-dancing contests, or maybe mechanical bulls in the back. I hate cowboys. They seem so English. Growing up, I'd never given much thought to French–English relations — I couldn't really give a shit — but somehow, the image of a cowboy always offended me. I couldn't understand what they were all about. All I saw were guys in stupid hats killing Indians. I guess if you know real Indians, then cowboys seem even more stupid. They were just adults playing dress-up, and it hit me right then that there's nothing more dangerous than a person believing he's something he's not.

We settle on one of those nondescript franchise taverns that try to appeal to everyone by putting up a lot of old crap on the walls so the interior looks like your grandfather's basement. There aren't any cowboys. We take a booth beside a window looking out onto one of the city's busy streets and quickly down a pitcher of Export. The guys make a big deal about drinking Canadian beer, like it's some kind of magic formula that makes them part of the country again. It makes me think there really are people whose only sense of Canadian identity comes from the brand they drink. Though I couldn't give a shit about it, I have to admit this is a beautiful country once you see it, and that's what should make a person feel good about living here. I consider explaining this to the guys — they really sound moronic going on about the beer — but decide against it. It won't do any good to insult them now.

It's somebody's birthday at the big table in the middle of the room, and the wait staff sing "Happy Birthday" to the poor fucker. I pick up our saltshaker, motioning as if to throw it over there. Rich and Serge laugh, but I'm dead serious. No one deserves to be happy right now. I'm not thinking selfishly; everyone else in the room is selfish. They're the ones who will look down on us for what we're about to do. "What was their fucking problem?" they'll say. "Why couldn't they just be happy?" I almost stand up and yell, "You're the ones fooling yourselves!" I've never thought so rationally before in my life.

The scrutiny is starting to wear me down. They see a greasy youth with long hair and immediately assume they know what I'm all about. I think again about dying in a public place. It's the only way; people will rush to help us but we'll just smile and wave from inside the car. I'll say everything is all right, and maybe some of them will finally get it.

Rich and Serge become quiet when I set down the saltshaker.

They drink and occasionally steal glances at people at other tables.

"Andre, when's your birthday again?" Serge asks. I actually have to think about it for a second.

"November 11."

"Remembrance Day? It's funny you'd forget it."

I flash back to childhood, when birthdays were always marked by sombre ceremonies at school and on TV. My brother used to tell me the minute of silence was because of all the shit I'd caused throughout the year. My parents did their best to make the day enjoyable, but I was always left with odd feelings of remorse — a sadness about something I didn't understand.

"I don't want to talk about birthdays," I say.

Our table falls silent again. Another pitcher comes and goes, but I barely touch it. Alcohol is a depressant, I tell myself. I'm not motivated to leave, though. Rich and Serge start talking about dumb TV shows and retelling old hockey stories, which gives me a chance to go over things in my head one more time. I will have to write one last letter to Sylvie and explain myself as best I can. That can be done once we get to a hotel room.

The idea of a will comes up again, too, and I begin compiling a list of my stuff. Too bad all of it is worthless. All I really have to give away are my records and books — a couple of boxes of crap accumulated over the years. Sylvie can have it all. Mario can have all my money as payment for the stress I've put him through. I wonder what they'll do with my clothes? My mother will probably want to keep a few things for sentimental reasons. Maybe Michel will steal some for himself. I can see him doing something disgusting like that. He'd steal a bum's last dime if he had the chance. All that's left is the car. But who would want it after what's going to happen? Maybe someone will put it on display, like the first rocket to the moon.

"From now on the car will be known as the Rocket," I say. I allow myself a smile, knowing the guys are caught completely off guard. They start laughing, and Rich asks if I'm wasted.

"No, I just feel we're on a mission again."

I have to win their confidence back by saying things like this. It means a bit of acting, although I can tell they're put off by how quickly my mood changes.

I buy another pitcher and try to join the conversation. But it's obvious I won't be able to tell them my plan when they're drunk. I suddenly regret letting them drink so much, as it's making the atmosphere too comfortable. It might take all night now to convince them of what needs to go down.

I never enjoy arguing. It's not that I always get my own way — more like the opposite. At some point in my life I must have accepted being deprived of things everyone else took for granted, so I never fought for anything. Sylvie could never understand that. She started the arguments, then got pissed off when I didn't fight back. Most of the time I was pretty wasted, but that didn't matter. I wasn't one of those Neanderthal guys who wanted a girlfriend to be a slave. I would walk away, knowing she'd eventually see that the whole thing was stupid. I only ever got mad when she dressed like a whore. It wasn't what she was, and I just assumed she did it for someone else besides me. A few times we argued about short skirts or too much makeup. Overall, I don't think it made me such a bad guy.

I force myself to stop rehashing this shit, and switch to mentally preparing for the inevitable confrontation with the guys. For the rest of our time in the bar, they keep up the chatter as I silently run through as many possible scenarios as I can. Eventually we have to leave, and I lead them, stumbling, back to the car. They're laughing and I'm resigned to finding a place to stay. Joanne made me see that staying in fancy hotels was a phony thing to do. The night we slept on the hood was uncomfortable as hell, but it was what I should have been doing all along. Cheap hotels are just plain unappealing, but it's the only option for the guys.

We have to drive to the outskirts of town before I find a reasonable motel. The process of checking in is almost automatic. I look forward to not having to live this way. The room we get is just like others we've been in: two identical beds side by side, a couple of chairs and tables, and a shitty TV. Rich heads right for the closest bed. Serge goes for the can to take a piss.

"Fuck man, I don't know how you can go on like this without getting tired," Rich says as he settles in. I'm sitting in a chair by the small window near the door, waiting for Serge's return.

"I've got a lot on my mind."

"Oh yeah. Hey man, I'm really sorry about that. I mean, we would've understood if you'd have told us." He thinks I'm still brooding over Joanne.

"No, I don't think you would've," I reply without thinking.

Serge sits on the other bed and turns on the TV with the remote control.

"I don't wanna watch TV," I say.

"Sorry, I guess it's just a reflex. What were you guys talking about?"

"I was telling Andre how we would've understood about Joanne," Rich says.

"Oh yeah, that's so true man. You should've told us. Things got really weird there for a while." Serge is really drunk and it's making me uncomfortable. But at least they're being honest.

"What do you mean?" I ask him.

"Well, I don't know if I should tell you this . . ." He looks at Rich who has his eyes closed. Mine are wide open, waiting for Serge to finish his thought. "I saw the two of you making out at the baseball diamond."

The news doesn't shock me. "Yeah, well, she's gone now. Forget about it. She just happened to be there and I didn't want to blow her cover. Maybe it was a mistake."

"Yeah, you're human after all," Rich says without opening his eyes. It makes me recall how he went gaga over that stripper in Toronto, and I feel a tinge of guilt for not taking him seriously then. He's had his heart crushed, too, but I've been too self-absorbed to consider how he was coping. These things aren't playing out the way I'd planned. Suddenly, I feel like opening up to my friends, but Serge breaks my train of thought.

"What are we gonna do here?"

"I don't wanna stick around much longer," I reply.

"Where are we gonna go then? Seattle?"

I've almost forgotten about Seattle. That was part of the original plan, but I was too concerned with getting back to Canada in one piece. It doesn't seem like a big deal now, since we don't have to worry about crossing the border. Seeing Kurt's home seems like the right thing to do. It's an attainable goal, and anyway, we're not ready for Vancouver. I still need more time.

"We're going to Seattle. Tomorrow," I finally answer.

"Cool. Where are you gonna sleep?" Serge asks.

"Why don't we talk for a while?"

"Aw, c'mon Andre, let's get some sleep. I'm too out of it." Still, curiosity finally gets the better of him. "What's on your mind?"

"It's about what we're going to do after Seattle, when we get to Vancouver." Serge's face sinks and Rich looks up for the first time. "It's been a long trip, but I haven't forgot what I want to do when it's all over."

"Don't start again," Serge interrupts. "We've been through so much. You can't say that we're the same people we were when we left. There's no reason for you to think suicide makes sense now."

I haven't thought about it that way. Am I different? No, I'm not.

"It's been my intention all along. You guys knew that."

"Yeah, but we didn't believe — I didn't believe — you'd actually do it." Serge glances at Rich, who stares at me with spooky, sleepy eyes.

"What do you guys think you'll do back home?" I ask. "There's nothing for us there. We couldn't even work in the goddamn mill, even if we wanted to. You can get your fucking degrees, but what good are they gonna be?" I focus on Rich. "Neither of you has a girl anymore. What have you got?"

"I don't know, but I've seen enough to give me an idea where to start," Serge says. "I thought that's what you told Sylvie you were going to do, find a place for you guys to settle down. I could stay right here if I wanted to."

"Bullshit. You couldn't make it on your own."

"Fuck you Andre! I'm sick of your fucking sob story. The entire world isn't against you." Serge is crying, real tears. "I can do whatever the fuck I want!"

I don't want to argue, and try to speak honestly. "Look man, do you want to end up pushing junk like everybody else? 'Cause that's what you'll be doing. You saw how easy it was for me. I know you guys. You might be able to get punch-clock jobs in the city, but that's it, you understand? Nobody owes me shit, that's why I wanna get out with a clean conscience."

"What about Sylvie?" Rich asks. It reminds me of writing the letter.

"She doesn't need me. It never would have worked out."

Serge has pulled himself together. "How can you know that?"

I snap back at him, "Because I've made up my mind, all right? You think this has been easy for me? I want her to be happy and she'd never be happy with me around. Don't ask me how I know, I just know. You can ask Rich. He knows what I'm saying." I need a second to compose myself, and I'm counting on Rich for support. He doesn't seem up to it.

All he can manage to say is, "You mean about Anne-Marie?"

"Yeah, and that stripper in Toronto."

"Oh yeah." He tries to sound like he doesn't think about her anymore. "She was a slut. She just wanted to get high all the time."

"See what I mean? Everyone's gonna let you down. Joanne let me down. Kurt let all of us down."

"So, you're not doing this for Kurt?" Serge asks. He doesn't seem drunk anymore.

It takes me a while to respond. I picture the guys who jumped off bridges in the days after Kurt's body was found, and the guys who offed themselves after the vigil. I'm not feeling like that anymore.

This is personal now. But does it matter?

"I'm doing it *because* of Kurt, not for him. He wouldn't want me to do it for him. He didn't want anybody to do anything for him, and I don't want anybody to do anything for me. I figured you guys would get it by now. Haven't you seen how shitty this world is? Rich, haven't you been screwed around with enough?"

"I don't know man, I just wanna sleep."

"No, you can't! I gotta know how you feel. Serge doesn't think we're serious."

"Serious about what?"

"Serious about making a statement. Serious about changing society."

"You're fucked," Serge says. "I knew this was going to happen. Why don't you just get it over with, so me and Rich can go home?" He starts crying again and it makes me mad. I want to slap him.

Rich has pulled the rat out of his shirt pocket and is trying to avoid the conversation, but I instinctively lash out.

"And you've gotta do something about that rat soon. I won't be able to sleep with that thing crawling around the room."

"Aw, he's all right. He stays with me."

"You don't get it, do you? Look at yourself. The best you can do is a fucking rat." I'm yelling at Rich now, and he's yelling back.

"Fuck you! Why are you coming down so hard on me?"

"Because you're even worse off than I am! You're Kurt-fucking-Cobain times ten! Both of you are! Killing yourselves would be the most productive thing either of you could do."

"You think if we do it we'll become some sort of heroes or something, don't you?" Serge says. "Well, you're wrong. There might be a few other freaks like you who think so, but everybody else won't give a shit. Have you thought about that? The majority of people out there won't care."

"I think they will. I mean, look at what we've done. Travelled across the fucking continent just to off ourselves. It's never been done before. Doesn't that count for something?"

"How are they gonna know? They'll probably think we were murdered."

This is the moment I've been waiting for.

"You wanna know how? Hold on." I run out to the car and grab my backpack. I return and triumphantly drop a black binder on Serge's lap. He cautiously opens it and sees my random thoughts jotted on the loose-leaf paper, along with the few doodles that have taken up my spare moments over the past few weeks. "It's all there. Well, most of it. Enough to let the cops know what we were all about. I was going to write my last letter to Sylvie tonight."

After flipping through all the pages, Serge passes the binder to Rich. "Don't let that rat walk on it," I demand. Rich gently picks up his pet and puts it back in his shirt. There's silence until Rich finishes reading. I want to know what they think.

"It's amazing," Rich says. "I couldn't have done that."

"But you did man. We're all a part of it." The binder sits on the bed between Serge and Rich and there's silence again. There is suddenly nothing more to say. I decide to start writing my letter to Sylvie.

"Why don't you two pack it in. We can talk more tomorrow if you want."

I grab the binder and sit back in the chair. Serge turns away. Rich simply closes his eyes again. Neither complains that the light is still on.

It takes me a long time to get started. I don't want it to be a sad letter, but it's so hard to sound happy without being phony. Most importantly, I want to apologize, but I can't get it right. I end up just explaining the plan, without going into too much detail, and assuring her she isn't the reason. I tell her she's the only thing that could make me stop now, but since we'll never see each other again, it's too late to turn back. Instead, she should find the thing that makes her happiest, and do that for the rest of her life. If she doesn't, I write, my ghost will come back to haunt her.

I run out of things to say after one single-spaced page. I find it better not to think too much when I write letters to Sylvie, and I know I'll screw things up if I think about this one. All she needs to know is that I love her and that I'm not crazy. I do apologize to her in the end — for lying before I left. When my words get sappy, I stop and fold it up. I don't even reread the letter. I probably should, since I've got such shitty grammar, but I can't bear to look at it anymore. I set the page aside, push the two cushioned chairs together and try to get some sleep.

I awake after a nightmare. Someone stole the car and I was frantically looking for it. My neck hurts like a bitch from the chairs, and it makes Serge and Rich look extra comfortable in their beds. It's all right though; they deserve it. I look out the window and catch a glimpse of the sunrise. The good weather is staying with us, and I silently hope it will keep up for the rest of the trip. I've heard it rains a lot in Vancouver. We'll have to wait for a nice day to go through with things if that's the case. I hate the rain.

I take advantage of the shower and attempt to wash out some of my clothes. I've given up on wearing underwear. The sound of the water unintentionally awakens the guys, and they're drowsily watching TV when I walk out in a towel. Neither acknowledges me, even when I remove the towel to get dressed. "You guys can clean yourselves up, too, if you want. I'm in no hurry." They look at each other before Rich makes the first move to the bathroom. I take his place on the bed and dry my hair with the towel, feeling surprisingly invigorated. Serge's face appears dark as he stares at the screen.

"So we're going to Seattle today, right?" he asks, as if trying to goad me into another argument. "You know you said a lot of stupid things last night," he continues.

"I was being sincere, man. I really believe this is something we should do."

"Why do you need me?"

"Well, I guess I don't. I thought from the beginning we were all in it together. We're brothers, man. We gotta go down together. Believe me, we're gonna make a difference."

"Yeah, right."

I don't care what he thinks. He's still coming along, and that's all that matters. He obviously wants to see how things turn out, not to mention the guilt he'll undoubtedly suffer if he lets Rich and me go without him.

I remember the letter to Sylvie. It's on the table where I left it, but I still can't bring myself to reread it. There's no time to be sentimental. I want to get moving again.

I wait impatiently while the guys get their shit together. It feels like the day we left Quebec City, as if all the stuff in between has just been a dream. The guys even play rock-paper-scissors for old times' sake. I stop at the first gas station to top off the tank, then mail the letter while the guys grab a snack. I have to force myself to walk away from the mailbox after dropping it in the slot. My last tie to Sylvie is gone.

I try to forget about it as I swing the Chevette onto another westbound stretch of highway. Rich was bright enough to pick up a map. I didn't even think about it. He ably guides me south to the Trans-Canada and we're through the mountains by late afternoon. Throughout the day, I notice several spray-painted messages on the rocks lining the road: *Will you marry me Susan? Tony + Jen 4 Ever, I Love You Kelly*. I'm having a hard time forgetting Sylvie.

The messages get to me, and at the next town I buy a can of red spray paint without telling the guys. I look for the right rock and then one appears, forcing me to pull over.

"What the fuck?" Serge says as I jump from the car. I shake the can furiously, heedless of the traffic that passes. No one but a cop can stop me. It's a beautiful piece of rock, but that doesn't prevent me from whipping off the lid and writing as fast as I can.

Cars honk their horns as they blow by and I convince myself they're giving a show of support. I get two words done before a van pulls over behind the Chevette. A large man with a beard walks toward me. I size him up but keep writing.

"What the fuck do you think you're doing?" he says. I ignore him and get three more letters done before he says, "You got a lotta fucking guts, pal. I'm not gonna let you get away with this."

One more letter. He grabs my arm and swings me around. He's about a head taller than me, but I'm filled with too much adrenaline. I flash the nose of the can in his face, and he loosens his grip. I quickly finish the last letter and bolt back to the car.

I hurl the paint can into the bushes as he chases me. I make it back, and he's trapped between my car and his van. I gun the engine and the tires tear into the gravel shoulder when I slam it into first gear. The fucker dives out of the way, and we hit the asphalt so fast I only catch a brief glimpse of my work.

Forgive me Sylvie

My eyes stay glued to the rear-view mirror. The van is behind us, but I have a good head start. I can't believe we're being chased again. This time it's more fun than frightening. Once Rich and Serge hear me joke about it, they calm down and keep their eyes on the van so I can concentrate on driving. We take the first exit, though I have no idea where we are. It turns out to be a short stretch that leads to a small ski village. The van hasn't followed, so we decide to chill out and grab a meal.

We all have cheeseburgers and fries. No more luxuries. I know exactly how much money we'll need from now until the end.

"Halfway there I think," I say, sipping a coffee.

"Where do we cross the border?" Serge asks.

"Vancouver. We'll probably have to put it off until tomorrow." They seem pretty sour after the day's drive. Neither talks much, and I hope it's a sign they've accepted our fate. I don't want to bring it up again. It's hard enough rationalizing things for my own benefit, especially with the letter to Sylvie on its way east. I imagine Rich has been thinking a lot about Anne-Marie too, but I know Serge is only thinking of himself. I don't leave a tip, and we get back on the Trans-Canada in the oncoming dusk.

The drive into Vancouver is uneventful. The mountains loom, swallowing the sun. I don't waste time looking for places to stay, stopping at the first motel after the *Welcome to Vancouver* sign. We're not in the mood for sightseeing or drinking. It's been one of the longest days on the road, especially for me, and I'm looking forward to sleep. I don't have to tell the guys this, and they allow me to have one of the beds.

I have another nightmare: Rich and Serge have left me. I'm lost in Seattle, searching for Kurt's house. I'm always lost in my nightmares. Lost and late. There's never enough time.

Rich and Serge are actually up before me in the morning. They seem quietly enthusiastic. Rich has the ghetto blaster in the room, and "In Bloom" is blaring for the millionth time. He plays with the rat on the other bed while Serge is in the shower. I'm awake in a hurry, and don't bother cleaning up.

"All right. Let's go." I feel a new clarity. We're actually here. No matter what happens, at least we've arrived.

The stretch to the border is short and we cross without incident. I assume the guards are used to characters like us. For once, I tell the truth, and it must be a common story. We're going to Seattle to see Kurt.

As we drive to the outskirts of the city, it doesn't feel like the America I've become accustomed to. It almost feels like home — small lumber towns filled with kids looking for a better way of life. Seattle is welcoming us with open arms, and it makes me hesitate with the thought that I might not want to leave.

11 Serge
Vancouver: May 25, 1994.

So this is it. Seattle. Fuckin' Mecca. Same as all the rest. It doesn't remind me of anything except what I once got from listening to its musicians. As we drive around and see the different shops and cafés, I look for the influence these places must have had on Kurt and the others. That might be the record store where he bought his first Pixies album. Or maybe that's the bar where Nirvana played its first show. That could be the apartment building where he first got high. The city seems so modern — at the same time, so full of ghosts.

Eventually we stumble upon Puget Sound, and spend a few hours chilling out by the water. It's a calm, sunny Saturday afternoon and the shore is busy with parents and little kids and seniors out for a stroll. Longhairs huddle around drums on the grass, the aroma of marijuana lingers. Nobody bothers them and nobody bothers us. For a long time we sit in silence, staring out at the ocean. We can't go any further.

"This town's all right, eh?" I say.

"I hear it rains a lot," Andre replies mechanically.

Rich is occupied with his rat, which has now taken up permanent residence in the pocket of his dirty flannel shirt. He wears it even on this hot day, and it fuels our general funk. Seagulls congregate. They must think we're statues. Andre's silence unnerves me. This is where he wants to be, and somehow I can tell he's wondering if it's worth all the trouble. I know this because I'm thinking the same thing. We've been wandering for too long, since the day we left, and it's time to find some kind of answer. We've come three thousand miles with a dead rock star as an excuse. It's like *The Wizard of Oz* — except we all want courage, brains and love. I feel like I'm the only one who understands that we've just been running away from those things.

"Let's get something to eat. We're wasting the whole day sitting here," I say. My body actually feels like a statue when I stand, the others following my lead without so much as a grunt. I limp like a cripple until the blood gets back into my legs. We drive downtown and park in a giant shopping mall's garage. It's been a long time since I've been in a mall, and I need to adjust to the cramped surroundings. The stores are boring, except for the one that sells imitation Indian stuff — jackets, moccasins, miniature totem poles. We spend a couple of minutes poking around before Andre leads us to the food court for pizza slices. There's a sea of kids wearing Nirvana T-shirts. Some nonconformers wear the names Soundgarden, Pearl Jam or Mudhoney.

I'm oddly comforted. I mention this to Andre, adding, "Maybe we should hang around a few days. We might meet some cool people."

"No man. Take a look. They're no better off than we are. They're just hanging on to some fucking thing that never existed in the first place."

I get angry. "Why the fuck did we come here then? All we've been doing is living out some fucking dream! *Your* dream. We've done everything you've asked."

"Don't you get it? It hasn't been a dream. It's reality. Our lives. All these kids think Kurt was some kind of symbol, someone who made it okay for them to skip school and get high. We know better. I mean, could you imagine going to high school here? Talk about fucking uniforms. These kids were probably issued flannel and ripped Levis in ninth grade. It's their world, and they're going to think like this for the rest of their lives. We don't belong here."

"Do you really believe there was more to Kurt than skipping school and getting high? People have been trying to make a big deal out of it, and you're beginning to sound like them."

"No matter what those assholes say, the point is, Kurt did the right thing. That's all I want to do, too."

I look to Rich but he's dropping crumbs of pizza crust into his shirt pocket, which writhes like a kangaroo's pouch. Andre is self-satisfied, like he's just perfectly summed up all his random thoughts.

"Now, if you're done bitching, let's find his house."

We probably could have asked anyone in the food court and got detailed directions, but instead we go in search of a cool record store, the kind Andre is convinced won't jerk us around. There's one a few blocks from the mall. Its front window is covered with posters of Kurt so that we can't see in, and small flower arrangements are laid among a collection of Nirvana CDs and magazines bearing his face on the covers, resting on a shelf at the base of the window. The store is populated by more bored mall kids. We sift through the racks for a bit, not looking for anything in particular. In the middle of one aisle, I overhear two girls talking about Kurt.

"I can't even look at his face anymore. I start to cry," one tells the other. I assume she's joking but she proves she isn't when I hear a loud, "Don't!" after her friend starts waving a copy of the *Rolling Stone* death issue in her face. I suddenly realize Andre isn't alone. This thing is bigger than the three of us, whatever it is. I guess it should be expected, since we're in the city where it all went down, but it makes us seem like the tourists we really are.

Kids here are dealing with the crisis in their own way, but all of us are being selfish beyond description. None of us knew the guy, but Andre could never be convinced of that. He thinks he knows Kurt because of the music. That's the part I could never understand. Why couldn't people leave the guy alone, let him just be a songwriter and musician? That's all he wanted, from what I can see. People like Andre and these mall kids pushed him. I'd probably kill myself too if I had to give up my normal life because every kid in the world thought I was telling them what to do. Everything Andre said in Calgary suddenly made sense. In some weird way he wants to tell these kids what Kurt wasn't able to.

I look around the store and see him, head held high like he owns the place. I go over and tell him in French what I'd just heard the two girls talking about, and he smiles as if he's already heard stuff like that a million times. He then casually walks over to the counter and asks the guy how to get to Kurt's house with as much of our French charm as I've witnessed since we left Chicago. The counter guy is a bit taken aback but replies kindly.

"Wow, where're you guys from?"

"Quebec. It's taken us three weeks, but we're here. We want to see where it's at with our own eyes, eh?"

Just as Andre suspected, the guy knows by heart where to direct us. He explains it as easily as if we'd asked where his own place is.

"I hope you guys think it was worth the drive," he says as we walk out the door. His words echo in my ears as Andre wheels the Chevette out of downtown and into the suburbs. His mouth is wide open in anticipation, and his head bobs around between the street signs and the record-store guy's crudely drawn map.

We can see our destination from a block away. Several groups of kids, many resembling the dopeheads in the park, are holding an impromptu vigil in the area surrounding a large, mostly hidden house. Andre parks the car on the street. We walk up and pass several tiny camps with radios playing Nirvana music at a modest volume. A couple of guys are sitting by themselves, banging on acoustic guitars. We aren't looking to make new friends and, again, nobody acknowledges our presence. When we get to the front gate we stare at the darkened windows on the top floor, the only part of the house visible over the immense hedge. I sense we're all picturing Kurt's headless body lying on the floor. I also wonder how many know he actually killed himself in the unseen greenhouse.

Eventually I'm distracted by a group of young girls sitting in a circle about five feet from where we stand. They're silent during the several minutes we stand at the gate, so when they start giggling, I assume it's at our expense. But as I face them, I don't feel self-conscious, I'm attracted to them for some reason.

"How long have you been here?" I ask.

"Since this morning," a girl with short hair, dyed blonde, responds.

I find myself flirting. "Mind if we sit down, we've had a long trip."

"Knock yourselves out." After that, the girls welcome us, and we gladly take swallows from one of their water bottles filled with vodka and orange juice. We find out they're from Oregon and had convinced one of their mothers to drive them up and pay for a hotel room for the weekend. Along with the booze and a handful of joints, they also brought some offerings of flowers, a ragged teddy bear, some candles for the encroaching darkness and the Xeroxed picture of Kurt that's taped to the fence.

We chat about Kurt for what seems like a long time. It's inane trivia mostly: videos, clothes, lyrics. To fill an uncomfortable pause, I eventually ask, "Do you think he's really dead?"

"How can you doubt that?"

"Well, I don't know, did you ever hear that story about Jim Morrison faking his death, then going off to live in Africa or somewhere where nobody knew who he was?"

"You mean that guy from The Doors? My sister likes them. He faked his own death?"

"I'm not sure. It's just a story I heard. I could see Kurt doing that."

"No way! Kurt's an angel and he's watching over us. All of us."

The blonde girl is upset at my words, so I leave it at that. She defiantly lights up a joint, which brings a security guard over to shoo us away. The girls form a new camp and we start to walk aimlessly around the neighbourhood. The initial awe begins to fade when it becomes clear there isn't anything particularly special about where he lived. He and Courtney had money, so they bought a secluded house on a quiet street. I don't know what I was expecting, but it sure wasn't a suburb where my family could have lived. Maybe that's another piece of the puzzle; these kids from the suburbs can identify with Kurt even more since he lived among them and blew his brains out in a place just like theirs, not in a crappy hotel room or a roach-infested apartment.

"Do you wanna go?" I ask Andre.

He takes a long look around before saying yes. It seems like a hard decision for him, but I can't tell if he's really disappointed. I'm not. I mean, what is there to see? It's just a house like any other, except it has a lot of kids sitting out front feeling sorry for themselves. I don't feel pity or guilt. I don't think any of the other kids do, either. There's only apathy, which Kurt would have wanted.

We get in the car and follow the route back through downtown before leaving the city. It's been another hollow mission, and the trip back to the border is a long and quiet one. No one mentions Kurt again. He's been exorcised.

"Let's stay in Vancouver for a few days," Andre says as we approach the border. "I hear it's a really nice city. Better than this shithole."

All I can say is, "Yeah, whatever."

This border crossing is pretty much an afterthought. It's late and there's no traffic. All the guard does is look around the car to check out, in fact, how we drove it all the way from Quebec. The engine sounds pretty rough now. Andre stops for gas and buys a map of the city. Fortunately, there's a kid working at the station who knows where the closest youth hostel is. There aren't any other customers, so he strikes up a conversation with Andre as if he's a regular tourist. I feel like saying, "No, I don't think we'll have time because, you see, we came here to kill ourselves." Andre would probably laugh the hardest.

We head straight for the hostel before its closes up for the night. I guess it's good that these places shut their doors early. It keeps out undesirables, but sometimes there's people, like us, who show up late and really need a place to stay. Andre parks the car outside the front door. There are lights on, but it's locked up. Andre beats hard on the door, until a rather manly-looking woman greets us about a minute later.

"You guys missed the curfew," she says.

The French charm works one more time. She happily lets us in after hearing our story, explaining that we're lucky it's Saturday night, since most of the regulars stay out late and crash at friends' places. Her name is Ramona, and her gut reaction to us for some reason prompts her to give us a personal history. She lived on the streets for several years, so she knows how to spot bullshit artists, she tells us emphatically, while being extremely gracious at the same time.

We choose our beds. I'm beyond fatigue but can't fall asleep for a while because Rich keeps playing with his rat, talking to it like he's its mother. Andre finally tells him to shut up and to keep the fucking thing in his pocket. That's my last memory of the day, Andre cutting into Rich about the rat. Throughout the night, I imagine it's crawling on me.

I awake sluggish and cotton-mouthed. I stumble to the bathroom in my underwear. Without warning I become lightheaded and lose my balance before puking my guts out. My first thought after collecting myself is that the rat has bitten me and passed on some weird disease. I sit against the cold concrete for a long time, gripped by fear until Ramona pokes her head in the open door and asks if I'm all right. I tell her yeah, and defensively try to explain that I don't know why I got sick, hoping she doesn't think I'm a junkie or a boozer or something. It doesn't matter if she buys my story; it's obvious she's seen a lot worse.

"You should clean yourself up and try to eat something. I'll have breakfast ready in a half-hour. I'm getting your friends up now."

Being around someone with a completely positive attitude, I'm suddenly invigorated. I realize anxiety has probably caught up to me and Ramona has instantly made it go away. She makes a vegetarian breakfast — fruit salad and toast — and sits with us to hear about the trip. Andre and Rich are pretty groggy, but I'm hopelessly smitten with her. I keep the conversation going on my own. I have no fear about the guys making cracks about her looks — at least you can tell she's a girl. I even help Ramona clean up — she's the only staff working on Sundays. I end up telling her little of what's really happened, apart from the day in Seattle. I try to pass off the pilgrimage as the main goal of the trip and have to consciously cut myself off when I start rambling on about the other stuff. I tell her we'll probably be staying a few days, and she says she'll keep our beds for us.

While I'm doing the dishes, Andre comes in and says we should drive around to check out some things. He won't elaborate, so I say I want to hang with Ramona instead. He doesn't argue, and I walk him to the car, where he rips up a parking ticket before driving off with Rich. I'm alone with Ramona and, much to my disappointment, spend the next few hours helping her with her chores. She maintains her great attitude, though, and I gladly obey her every whim. Around noon, she finally takes a break and we walk down to the coffee shop on the corner, where I have my very first café latte.

"You never told me why you came to Vancouver," she says, as we sit down at an outdoor table.

There's a pause while I absorb the moment before answering, "We came to see Seattle, but we'd heard so much about this city we had to see it too, I guess."

Ramona laughs. I've almost caused a spit-take.

"Sorry. I didn't mean to laugh," she says. "But if I had a dime for every kid looking for some answer out here, none of my friends would need student loans. You said you were just in Seattle yesterday? What did you think?"

"We found Kurt's house. It didn't look that special."

"That's right. That's what I've been telling all the kids who want to kill themselves because of that guy. He wasn't special. In fact, from what I know, he was more fucked-up than half the kids who listened to him. They were his therapy. He probably would have killed himself a lot sooner if he hadn't felt that millions of kids were inspired by what he was doing. It's okay to relate to what he sang, but to feel that he was going to solve anyone's problems is totally wrong. Please tell me you're not one of those guys."

I feel a strong twinge of anxiety and the sense that she's reading me like a book. I choose my words carefully. I can only speak for myself, after all.

"No, I'm just a fan."

"What about your friends?"

"They're bigger fans than me. It was actually Andre's idea to go to Seattle. It's his car, too."

"How long were you going to stay in Vancouver again?"

"I don't know. At least a few days. I like it here."

"Yeah, it's beautiful. Even when I was on the street myself it made me feel better just to go down to the beach for a couple of hours. Now that I've got this job, I love it even more. The only thing I tell these kids is to look around while they're out there. There are so many beautiful things in this city, it can make you love life, no matter how down you are."

I know exactly what she means, and I decide I won't listen to Andre anymore. It's not that I'm falling for her or anything; it's just that things suddenly look different.

As we walk back to the shelter, Ramona keeps me entertained with horror stories about her life on the street. Like the time when she was fifteen, and her boyfriend broke up with her while she was peaking on acid. He said afterward that he could only tell her how he felt if she was dosed. He ended up tripping, too, and the two of them spent the rest of the night holding onto each other as they came down.

Then there was a funny story about the first meeting between her best friend and her mother in the emergency room, after Ramona had OD'd on acid and vodka and had to have her stomach pumped at three in the morning. Her mother was freaking out, but her friend joked around as if this kind of thing happened all the time. It was soon after that incident that she left her house for good.

We spend the rest of the afternoon sitting in the shelter talking about the city. After a while, I clumsily tell her I could see myself living here.

"You should. You guys would love it here. It's really not that hard to find a job. Most street people are just too messed up on drugs and shit."

"I don't think my friends would like it."

"Why not?"

The weight of my guilt over being part of Andre's plan suddenly hurts. I have to tell somebody, and Ramona is the only person in the world who could possibly understand.

Still, my English fails when I try to explain that he wants us all to kill ourselves in the name of Kurt Cobain. I know if I tell her, she'll want to stick Andre and Rich in a mental hospital or something, and they'd never forgive me.

"We're used to snow," is all I say.

The guys return about an hour later, looking weary. They've obviously had a conversation of their own. I feel relieved to see them anyway.

"So what do you want to do tonight?"

Andre seems on the verge of passing out. "I don't know man. I think I'm gonna catch up on some sleep."

"So maybe we can check some things out tomorrow?"

"Yeah, sure."

After hearing this, I feel better. At least we have some time.

Surprisingly, no one else has come into the shelter by dinner, so Ramona prepares a feast for us from what's lying around. The weekly rations are due early the next morning. We clean ourselves up while she makes the beds. Andre follows her into the sleeping area, and I don't see him again until the next morning. After we eat, Ramona has to stick around to play hostess to some new arrivals, so I take Rich out for coffee at the same place Ramona took me to lunch. He looks just as tired as Andre, but I figure Rich will appreciate me wanting to spend time with him. The sun is still hanging in the sky, so we sit on the patio. He buys a bagel so he can feed his rat. I ask him what they'd done.

"We drove around. You know, just lookin' at stuff." I know there's more. We're not really tourists after all.

"What did you see?"

"Oh, some totem poles and shit. Cruised the beach and looked at chicks. Didn't see many hot ones, except these two who I could have sworn were Sylvie and Lise. We lost them in the crowd, though." For a moment, I entertain the odds of such a coincidence, until Rich brushes it off.

"We were probably hallucinating. What were you doing all day with Ramona?"

"Nothing much. Just shooting the shit. She's really cool."

"She looks like a dyke." I ignore him. He's looking more exhausted by the minute.

"Why are you guys so tired?"

"We were looking for something."

"What?"

"Andre was checking out storage places." It takes a second for this to register. I set down my coffee, and my mind flashes on how things will go down. This is it. It's going to happen.

"Did he get a place?"

"Yeah."

"For how long?"

"A week. We're getting the key tomorrow."

"So you're cool with all this?" I don't know any other way to put it.

"What do you mean?"

"Come on man, I mean about going along with Andre's plan. You're really going to do it?"

"You mean you don't want to? What the hell have we been doing all this time? That's what this whole trip has been about, making a statement, changing the world."

"But these are our lives we're talking about. What the fuck happened to you? What did Andre say today?"

"Nothing, man. I've made the decision myself. That's it. We can't go home."

"We don't have to go home. We can do whatever we fucking want, but we don't have to die. Why do you want to die?"

"Why not?"

I can't believe *I've* become the voice of reason. Rich starts spilling his guts. He's probably been waiting a long time for this opportunity, so I sit back and let him talk for as long as he wants.

Most of it is stuff about Anne-Marie I've already heard, but he eventually gets into what Andre has been feeding him all day.

"He made me see that there's really nothing for guys like us to believe in. I mean, some guys fought in wars and came back heroes. They were set for life. Other guys got to go off on ships and explore the world. What do we get? Fucking computers. It's too late for us to form a rock band; we'd probably never get a gig anyway. And there's no way we could become astronauts and all that shit. Man, dying's the final frontier."

I can't bear hearing my best friend ranting like a maniac, but I can't think of anything to do about it beyond running away. That would be easy. Just hop on the next bus out of town. But they're my friends. I can't leave them. I picture the scene, the cops asking me why I didn't stop them. I can't imagine what my answer will be.

As I'm agonizing, he relates a story Andre told him about two kids from a farm in Saskatchewan who were so bored one day, they decided to jump into the grain vat just to see if they'd die. Of course they did, their small bodies sank to the bottom and the grain filled up their lungs like seawater. All they wanted was to find out what it was like. Rich has reached that point, too, and it's clear nothing I can say will change his mind.

I buy him more coffee to keep him awake. After a while, he seems to be slipping in and out of consciousness. Of course, he isn't making sense. People actually start looking at us as Rich's voice grows louder and his French becomes slurred. I understand when the waitress asks us to leave.

"He's not a bum," I say, not knowing if anyone hears me.

It's dark when we get back to the shelter. I'm practically carrying Rich. There are a lot of people there hoping to settle in for the night. It makes me a little nervous as they stare at the two of us heading straight for our reserved beds. I tuck in Rich, and even make sure the rat is comfortable, before nodding off myself. I don't bother checking on Andre. The voices and scuffling of the new-comers keep me up for a while; any one of them could be a thief or a rapist. As I doze, I'm overwhelmed by paranoia. Several times I think of getting up and leaving, but each time I'm stopped by my desire to save my friends' lives. I think of sabotaging the car, or alerting someone. I even ponder the consequences of tipping off the cops, or simply getting on my knees and begging them not to do it.

These thoughts fill my head all night, and consequently, I don't sleep. At first light I check on the guys. They're still asleep, so I go to the bathroom and splash water on my face. I get dressed and go in search of Ramona. My heart is lifted when I see her at the front desk. I guess she doesn't sleep either. She's equally surprised to see me.

"What are you doing up?"

"I couldn't sleep."

"Why? Was somebody making noise?"

"No, I just get nervous in these places."

"Well, at least now you can help me when the food truck gets here."

"Yeah, sure." My brain doesn't translate what she says until the truck shows up and I'm carrying boxes of canned soup. The heavy lifting doesn't matter; Ramona restores my sanity.

"What're you guys gonna do today?" she asks after the truck departs.

"Oh, I don't know."

"I've got the afternoon off. I could show you around if you want."

"Yeah, that would be nice." I want to leave with her now, before everyone wakes up, but we have to wait until breakfast is served. Andre and Rich are silent when I see them in the dining room and I don't say anything to them either. I know they have to get the garage key, so I don't mention going out with Ramona. When they finally tell me the plan, I respond casually, "Oh, okay, have a nice day." Andre becomes visibly unhinged. He starts to make a move to question me, then walks out with Rich, disgusted. I hope this won't be the last time I see them.

"What are they gonna do today?" Ramona asks when she notices them leaving.

"Um, I think they're going to get the car looked at. It's still got to get us home."

Ramona and I spend the whole day travelling around the city; I'm exhausted when it's all over. Hopping on and off crowded buses and the Sky Train only reinforces what I've started to feel. I actually could live here.

We spend a good part of the afternoon at Stanley Park. She admits it's kind of touristy, but it's still a place I need to tell people I've seen. I'm feeling extremely close to Ramona and the pressure to tell her about the guys builds until my head starts throbbing. I can't see what she could do about it, though. I almost tell her during one coffee break, but instead I ask her if any of her friends had committed suicide.

"Oh yeah, several," she answers. "It's always an option when you're on the street. With a couple of people I knew, I don't think they wasted much time thinking about it. They just got up one morning and said, 'This is it, I don't want to live anymore.' I even tried it once myself one night. It was right after I'd accidentally done heroin for the first time. I was told it was an opium joint, but that's a whole other story. What happened was, after I came down, I got all paranoid thinking I was a junkie now. I knew a lot of junkies, and I didn't want to become like them, so I thought it was a good excuse to kill myself and get it over with. I tried slashing my wrists — it was in the shelter actually — but Annie, the supervisor, heard me screaming and fixed me up. She helped get my life together after that and got me my job."

"How did she change your mind?"

"She made me see that all I really wanted was to help others, but I had to learn how to help myself. Once she gave me a goal, it was easy. I wasted five years on the streets to find myself, but in the end it was worth it, you know?"

I don't feel better, hearing her story, because I know now she can't help Andre with such simple logic. Death is the only thing he wants. I expect her to ask about me, but she keeps talking about herself. My thoughts are with the guys, so I stop listening.

We get back to the shelter in time for dinner, even though Ramona doesn't have to work. She wants to be there anyway, for my benefit. Andre and Rich are back, and I'm surprised to see them chatting with a small group of regulars. They're in good spirits, and acknowledge me when I sit down. When the group gets up to be served from the big soup cauldron, Andre holds me back.

"We're gonna take the ferry over to the island tomorrow," he says. "You coming, or you gonna hang out some more with your girlfriend?" The sense that he might be changing his mind prompts me to say yes immediately.

Some of the tension is eased during dinner, but when we're done I purposefully get Andre alone in one of the meeting rooms.

"What about Rich?" I ask point blank.

"What about him?"

"Don't you think he's starting to lose it? He's turning into a babbling idiot."

"Nah, he's all right. He's just getting homesick. That's why I wanna go to the island tomorrow. We'll chill out, get a fresh perspective." I'm encouraged even more hearing Andre say this.

"So what about the plan? You thinking of changing it at all?"

"Maybe."

The word hangs in the air like a life preserver on its way to a drowning man. I can't hold back a sheepish grin, and Andre returns it. We stare at each other in silence, until Andre extends his right hand. Our palms connect and thumbs entwine, but I'm moved to go further and throw my left arm around Andre's neck.

The mistrust melts away as we embrace. I'm rejuvenated, and seek out Ramona after Andre goes to Rich. Ramona tells me she's going out with friends. I'm welcome to come along, but I tell her I'll be all right with the guys. She clearly notices my enthusiasm, giving me a strong hug before saying goodnight.

There's not much to do at the shelter, so we roam around the neighbourhood before curfew, stopping occasionally for beer, fast food and video games. Rich seems stable again, and we're back to being three friends, without Andre's darkness dominating our actions. When we return to the shelter, I eagerly fall asleep in anticipation of this being our first step toward going home. I'm still soundly unconscious when Andre shakes me.

"Let's go."

I'm surprised to find he and Rich fully prepared for the day ahead. They're both wearing wrinkled Nirvana T-shirts under flannel jackets, and their familiar torn Levis. Andre is rushing me, but I don't complain.

The sun is barely up and there's no movement in the shelter. There isn't even anyone at the front desk when we walk out the door. The entire city seems empty. The car is parked in a lot around the block and turns over, barely. I call shotgun and Rich doesn't protest. At that point, I notice his eyes are blank and his movements are slow. His jacket pocket still bulges with the body of the rat, although it's not moving.

I try to make small talk as the engine warms up, but it's only answered by grunts and snorts from Andre, whose eyes remain trained straight ahead. At the moment he puts the Chevette in gear, Rich grabs both my arms, holding them behind the passenger seat while quickly tying my wrists together with something. The move comes as such a shock, I don't react until I realize what's going on.

"You fuckers! You can't do this! I'm not gonna die with you!"

I keep yelling all the way to the self-storage complex, not eliciting a response until Andre pulls in and screams directly in my left ear.

"Just shut the fuck up! It'll all be over soon!" I'm breathing heavily anyway, so I try to assess my options as rationally as I can.

The engine slows to a low growl as the car homes in on Andre's spot. The identical garages resemble tombs, though most probably hold the common belongings of normal people. Andre finds his space and I recognize some nervousness as he gets out and fumbles for the key. This is my opportunity to try to reason with Rich, even though I can't see him.

"Don't let him do this to us, man. Don't let him do this to you. Just let me go, and we'll get back home. I'll make things better for you, I fucking promise!"

I'm crying by the time I get through my plea, and lose control even more as Rich ignores me. I can't tell if he's crying, too; my only sense that he's back there is the distinct smell of a magic marker and the sound of him using it on something.

Andre returns and pulls the car into the garage. He gets out again to lower the big steel door, after methodically locking all the car doors except his own. I can see him in the rear-view mirror carrying a long section of hose, which he fastens to the tailpipe and hangs through his slightly opened window. The car is running the whole time, and the interior quickly fills with choking fumes. Andre jumps back into the driver's side, not bothering to look at me, and sits back with his eyes closed. We start coughing uncontrollably and I feel my vision going. Rich is no longer concerned with my struggling, and with a last ditch effort, I manage to squeeze one hand free of his crude knot. I take a look back through the fog and see his body splayed across the back seat, his jeans covered in magic marker scribblings. I instinctively reach to shut off the car. Andre looks unconscious, until he notices my hand grasping for the key and grabs my arm with both of his hands. His grip is still strong, and I struggle to hold my breath. Our eyes lock in a hazy battle of wills, but after an eternity, the fumes are too powerful. In a single action, he releases my arm and slumps backward in his seat. I shut off the car, then summon the strength to open my door and tumble out to the concrete. I remain face down for several seconds, gasping for the less-contaminated air inside the garage. I haven't forgotten I'm still trapped, although I question if I have the strength to open the large door. My only thought is to try to make an effort to save them, so I stumble over to Andre's door and pull the hose out through the window while straining to work the handle. His face is blue, and I can't feel a heartbeat. I've lost all track of time. I frantically check Rich next. He hasn't moved either and his face is a mirror of Andre's. I'm powerless and terrified, but still more afraid of slipping out of consciousness myself. My fear propels me toward the garage door. With one desperate thrust I manage to open it enough to roll myself out into the fresh air. I lay in the alley for a long time, staring at the sky and getting my breath back. I can't think of the guys until I feel coherent enough to tell someone what just happened. I don't know where I am, I can only choose a direction and run. I end up lost in an industrial plaza, forcing me to backtrack to where I assume we had entered. The running saps nearly all of my wind.

In a daze, I decide not to call the cops or an ambulance. The only person I want is Ramona. I check my money and figure I have enough to take a cab back to the shelter, so I nearly throw myself in front of the first one I see. I arrive at the shelter exhausted and Ramona immediately runs to me when I stagger in.

"What the fuck happened?"

"I wanted to tell you but I couldn't. It's too late." My English nearly fails me. "They're dead. They killed themselves."

"Who? Andre and Rich?"

"Yeah. I wanted to tell you but I couldn't."

The rest of the day is a blur as I tell the story several times to several different people. After Ramona, it's the paramedics, then the cops. I don't see them haul the car out of the garage, but by nightfall, the story has been leaked to the media and the shelter is crawling with reporters who want to talk to me. None of our parents know yet, so Ramona and the cop who has been with me all day don't let anyone get close. They make me call home from the police station after they finish their questioning.

/

It's all a bad dream, with no conceivable end. I don't remember anything about the conversation with my mother. The cops call the other guys' houses. I guess they're satisfied with what I tell them, because they put me on the next plane back to Quebec City after I say I want to go home. I don't see Ramona again. I don't even care that my mom is crying her eyes out when she meets me at the airport in the morning.

12 Marcel
La Forest: September 6, 1994.

I guess word started getting around the morning after it happened. I woke up to the phone call. It was my mom at work saying she'd just heard on the radio that two local boys were found dead in Vancouver. I knew instantly that it was them, and after the initial chill passed, I was forced to grapple with the question of why two and not three? I wondered if my mom had got it wrong, or maybe the report was wrong. The cops would not have miscounted the bodies.

The shock hit me again as I went back to bed. This time it came a lot harder. The confusion didn't matter — they were dead, and I knew I'd never see Andre again. More phone calls came in the next few hours and I made a few myself. I learned with relief that Serge was still alive, and many of the conversations centred on who would make the first move to talk to him. Plans were made to get together at the youth centre that night, but nobody was really sure what to do. Nobody had seen the guys in weeks, so I didn't get a sense of how the news was affecting everyone. I didn't really grasp it until I arrived at the youth centre that night and saw all of our friends gathered. At that moment, everything became painfully clear: two of us were gone. Someone started crying, and the feeling soon spread through the room like a brushfire.

What made things worse was that the one person we all wanted to be there, Serge, wasn't. Everyone wanted to know the truth, but the outpouring of love toward Serge was stronger. There was another buzz in the room because Sylvie wasn't there.

I'm sure, like me, everyone was wondering how she would learn the news. Did her parents know how to contact her? Maybe the story was on national TV, and she was on her way home at this moment. Maybe she had actually met them in Vancouver and had been there when it happened. Maybe she was the reason it happened. The questions came in waves the more I spoke with the others. Unravelling the mystery kept the pain away.

Eventually, as we all started speculating, the shared emotions quickly shifted from sadness to a thirst for information. Then, someone decided to go to the DJ booth and put on *Nevermind*, which made some of the girls lose it again. I could clearly see some of the guys taking advantage of the situation, lending a shoulder to cry on. I would have judged these little moves to be in bad taste at any other time, but it was obvious even the sleaziest guys were at least a bit sincere in their intentions.

I wasn't in the mood to comfort anyone, so I searched out the older guys. Mario rarely left his house, which was now commonly known to be his lab. I didn't expect to find him. I also didn't expect to find Michel — it only made sense he should have been at home with his parents. But as I headed toward the bathroom in the back, I saw him huddled in a corner, blowing a joint with two other guys. I quickly thought of something to say while I was in the can, and after I exited I cautiously moved in, hoping he would recognize me. I stood behind him for an eternity before one of his friends tapped Michel on the shoulder.

"Oh Jeez, I thought it might have been a cop," he said half-jokingly.

I hadn't seen him up close in a long time. His face looked puffy and wrinkled, and his expression showed no signs that he'd just lost his brother. He was obviously stoned. He was smiling at me, and I had forgotten what to say. All I could think of asking was if he'd heard anything more about what had happened.

"Nah, the cops just said they're gonna ship his carcass back tomorrow. He could never do anything the easy way."

I was amazed, hearing him talk like this. Even though he was stoned I wanted to tear him apart, but I somehow kept my cool.

"Um, when's the funeral?"

"Fuck, I don't know. Nobody tells me anything. The old man just said they're shipping him back tomorrow. You want a hit?"

I declined and walked away, still trying to suppress the urge to grab Michel by the throat and pound the significance of what was happening into his moronic skull. It wouldn't have done any good. I'd learned, partially through Andre, that you can't make guys like Michel care about anything. They're selfish to the extreme, and proud of being fuck-ups.

I finally felt Andre's absence. I saw that he wasn't a fuck-up. None of us were. At least, not those of us who wanted to get out of this place. I looked around the room and recognized all the shattered spirits. Michel would have been here getting high even if it wasn't a gathering to honour his brother. But the rest of these kids, even the ones who didn't know Andre that well, were losing it because, like me, they were jealous of him and Rich and Serge getting out of this shithole. I recalled the handful of nights Andre's band played in this same room. I now understood that most of the kids went to hear those clumsy but heartfelt attempts at Kurt Cobain's songs because Andre was the closest any of them would ever get to Kurt. Andre looked more like him, sounded more like him and tried to live more like him than anyone else, and those memories were what had brought everyone back together one last time. At that moment, he was as close to being a real-life hero as anyone ever had in this town, and the thought made me cry openly. I wept and didn't care. It didn't matter who saw me — I just cried.

I felt hands patting me on the back, then someone helping me to a chair. I didn't look up to see who it was. I was overwhelmed by the pain — my pain, Andre's pain, Rich's pain, everyone else's pain. I was under attack from all sides.

I must have remained in the chair for a long time, because the next thing I knew, Jean-Jacques was shaking me and asking if I was all right. I struggled to tell him that I was, and he replied that most of the others were going home. The plan was to get everybody together again for a bush party after the funerals. I told him I'd be there.

I hadn't pictured I'd be alone when the night was over, but I was.

It wasn't as late as I'd thought, and my parents were still up when I got home. My mom started crying when she saw me.

"I'm so sorry. If you want to talk, we're here, okay?" my dad said, holding her hands in his.

"It's all right. I wasn't that close with those guys."

"Please, don't keep anything bottled up. It's not healthy," Mom called after me as I walked down the hall to my room. Her voice was cracking with emotion, and it shook me hearing her sound so desperate. I could have told her she didn't have to worry, but I figured everything would be okay once the whole story came out.

When I awoke, the cloud of confusion had momentarily lifted. After a big breakfast, I set about planning my day. First I went back to the youth centre to see who was hanging around. Jean-Jacques, Claude and some other guys were there. Apparently, the logging companies had given anyone who said they knew Andre or Rich the week off.

"Hey guys."

"Hey Marcel, what's up?"

"You hear anything else about what happened?"

Jean-Jacques stepped up and said he'd heard they'd gone to Cobain's house, then sucked on the tailpipe right after. "They're back now, I guess. We're going to see them tonight."

"When's the funeral?" I asked.

"Friday, I think. Well that's when the bush party's gonna be anyway. Oh yeah, you missed it. There were some CBC reporters here about an hour ago asking us what we thought about all of this."

"What'd you tell them?"

"Couldn't really say much. They were asking about this journal or something the cops found in the car. We didn't know anything about it."

"What kind of journal?"

"That's what I asked the reporter. She goes, the cops found this book in Andre's bag filled with stuff he'd written about what they'd done. There were drawings in it, too, I guess. The reporter wanted to know if we knew anything about it."

"Why?"

"Well, she said he wrote some pretty intense stuff about killing themselves in Kurt's name and wanting to show how impossible things are for people our age. I told her I had no idea he thought that way."

Our conversation faded, and I became consumed with thinking about what Andre wrote. The funny thing was, it all made sense somehow, even though he'd never showed any inclination to document his life apart from the few songs he'd finished. But then, Andre never did anything without a purpose. I recalled those nights at Mario's when Andre would drink and philosophize, convincing us that the world was completely fucked up. And that he could change it — if he wanted to. I thought all of that had passed after he had moved to the city, but now I understood being on his own had only made him more determined.

"Yeah, we gotta watch the news tonight man, we're gonna be on TV," Jean-Jacques said, trying to hide his enthusiasm, although it was plain he wanted everyone to know that this was his 15 minutes of fame. I didn't hold it against him.

I told the guys I'd see them later, then went to the donut shop for lunch. All the moulded plastic chairs were taken up when I got there, and the room buzzed with astonished, adult commentary about what had happened. I took one of the few remaining stools at the counter and ordered a black coffee. On my left, a couple of road-repair guys on their break were locked in a sympathetic conversation about Andre's motives. On my right, a QPP officer scanned the newspaper. He eventually noticed me stealing frequent glances over his arm and graciously opened a line of communication. I found myself involved in my first casual chat with a police officer, something that took a bit of adjustment. He did most of the talking though, sensing my fragile state.

"Did you know these boys?"

"Yes sir. We went to high school together."

"This must be very difficult for you." He tried hard to show me his guard was down, and that he wasn't looking for incriminating information. I wasn't sure if I should spill my guts or not.

"Yes, it's been hard. I'm sorry, but I still don't know everything that happened and that's the worst part about it."

"I can tell you what happened, if you want me to."

He suddenly wasn't a man in uniform with a gun anymore, but the person I'd been searching out for the past two days. I warmed up to him.

"How did you find out? The BC cops?"

"Well yeah, mostly. They had to contact us to get a positive ID, so we were filled in. I was just reading the paper now to see if they got the story right. Anyway, some of it might be a little gruesome, so stop me if you don't want to hear any more."

"No, I want to know everything."

"Okay. Well, you probably know that they suffocated on exhaust. That means there wasn't any pain, if it's any consolation. The third guy there . . ."

"Serge."

"Serge. He bailed out at the last minute and tried to get help."

"What about the journal?"

"Well, the journal was what explained everything that Serge couldn't say when he was interviewed afterward. This whole thing was really something I'd never heard of before. I don't think anybody had."

Over the next half-hour, the officer told me all he knew of what was in the journal. There was the concert in Quebec City, the drug dealing in Montreal and Toronto, the border crossing, the bad deal in Detroit, picking up the girl passing herself off as a guy in Chicago, the day at Cobain's house and, of course, the reams of pages containing Andre's musings on life and what he wanted to accomplish by killing the three of them. The cop noticed I was drifting.

"Are you okay hearing this?"

I snapped back. "Yeah. I was just thinking, what did they do with the journal?"

"Well, we're holding it as evidence right now because it's got some information we might want to investigate further, but in the end, I suspect we'll give it to his parents."

"What about their other things?"

"I don't think there was much more to speak of. The other guy . . ."

"Rich."

"Yeah. He . . . I'm not sure you want to hear it."

"No, what?"

"Well, when they found him in the back seat, it looked like he was in the middle of writing a will on his jeans, but what he was writing kind of trailed off as he went under, so nobody really knows what to make of it. Did you know him well?"

"Not as well as Andre."

"They also found a rat in his shirt pocket. What do you think of that?"

"It doesn't sound like him."

I got distracted again by this, and our conversation ground to a halt. After a minute, the cop repeated his condolences before getting back to work. I gathered his discarded newspaper and quickly scanned the front page, which was covered from top to bottom with stories about the guys. There were pictures of them taken for the high school yearbook and pictures of Rich and Serge posing in their hockey equipment. There was a picture from Vancouver, too, and for the first time, I got a clear idea of what happened. There wasn't really much in the photo actually. Just a shot of the garage with the big door raised enough so that the rear end of Andre's Chevette could be made out. Cops from BC milled around it, holding what could have been the guys' knapsacks.

The reporters didn't add much to what the QPP told me, so I turned to the obituaries. They were easy to find, as they were also decorated with the yearbook photos. I studied their young faces and wondered if they really had looked like that at one time. Their hair was unnaturally clean and brushed, Rich's smile seemed forced, and in Andre's case, his serious gaze suggested a guy with dreams of ruling the world. No wonder people are so nostalgic about high school — all you have to do is look at the pictures. People in yearbooks look indestructible.

I became concerned with seeing that the obits got everything right. There was no way they could have, of course, since the parents probably wrote them in a moment of intense pain. Rich's appeared first, and it glorified his accomplishments in school and on the ice. It was pretty much what I'd expected; Rich wasn't a model kid, but from what I knew, he and Serge did well for themselves. I mean, most of the guys who played on the all-star team were a tight-knit group who purposely ignored the rest of us. Only Rich and Serge really seemed to make an effort to distance themselves from being jocks, and that's what must have attracted Andre to them. I guess at that moment, most people in town would say, "Look where it got them." But sometimes a person's mind and body exist in two different places. Rich's body was here to play hockey but his mind was here to do . . . well, anything but.

The rest of his space was filled with a list of all those he was leaving behind. I realized that if I hadn't known him, I really wouldn't have much of an idea of what Rich was all about. I prepared for the worst in Andre's space — I knew his parents didn't know him at all. I had a brief flash that they, like Michel, didn't even care that he was dead.

I scoured every word for significance. ". . . was taken from us unexpectedly in his twenty-first year . . ." He wasn't taken; he went willingly. ". . . loving son of Jean and Collette, beloved brother of Michel . . ." Bullshit; 100 per cent bullshit. I couldn't take anything after that seriously, but there wasn't much more to read anyway. Andre's piece was about half the size of Rich's. There was no mention of the band, or Sylvie. I imagined Andre reading this and being thoroughly disgusted. I'm sure he would have wanted the trip to be listed as his greatest accomplishment.

I did learn that their bodies would be on display at the funeral home that evening, and that the funerals were on Friday. I shifted on the stool and took a deep breath, picturing the scene. Serge hopefully would be there; maybe Sylvie, too. I thought about what I'd wear. My Sunday suit, obviously. The hardest thing would be what to say. This was the first funeral I'd be attending for someone outside my family, and it meant I was an outsider. I'd just be expected to pay my respects and keep quiet. But I didn't want to keep quiet — too many people there wouldn't know the truth. I guess I didn't know the truth either, but I knew enough. It was pointless, but all the bullshit kept making me more and more angry.

The feelings subsided by the time I got home. I'd found out all I needed to know so I spent the rest of the afternoon watching TV to keep from over-analyzing. I settled on MuchMusic as usual, hoping my favourite bands would eventually appear. In the aftermath of Kurt's death, the station had done a good job at summing up his life and influence, as well as serving as a kind of sounding board for confused kids. When a Nirvana video eventually came on, I felt like calling up the station and telling whoever was there what I was going through. Somehow, I thought they might understand.

I didn't call. I don't think even the smoke alarm could have got me out of the La-Z-Boy. I was completely focused on the screen and the barrage of images it threw at me as my thumb spasmed on the remote control's buttons. There were soap operas, talk shows and tragedies from all four corners of the world. The guys were in there somewhere, and they would be soon forgotten — like everything else. That thought struck me when I landed on the 24-hour news channel and saw the story for which Jean-Jacques was interviewed. It was the first time I'd seen a recognizable part of my life on TV, and it was shocking how the front of the youth centre stood out in the background. After hearing Jean-Jacques struggle with the reporter's questions, I felt a burning regret for not having the foresight to be there, too. I would have set the record straight, but I'm sure it wouldn't have been what the reporter wanted to hear.

The story ended, and I changed the channel before the anchorwoman moved on to the next item.

My parents returned from work. The afternoon had passed unbelievably fast. My mom instinctively came to me and asked in a concerned tone what I'd done that day. I told her about the news being at the youth centre, and about my conversation with the cop. She said that everyone she worked with at the hospital was shocked by what had happened. She was always going on about what people at the hospital were saying.

I didn't respond. As usual, she was only interested in hearing herself talk. I didn't hate her for it, I hated that this was no longer my own crisis. But I figured I had to get over the ego trip. In a few hours I would be at the funeral home among people who were suffering ten times more than I was.

I ate dinner, then showered and pulled out my suit. It was boring and it was brown, not black, but I assumed it wouldn't matter; there would be many people there who didn't even own a suit. My mom started crying when she saw me. I'd heard her cry more in the last two days than I ever had, and I was truly getting sick of it. I told her when I thought I'd be home, and was relieved to feel a humid breeze hit me as I walked out the door.

But the heat soon became a burden on the walk to the funeral home. By the time I arrived, I felt damp and a little embarrassed. The parking lot was completely full, and there were even a few bikes chained to nearby trees. Not finding anyone in the foyer, I followed a simple sign to the room where the guys were lying. I hesitated, hearing voices in a large reception room. It took a few seconds for me to enter, where I found most of the people I expected to see standing around talking in hushed tones, while others looked completely out of sorts.

I gravitated toward a small group that included Jean-Jacques and Claude — they both looked sweaty in their suits, too. They greeted me cordially, yet coolly, in keeping with the sombre atmosphere. As I made small talk, my eyes darted around for a glimpse of Serge or Sylvie, or even Anne-Marie. I found Andre's parents first. They had entered from an adjoining chamber, where

I assumed the caskets were. They looked old and beaten, Andre's dad worse than usual — a recent drinking binge, obviously. Michel followed them, his long hair obscuring his downturned face. They didn't speak to anyone, and no one bothered them.

The first hour turned out to be more of a high school reunion than anything else, even though I still bumped into most of these people on a regular basis. After a while, someone asked if I'd seen the bodies, and I finally summoned the strength to go in. I didn't want to do it alone, though. I grabbed Jean-Jacques, and he led me to the chamber where both coffins sat. I prepared again to gaze upon their faces as we entered the room, but what I saw took me aback. There was Mario, sitting alone, beside Andre's coffin, staring at the floor in silent contemplation. He was so still I was afraid to disturb him. He looked up when he heard our steps.

"Hey," he said, in a barely audible voice.

All I could think of saying was what the cop told me about Andre's journal, about how they wanted to investigate the drug dealing. I swallowed hard before asking if anyone had questioned him.

"Yeah, I figured as much when I heard about the journal. Andre wasn't dumb enough to name names. If they do catch me, what the fuck, eh? I've got nowhere to go."

He seemed on the verge of breaking down, so I turned to look at the coffins. Andre was laid out in a suit and looked far too clean. I don't remember my initial reaction, aside from thinking the body looked nothing like him. It was like a sculptor's rendering of him, except he wasn't made out of stone, but clay or playdough. I glanced at Rich, and he looked much the same. They both appeared restless, as if at any moment they could sit up and rip off their ties.

More people started coming in, relatives from the looks of them, so Jean-Jacques and I retreated to the common area. The evening wasn't turning out the way I'd hoped. It was just like a night at the youth centre, only a lot more stressful. I'd seen the guys, but there wasn't really anyone there I wanted to talk to, so I made an early exit.

All the way home I wondered what Serge was doing. I thought about calling him when I woke up the next day but as we weren't that close it didn't seem like the right thing to do. I went back to the funeral home the next two nights, hoping to see somebody, and finally encountered Anne-Marie. She told me Serge and Sylvie had been coming during the day, when nobody was there. They didn't want to talk to anyone.

I realized it was rude asking Anne-Marie what they were doing, but she didn't take offense. She was strong by nature and said she was coping well. She was actually there to comfort Rich's mother, who seemed on the verge of collapsing. It was difficult talking to Anne-Marie; she seemed almost apathetic about losing the guy who loved her. She'd built a wall around herself. Nothing I said could penetrate. I really didn't even want to; it made me think Rich was better off without her.

Now that I knew Serge and Sylvie were around, I prepared myself for the actual funerals. I expected the weather to be gloomy, but it turned out to be another bright, humid day. The services were held in the morning at the largest church in town. Nearly everyone was there. It was an amazing sight. I felt lost in the crowd, until Andre's mother spotted me and asked in a trembling voice if I'd be a pallbearer. There was obviously no way I could refuse, so I gratefully left my parents and sat with the other pallbearers in the first row of pews. They included, to my surprise, Michel and Mario and some of their friends. It made me painfully aware how few Andre had of his own. At least the two of them didn't seem wasted.

The priest talked about Andre and Rich equally, and random wailing broke out at the mention of certain things. All of Rich's hockey teammates were there wearing their jerseys. Except for Serge. I finally noticed him after a burst of sobbing seemed to come from directly beside me. He was sitting in the same row, across the aisle, wearing a suit and listening intently to every word. I was momentarily distracted as I watched him, longing for him to turn my way and just say hi. His face was stony and his neck was rigid. He seemed to be fighting something, but his will was keeping it in check. I felt an overwhelming sense of pride and tried to rally some inner strength of my own as I returned my attention to the priest.

I soon realized the sobbing was coming from behind me, and that it was a girl. It became more intense. I resisted the temptation to turn around.

The ceremony ended with a prayer, and I focused on the duty of carrying Andre to the hearse. I was afraid of screwing up, and watching Michel and Mario fumble with their positions didn't help. Nobody really knew what to do; it made me want to hide in shame. Michel and one of his drug buddies actually started laughing at the absurdity of the situation. The rage I'd had at the youth centre briefly flared up again, but in the end, we all managed to find our places and strained to exit the church. I closed my eyes and imagined I was holding Andre's hand. It was corny, but it was the only thing that got me down that aisle.

I didn't open my eyes until I felt a rush of hot air as we passed through the big wooden doors and faced the imposing stone steps leading to the hearse. I was then ushered into one of the limos with the other pallbearers and driven the short distance to the cemetery. It was no longer a place where we used to play as kids, or made out with girlfriends.

We struggled again as we laid the casket onto the device that lowered it into the ground. Andre's plot was about 50 feet away from Rich's, so I lost track of Serge. As the priest was giving last rites, I saw Sylvie standing with her parents. She wore a long black dress and a black hat that shaded her face. I had to reunite with my own parents when it was all over, so we didn't have a chance to talk. I wouldn't have known what to say anyway. I just stood and watched her walk back to the car while my mother again asked how I was holding up.

The bush party was that night and I didn't feel like going. I decided to stay put until somebody called. Jean-Jacques finally did, and even offered to pick me up, so I couldn't refuse. I became unsettled when we turned onto the trail which led from the cemetery to a large clearing where all the best parties were normally held. The town once tried to cordon it off, but there was no fear of this party being broken up. There was already a small fire going by the creek, and most people sat quietly around it, drinking from all manner of containers. Several joints were also making the rounds. I hadn't brought anything myself, but Jean-Jacques carried one of the twenty-sixers of Southern Comfort his dad had smuggled from the States. He generously offered me as much as I wanted. There was plenty more in the car, he said.

There was silence for the longest time. People seemed able only to drink and inhale, or, I reasoned, no one was willing to speak out of turn in fear of reopening someone else's wounds. As expected, Serge and Sylvie weren't there, and the urge to leave again came quickly. Someone brought out a copy of the new Nirvana *Unplugged* tape, so I stayed to hear it. The music was transcendent, the surprisingly mellow side of Kurt blending perfectly with the mood in the clearing. Everything stopped when one song began, "Where do bad folks go when they die? They don't go to heaven where the angels fly."

My English couldn't make out every word, but the important ones cut to the bone. We'd all heard of the "lake of fire" in Sunday School, and I knew everyone was thinking Andre was probably there. No one met my gaze as I looked around the bonfire. Everyone was in their own world.

A rustling came from the trail, and a figure emerged in the fire's glow. Everyone turned. It was Serge. Some rose to greet him, but others remained seated, as if they were expecting him. Claude offered him a beer and Serge carefully opened and drank it as he approached the fire. We all waited for him to speak — a million questions hovered in the air.

"It's really nice that you all got together like this," he eventually said. "It means a lot to me, I guess."

"No problem, man. We, um, can't believe it happened," Jean-Jacques replied.

"I can't either," Serge said. "Just . . . don't listen to what everyone's saying about it." He spoke deliberately and his will seemed as strong as I'd seen it in the church. "Andre and Rich weren't nuts."

There was silence, and Serge stared at the flames, oblivious to those around him. I couldn't resist the urge to go over and put my arm around him. It didn't last long, but after I withdrew, Serge turned to me and gave a broad smile.

"I've been wanting to talk to somebody for the past three days," he said, tearing up.

"Anytime, man."

We each grabbed fresh beers and sat side by side on a log away from everyone else. He began telling me everything in detail, and a few people cautiously gathered to listen without intruding. About halfway through the story, Serge reached into his jacket and removed a folded notepad, which he flipped through. For a moment he was lost in the words on the small pages until finally he said, "This is my journal from the trip. I was gonna burn it here tonight, but I think I'm gonna give it to you instead. Everything's there; I can't tell you all of it tonight."

I took the notebook and tried vainly in the dim firelight to make out his scribbling. Instead, I asked him about Andre's journal.

"Yeah, the cops told me they found it," he answered. "I only saw it once. I didn't think much of it at the time, but I guess that's what he meant by leaving something that would explain everything. They said Rich wrote some stuff, too, but I never saw it. They would have taken my journal but I kept it hidden. They figured I'd be able to lead them to some drug kingpin, I guess. I didn't say anything. Anyway, you can do whatever you want with it. I don't want to be reminded."

It was hard to change the subject, but I managed to ask him what he was planning to do next.

"I'm going back to school, I guess," he answered. "I've gotta find a new place to live, meet some new people. What are you gonna do?"

I thought about it for a moment as I stared at his journal in my hands. My marks weren't good enough to get into university, and I'd spent the past year taking night classes and summer school trying to upgrade. I honestly couldn't tell him what I was going to do. Serge smiled when I said this. It was a smile that masked the pain of having too much freedom.

"Well, if you ever make it to the city, you can stay with me."

We left it at that, and I left Serge to speak to other people he knew. Jean-Jacques ended up getting too plastered to drive, so I took him home in his car.

I spent the next few days going through Serge's journal, lingering on certain passages and rereading others several times. Most of it was unbelievable, especially the description of the day they died, which was written on the flight home. He was, I assumed, in shock at the time. I visited Andre's grave regularly before the end of the summer, and took Serge's journal with me. These visits eventually became a source of inspiration. Sometimes I would read from the journal, pausing to compliment Andre on his tactics; other times I would just sit in silence. In August, I happened to arrive at the cemetery when Sylvie was there, too. She had flowers and a note, which she buried just beneath the sod near Andre's stone. I gave her a moment before I called out, and she waved me over.

"What's it like being a widow?" I asked, hoping she'd laugh. She did.

"I don't recommend it. I hear you come here a lot, too."

"Yeah. He's still my best friend, I guess."

We spent the next few hours at Andre's grave, engaged in the timid conversation boys and girls often have. We talked about putting things behind us, while still holding onto our rapidly fading youth. Eventually, Sylvie opened up about her trip to the coast to find him. It had been a desperate plan, she admitted, but she no longer regretted doing it. Once she realized he was gone, Andre's final words to her sunk in. She had to move on and make something of the opportunities he never had. At the end of the month, she was moving to Vancouver and starting classes at UBC. She wasn't going to let her pedestrian English stand in her way, either.

I told her I'd recently had similar revelations. I said my parents were worried that I had developed suicidal tendencies, that they were encouraging me to go to church all the time.

"Yeah, my folks were like that, too. They wouldn't let me out of their sight for the longest time. I mean, the thought did cross my mind, but I know now that there's a place for me out there. I don't know if I would have seen that if Andre hadn't shown me."

I cried, as Sylvie's words made me understand that I felt the same. We embraced, fully aware of our newly forged bond, one we know will remain, even if we never see each other again.

Her words still echo as I prepare now to move to Quebec City with Serge. I'm not sure what's going to happen to me there. Serge says he'll help me get a job, then get into school if I want. My parents say they'll help me out, too. I think they're glad just to see me doing something.

I told Serge about my talk with Sylvie. Her words have become our mantra, our secret code. No one can believe how we act when we're together now, but it doesn't matter. They have a long way to go to get to where we are.

"I wanna live."

"Me too."